Artfall

Betsy Tate

Published by Betsy Tate, 2024.

This is a work of fiction. Similarities to real people, places, or events are entirely coincidental.

ARTFALL

First edition. November 11, 2024.

Copyright © 2024 Betsy Tate.

ISBN: 979-8227580948

Written by Betsy Tate.

Chapter 1: The Storm Within

The thunderstorm rages outside my New England cottage, its fierce winds howling like a pack of wolves, an untamed force echoing the chaos swirling inside me. Each crack of lightning illuminates the dim interior, casting dramatic shadows that dance across the walls, shadows that seem to taunt me as I prepare for the opening of my art gallery. I stand amidst a chaotic sea of canvases, brushes, and half-finished sculptures, my pulse racing like the storm outside, an unsettling rhythm that drives me to distraction.

My heart thrums in sync with the tempest, the anticipation and dread swirling together into an intoxicating cocktail of excitement and anxiety. The gallery, my sanctuary and battleground, is set to unveil my latest collection—pieces that breathe life into my emotions, raw and unfiltered. Each brushstroke captures fragments of my soul, but the thought of Liam Sinclair lurking in the wings makes my stomach twist.

With a fierce crack, the door swings open, slamming against the wall, rattling the frame like an angry guest refused entry. There he stands, Liam Sinclair, tall and infuriatingly handsome, with tousled dark hair that glistens as the rain-soaked tendrils cling to his forehead. His stormy blue eyes, like shards of ice and the tumultuous sea combined, search my face, and for a fleeting moment, the air hangs heavy with something I can't quite place—curiosity, perhaps, or a challenge. The last thing I need right now is a face-off with my greatest rival.

"What a charming welcome," he quips, stepping inside, his tone dripping with sarcasm as he wipes the rain from his brow. "I see you've decided to invite the elements to your little soirée."

"Better than inviting you," I shoot back, unable to resist the instinct to volley back. The tension crackles, and though my voice is sharp, there's a flicker of humor beneath it, one that I can't quite conceal.

He chuckles, an easy, magnetic sound that somehow cuts through the noise of the storm. "A pleasure as always, Elara. Though I must say, you could use a few more candles. It's practically a cave in here."

"Who invited you to critique my ambiance?" I snap, but the warmth of my smile betrays the fire in my words. Our rivalry has always been a dance, sharp and quick, with playful jabs that mask something deeper, something that sizzles beneath our competitive banter.

"I figured someone had to rescue you from your self-imposed exile. I can't believe you're still holed up in this place." He gestures around, eyes roaming over my eclectic collection of unfinished pieces, the remnants of late nights spent wrestling with my imagination.

"I'll have you know, this 'exile' has produced some of my best work," I reply, my pride prickling. "And I'd rather be here than at one of your extravagant openings, where everyone pretends to love your work while secretly wondering if they'll trip on their own pretentiousness."

"Ah, but at least my pretentiousness comes wrapped in awards and accolades," he retorts, stepping closer, his presence almost intoxicating, electrifying the air between us. "Your bitterness, however, is just that—bitterness. You should try it sometime; it adds flavor."

My heart races, caught between annoyance and an undeniable attraction. This rivalry has become an elaborate game of chess, and each encounter feels like a new strategy, a calculated risk where neither of us wants to lose the upper hand. Yet, beneath the sharp wit and feigned animosity, I sense an unspoken understanding, a hidden camaraderie that tugs at the edges of my consciousness.

"Is this really the time to debate our artistic merits?" I ask, struggling to keep my focus, my thoughts drifting dangerously close to the possibility that maybe, just maybe, there's more to him than the rival I've crafted in my mind.

"Why not? It's a stormy night, and what's a little verbal sparring between old foes?" His smirk deepens, making my heart flutter and my resolve waver.

"Because I have an opening to prepare for," I insist, forcing myself to sound firm as I begin to gather my brushes, a futile attempt to retreat into my art, to escape the simmering tension between us. The truth is, beneath the layers of competition, a flicker of admiration has sparked—a recognition of talent that unnerves me more than I'd care to admit.

"Are you worried I'll overshadow your big night?" he asks, his voice dropping to a conspiratorial whisper.

"I'd say your ego is more than capable of overshadowing a few canvases," I shoot back, but as the words leave my lips, I can't help but notice the subtle shift in his expression. For a moment, the mask of rivalry slips, and I catch a glimpse of something vulnerable, a fleeting moment that makes my breath hitch.

Outside, the storm intensifies, rain lashing against the windows, mimicking the tumult of our conversation. In this cocoon of chaos, our shared animosity feels strangely intimate, a world separate from the usual clamor of competition and envy. Yet, with each heartbeat, the undercurrents of something deeper pull me in, drawing me closer to the very man I've spent years trying to outrun.

"What if," he proposes, leaning closer, "we set aside the rivalry for just tonight? I could help you with the gallery opening. You know, a little collaborative effort might create quite the buzz."

"Is this your idea of a joke?" I laugh, the absurdity of it sparking a flicker of disbelief. "You and me, collaborating? That's rich."

"Why not?" he presses, his gaze steady, unyielding. "We both know how much this opening means to you, and I have some ideas that could elevate your work."

An unexpected thrill courses through me, tempting and dangerous. "And what's in it for you, Liam? A chance to gloat about how you saved me from myself?"

"Maybe I just want to see you succeed. Or maybe," he adds, a mischievous glint in his eyes, "I'm intrigued by the idea of shaking things up in the art scene."

The prospect hangs heavy in the air, a tantalizing invitation to cross the invisible line between rivals and collaborators. As the storm rages outside, I find myself at a crossroads, caught between fear and excitement, drawn toward a possibility I never expected. The thunder booms in the distance, a warning of the storm within and around us, but as I look into Liam's captivating eyes, I can't help but wonder if this tempest might lead to something unexpected—a storm of a different kind.

"Collaboration?" I scoff, trying to maintain a façade of indignation while my mind races with the possibilities he's just thrown at me like a curveball. "And what exactly would that entail? You, the prodigal artist, swooping in to save the day with your glossy reputation?"

He smirks, that infuriating, charming smirk that's as much a part of him as the talent I both admire and envy. "Let's not pretend I'm doing this out of the goodness of my heart, Elara. I'm here because I know you have something special. Something the world needs to see, and quite frankly, it might be fun to watch you squirm under the spotlight for once."

"Fun for you, maybe," I retort, folding my arms defiantly. "And just to clarify, squirming is not typically on my list of opening-night activities. If I wanted that kind of entertainment, I could watch paint dry. You know, like how you treat your canvases."

His laughter is unexpected, and it resonates like the distant rumble of thunder, shaking the tension in the air. "Oh, come now. You're telling me you've never been curious about how your work might be received if it had a little... polish?"

I hesitate, the flicker of temptation undeniable. Deep down, I know that the upcoming opening isn't just about showcasing my art; it's about validation. It's about proving to the world—and perhaps to myself—that I belong. The prospect of having someone as experienced as Liam on my side is alluring, yet the thought of lowering my guard around him makes my skin prickle.

"I don't need you to come in and wave your magic wand over my work," I finally reply, striving for nonchalance. "I built this from the ground up. It's mine, and I won't let you tarnish it with your ego."

"Your ego might need a little polishing too," he shoots back, raising an eyebrow, a playful challenge igniting the air between us. "Look, if we're going to go down this road, we should at least make it entertaining."

I shake my head, a reluctant smile creeping onto my lips. "Entertaining? Is that your definition of art? Because I always thought it was supposed to evoke emotion, not just provide a spectacle."

"Emotion, spectacle—what's the difference? A little drama never hurt anyone. Besides, it could give you the edge you've been missing." His eyes gleam with mischief, and I can't help but feel a flicker of curiosity. What would it be like to see my work through his eyes?

"Fine," I say, the word spilling from my lips before I can stop myself. "But this doesn't mean I trust you. The last time I let you near my work, I found paint splatters in places I didn't even know existed."

"Ah, memories," he replies with mock nostalgia, his tone dripping with amusement. "That was an experiment in mixed media. And it worked, didn't it?"

"Only because I spent the next three hours cleaning it up," I counter, my resolve beginning to soften. "You're impossible."

"I prefer the term 'challenging.' It's got a better ring to it." He takes a step closer, the tension between us thickening like the humidity in the air. "So, what do you say? Let's make a masterpiece."

The rain drums steadily against the roof, a steady rhythm that matches the quickening of my heartbeat. Part of me screams to retreat, to lock him out of my creative space, but another part—one that thrives on the thrill of pushing boundaries—beckons me forward. I nod, albeit reluctantly. "Alright. But I'm still in charge here."

"Of course," he agrees, his eyes sparkling with mischief. "I wouldn't dream of taking the reins. Just know that when the crowds see your work and rave about it, you'll have me to thank."

"Is that a threat or a promise?" I ask, trying to mask the fluttering in my stomach with sarcasm.

"Why not both?" He winks, his expression delightfully infuriating.

With a resigned sigh, I start to gather my materials, knowing full well that inviting Liam into my creative process means inviting chaos. And perhaps, just perhaps, a little magic. The room buzzes with an electric energy, a strange mix of dread and anticipation that sends shivers down my spine.

"Now," he says, pulling on a pair of rubber gloves with exaggerated seriousness, "what do you want to tackle first? The emotional turmoil of unrequited love? The struggle between light and dark? Or should we focus on your fear of letting anyone see the real you?"

I shoot him a glare that could curdle milk. "You think you know me?"

"Oh, I know you," he replies, his voice dropping to a conspiratorial whisper. "And I can smell the fear behind that bravado of yours. It's almost charming."

"Charming is the last thing I'd call you," I huff, though a part of me warms at his perceptiveness. "I'm an open book. I don't hide my feelings."

"Really?" He raises an eyebrow, clearly skeptical. "Tell me, what does this particular piece convey?" He gestures toward a canvas covered in a riot of colors—chaotic swirls of crimson and deep blues, a stormy depiction of my emotions, crafted during one of my darker moments.

"That's about anger," I explain, crossing my arms defensively. "It's messy because it's raw. There's beauty in chaos."

He studies the canvas, his brow furrowing in concentration. "I see it. But what if we could amplify that chaos? Channel it into something more cohesive? A true storm rather than just splatter."

I find myself intrigued. "How do you suggest we do that?"

"Let's combine your emotions with some structure. Create a narrative within the chaos." His voice is almost hypnotic, coaxing my creative spirit to rise to the surface. "Tell a story."

"A story? Like an artist's narrative?"

"Exactly. What if you infused your work with a personal experience? Something that feels tangible, relatable?"

As he speaks, I can feel my defenses softening, the walls I've built around my creativity beginning to crumble. "You want me to expose myself to a crowd?"

"Isn't that what art is all about? Revealing truths that are often uncomfortable?" His eyes bore into mine, filled with genuine curiosity. "Your audience wants to connect, Elara. They want to feel."

"But what if they don't like what they feel?" The vulnerability stings, but I can't help but probe deeper. "What if they see something they don't understand?"

"Then you've done your job," he insists, his voice steady and reassuring. "You've stirred something within them. If you can provoke thought, stir emotions, then you've succeeded."

His passion is contagious, igniting a spark of inspiration I thought I'd long extinguished. Maybe there's something to this reckless idea of collaboration. Maybe allowing him into my creative sanctuary won't destroy everything I've built, but rather, expand it.

"You know," I say slowly, a smile tugging at the corners of my mouth, "you might just be full of surprises, Liam Sinclair."

"Careful," he warns playfully. "You might just start to like me."

"Let's not get ahead of ourselves," I counter, trying to mask the warmth blooming in my chest. "We still have a gallery to prepare for."

"Then let's make it unforgettable," he says, and I can't help but feel the gravity of that promise. In this storm of colors and emotions, perhaps the most unexpected masterpiece lies ahead, waiting for us to bring it to life.

The thunder continues to rumble outside, a cacophony of nature's fury that seems to mirror the rising intensity in the room. Liam stands across from me, arms crossed, an amused expression playing on his lips as I prepare my materials, the swirl of colors and textures almost dizzying in their chaos.

"Are you always this organized, or is today special?" he teases, glancing at the scattered brushes and the half-finished canvases that crowd my workspace.

"Let's just say I like my chaos to have a method," I reply, setting a few tubes of paint aside with more force than necessary. "But I can't expect you to understand. You thrive in your own brand of pandemonium."

"Touché," he concedes, his tone playful. "But you're forgetting that sometimes, a little pandemonium can spark creativity. How about we start with your most chaotic piece? It might just need the Liam Sinclair touch to elevate it."

I shoot him a skeptical look, crossing my arms over my chest. "And what exactly is the 'Liam Sinclair touch'? A coat of charm and a sprinkle of arrogance?"

He grins, unfazed. "Let's call it confidence. A fearless approach to color, a dash of unexpected—"

"A touch of pretense?" I interrupt, raising an eyebrow.

"Okay, you caught me there," he laughs, the sound infectious. "But seriously, what's the worst that could happen? We mix your storm with my... flair? It could be a disaster or—"

"Or it could be a masterpiece," I finish for him, a glimmer of intrigue creeping in. The thought of combining our talents, chaotic as it may be, sends a ripple of excitement through me. I can't ignore that idea, however reckless it sounds.

"Precisely," he says, stepping closer, a challenging gleam in his eyes. "So, what do you want to do first? Or should I just dive in and make a mess?"

"Please don't touch anything before I give you the green light," I warn, smirking as I pull out a canvas that features jagged lines in shades of red and black, an embodiment of frustration and unrest. "This one could use your 'fearlessness.' It's called 'Rage in Abandon.'"

"Lovely title," he remarks, eyeing the canvas appreciatively. "You really aren't afraid to wear your emotions on your sleeve."

"Trust me, I'm just as afraid of them as anyone else. But that's what art is for, right? To spill your guts out where everyone can see."

"Exactly," he says, nodding with fervor. "Let's give them something they can feel. When people stand in front of your work, I want them to think, 'This is real. This is raw.'"

A surge of excitement rushes through me, an unexpected thrill at the thought of someone else seeing my vision and believing in it, even if that someone is my greatest rival. "Alright, fine. Let's do this."

As we start to work, the atmosphere shifts. We move rhythmically, Liam mixing colors while I layer strokes of paint onto the canvas. Our dialogue flows easily, filled with laughter and light-hearted jabs, as if the storm outside has imbued us with a creative energy that refuses to be contained.

"I have to admit, this is surprisingly pleasant," I comment, stepping back to assess our progress. "I didn't think I could enjoy anything while sharing my space with you."

"Don't get too used to it," he teases. "Once the opening is over, I plan to go back to being your greatest nemesis."

"Perfectly fine with me," I reply, tossing a brush at him, which he dodges with exaggerated flair. "Just remember, you'll need to give me full credit for this masterpiece."

"Only if I get to take half the credit," he counters, a mischievous twinkle in his eye. "After all, we wouldn't want the world thinking you're a one-woman show."

"Touché," I acknowledge, fighting back a smile. There's an undeniable chemistry brewing between us, a playful banter that blurs the lines of our rivalry. As we continue painting, the sound of the storm outside fades into the background, becoming a mere whisper to the laughter and lightheartedness in the cottage.

But as the night wears on, a darkening shadow looms on the horizon—an uninvited thought creeping in like the clouds gathering for the next wave of the storm.

"Liam," I begin cautiously, wiping my hands on a cloth and suddenly feeling vulnerable, "why did you really want to help me? I mean, we're not exactly friends."

He pauses, his expression shifting from playful to serious, the air thickening with unspoken tension. "Maybe I see something in you that others don't. You have talent, Elara, and it deserves to be seen. Perhaps I also just enjoy a challenge."

"Is that all?" I press, needing to understand his motives, trying to separate the truth from the bravado. "I find it hard to believe you'd do this without any strings attached."

"Maybe you're just too accustomed to seeing the worst in me," he says, his tone softening. "What if I genuinely want to see you succeed?"

The sincerity in his voice pulls me in, and for a moment, I'm thrown off balance. "And what if you're just playing a game?"

"Ah, always the skeptic," he replies, a hint of admiration in his gaze. "But I'm not here to play games with you. Not this time."

Before I can respond, there's a sudden crash of thunder that shakes the very foundations of the cottage. The lights flicker, plunging us into momentary darkness, and I feel a chill creep up my spine.

"Just a little thunder, don't let it get to you," Liam says, attempting to inject levity into the moment, but there's an unmistakable edge to his voice.

"It's more than just thunder," I whisper, anxiety tightening my throat. "It feels like something else is brewing."

He steps closer, his shoulder brushing against mine as we stand in the darkness, and for a heartbeat, the air thickens with the kind of tension that electrifies. "Let's not forget, Elara, storms can be beautiful, even in their chaos."

"Beautiful or not, they can also destroy," I murmur, my voice barely above a whisper.

Just as he opens his mouth to respond, the lights flicker back on, casting an eerie glow around the room, illuminating the canvas we've been working on. The colors seem to pulse with a life of their own, vibrant and almost threatening, an embodiment of the storm raging outside.

Suddenly, I catch a glimpse of something at the edge of my vision—movement. My breath hitches as I turn, the hairs on the back of my neck standing on end. "Did you see that?"

"See what?" he asks, glancing around, a frown forming on his handsome face.

"There was... something. I swear I saw movement by the window."

He steps toward the window, peering out into the inky darkness, the storm still howling as the rain lashes against the glass. "It's probably just the wind. You know how storms can play tricks on your mind."

But as he speaks, an uneasy feeling settles over me, creeping like the shadows pooling in the corners of the room. The night feels charged, as if it were holding its breath, and I can't shake the sensation that something—or someone—might be watching us.

Before I can voice my concern, a loud bang echoes from outside, the sound resonating through the cottage. My heart races, and I can feel the heat of Liam's body next to mine, his presence both comforting and electrifying. "What was that?" I ask, fear threading through my voice.

Liam's gaze is sharp, assessing, and for a moment, he seems to be grappling with his own emotions. "Stay here," he says, his tone suddenly serious, the playful banter gone. He strides toward the door, tension coiling in the air like a tightly wound spring.

"Wait!" I call out, but he's already opened the door, a blast of wind rushing in, rattling the frame. My instincts scream at me to grab him, to pull him back, but he's gone before I can react.

I stand frozen, anxiety thrumming in my veins as I watch him disappear into the dark storm, the door hanging ajar like an invitation to the unknown. Outside, the wind howls, and I can feel the storm intensifying, the air thick with anticipation.

"What are you doing, Liam?" I murmur to myself, but deep down, a nagging feeling warns me that whatever is waiting in the storm is far more sinister than we could have ever anticipated. Just as I muster the courage to follow him, a flicker of movement catches my eye again—this time, right behind me.

I turn slowly, dread pooling in my stomach. The light casts strange shadows across the room, distorting the shapes, but there it is, a figure lurking at the edge of my vision, hidden in the darkness. A heartbeat later, a chilling whisper fills the room, echoing like the very thunder that rumbles outside.

"Elara..."

My heart stops, and in that moment, I realize that the storm we had thought was just outside might be the least of our worries.

Chapter 2: Collisions

The gallery thrummed with energy, a living tapestry of laughter and the soft hum of chatter interwoven with the occasional clink of crystal glasses. My heart raced, a chaotic symphony echoing in my chest, as I navigated through clusters of art enthusiasts, their polished shoes gliding over the marble floor. The walls, adorned with vivid splashes of color, spoke in hushed tones, each piece vying for attention in the warm glow of strategically placed lights.

I could feel the pulse of excitement in the air, a mingling of scents—fresh paint, aged wood, and the intoxicating aroma of rich hors d'oeuvres that wafted through the space. I had spent weeks preparing for this moment, crafting the perfect evening that would showcase not just the art, but also my passion for it. As the curator of this gallery, it was my job to ensure everything went flawlessly. But of course, chaos had a way of worming its way into even the best-laid plans.

"Amelia! You have to see this piece!" A voice broke through my reverie, and I turned to find Chloe, my enthusiastic intern, waving her arms as if she were trying to attract a wayward bird. Her excitement was infectious, and for a brief moment, I felt the weight of my responsibilities lighten.

"Which one?" I asked, stepping closer to her, feeling the warmth of the crowd pressing around us.

"The one with the gold leaf! It's stunning!" she exclaimed, eyes sparkling.

Just then, amidst the vibrant chatter, I caught a glimpse of him—Liam Sinclair, the enigmatic artist with a reputation for both his brilliant work and his infuriating arrogance. He stood near the bar, effortlessly charming a group of admirers while casting lingering glances my way. I could feel my pulse quicken, a strange mix of irritation and undeniable attraction swirling within me.

"Liam?" I muttered under my breath, the name rolling off my tongue with an edge of annoyance.

"Amelia! Come on!" Chloe tugged my arm, dragging me toward the painting.

As I glanced back, Liam's gaze locked onto mine. His smirk was maddening, and I had to resist the urge to roll my eyes. We had shared a complicated history, one laden with competitive tension and playful banter. Our last encounter had left a bitter taste in my mouth—his smugness had been unbearable, yet there was something in his eyes that hinted at a deeper connection.

"Amelia, are you coming or what?" Chloe's voice jolted me back to the moment, and I followed her, feigning interest in the artwork while trying to ignore the disconcerting way Liam's presence lingered in the back of my mind.

The piece was indeed magnificent, with gold leaf glinting under the lights, casting a halo around it. I admired it, letting Chloe's enthusiasm wash over me, but my thoughts were elsewhere. As the evening progressed, I found myself dodging Liam's attempts to engage me in conversation. Each time our paths crossed, the air crackled with an unspoken challenge, a duel of wits that neither of us was willing to back down from.

"Nice to see you haven't managed to trip over your own ego tonight," he quipped, appearing at my side as I attempted to catch my breath by a particularly striking abstract piece.

"Funny," I shot back, crossing my arms. "Coming from someone who uses charm like a weapon."

"Is it working?" His gaze was mischievous, and I had to fight the smile threatening to break free.

"Hardly," I replied, though my heart betrayed me, fluttering like a moth around a flame.

But before our verbal sparring could escalate further, a sudden commotion near the entrance pulled my attention. The crowd shifted like a wave, and I could hear snippets of frantic conversation. Something was wrong.

A voice rang out, cutting through the noise. "The painting! It's gone!"

Panic surged through the room. I exchanged a look with Liam, and in that moment, the atmosphere shifted. Our rivalry felt trivial compared to the gravity of the situation.

"What do you mean it's gone?" I pushed through the crowd, adrenaline spiking. Chloe followed closely, her eyes wide with confusion.

"Someone just stole it! The gold-leaf piece!"

The gallery erupted into chaos, whispers and shouts ricocheting off the walls. I scanned the room, spotting the security personnel rushing toward the scene, their expressions a mix of disbelief and urgency. I felt a strange mixture of fear and determination; this was my gallery, my responsibility.

Liam moved closer, his expression serious for the first time. "We can't let them get away with this," he said, a glint of resolve in his eyes.

"What do you propose we do? Sit around and hope they magically return it?" I snapped, but beneath my irritation was a flicker of agreement.

He smirked, that familiar arrogance returning, but there was a new layer to it now—an understanding that we were both in this together. "No, Amelia. We're going to find it."

The competitive spark ignited between us once more, but this time it felt different—urgent, electric. We were no longer rivals in a game of art and charm; we were partners, albeit reluctant ones, thrust together by circumstance and the pressing need to reclaim what had been stolen.

As we raced toward the exit, I could feel the weight of the gallery behind us—the art, the memories, and the potential loss that lingered in the air. Our banter had transformed into an unspoken alliance, and for the first time, I found myself appreciating the unexpected thrill of working alongside Liam Sinclair.

The chaos of the gallery spilled out into the night, an almost palpable tension hanging in the air. As we darted through the crowd, the warm glow of the gallery's lights cast a surreal ambiance against the darkening sky outside. My heart raced not just from the thrill of pursuit but also from the presence of Liam at my side, his energy crackling like electricity. There was a strange comfort in the chaos; in a room full of unfamiliar faces, we were both outsiders now, united by a shared goal.

"Do you have any idea who might have taken it?" I asked, my voice slightly breathless. The weight of responsibility bore down on me like a heavy cloak, but I was determined not to show any weakness, especially not to Liam.

He shrugged, the casual gesture doing nothing to mask the sharp intelligence in his eyes. "In a crowd like this? It could be anyone. A jealous competitor, an aspiring artist, or maybe someone just looking for a thrill. But I can't shake the feeling that it was someone inside—someone who knew exactly what they were doing."

"Great, so we're looking for a mastermind among the masses," I replied, half-joking, trying to lighten the mood despite the gravity of our task. "Any leads, Sherlock?"

He smirked, that infuriating, cocky grin that set my heart racing. "Well, Watson, I believe we should start with the last few people who were admiring the painting. They might have seen something."

I rolled my eyes at his theatrics, though a smile tugged at my lips. "Fine, but let's make sure we do it quickly before this whole evening becomes a gallery of disaster."

We slipped through the throng of guests, their conversations turning from art appreciation to speculation about the theft. Each whispered theory only heightened the urgency in my chest. The last thing I needed was a scandal tarnishing my gallery's reputation, especially not on opening night. The walls felt like they were closing in, each piece of art a silent witness to the unfolding drama.

We approached a couple who had been admiring the gold-leaf piece just moments before its disappearance. A man with tousled hair and a woman dressed in a striking red dress were deep in conversation, their expressions a mix of confusion and concern.

"Excuse me," I interjected, my tone firm but polite. "Did either of you notice anything unusual just before the painting went missing?"

The woman looked startled, her hand instinctively clutching her purse. "We—uh, we just admired it for a moment. I thought it was so beautiful. Then we turned to discuss it, and when we looked back... it was gone!"

"Did you see anyone near the painting?" Liam pressed, his gaze intense.

The man shook his head, clearly distressed. "No, but there was a man in a dark coat who lingered nearby. He seemed out of place, but I thought nothing of it at the time."

"Dark coat?" I echoed, feeling a knot form in my stomach. "Do you remember anything else about him?"

The woman frowned, her brow furrowing in concentration. "He had a beard, I think. And he was looking around a lot, almost like he was waiting for something."

Liam and I exchanged a look, the same thought flashing between us. "We need to check the security footage," I said, determination hardening my voice.

"Right," he replied, and his tone shifted, becoming more serious. "Let's get to the security room. It's at the back of the gallery."

We maneuvered through the crowd once more, and I couldn't shake the feeling that we were racing against an unseen clock. The laughter that had filled the gallery earlier now felt tainted, like a cruel reminder of how quickly everything could change.

Upon reaching the security room, I was relieved to find the door unlocked. A young technician sat at the monitors, the flickering screens illuminating his anxious face. "What's happening?" he asked, glancing between us.

"A priceless painting has been stolen. We need to see the footage from the last hour," Liam said, his tone leaving no room for hesitation.

The technician nodded, fingers flying over the keyboard as he pulled up the recordings. Images flickered on the screen, revealing snippets of the evening—guests laughing, admiring art, and, among them, the shadow of the elusive thief.

"Here," the technician said, pausing the footage. "This is the moment the painting was taken."

The screen showed a figure in a dark coat slipping between the throngs of guests, his movements quick and purposeful. My heart raced as I watched, the seconds stretching into an eternity. The figure paused, glancing around, and then with a swift motion, lifted the painting from its place and disappeared into the crowd.

"Can you enhance that?" I asked, urgency thrumming in my veins.

"Give me a sec." The technician manipulated the footage, and the figure came into sharper focus. I leaned closer, squinting. "There! That's definitely not a typical guest."

"Definitely not." Liam's voice was low, almost a growl. "We need to find that man."

Just then, the technician's face turned pale. "Uh, I think I know who he is. I've seen him before at other galleries. He's... a known art thief."

My breath caught in my throat, and I shot a glance at Liam, whose expression mirrored my concern. "What's his name?"

"I'm not sure, but he's been in and out of the scene for years, always managing to slip through the cracks. I can pull up a database of previous incidents."

"Do it," Liam ordered, his tone sharp as he turned to me. "We need to get ahead of this."

As the technician hurried to gather information, I felt a sudden sense of urgency wash over me. My gallery, my vision, was at stake, and the thought of it slipping away due to one man's greed was infuriating.

"Okay, let's think this through," I said, trying to piece together our next steps. "We need to alert security, but we also need to gather more intel on this thief. If we can anticipate his next move..."

"Then we might have a chance to catch him," Liam finished, his eyes narrowing with focus.

"Right. And perhaps even get the painting back," I added, determination flooding my voice.

Liam smiled, a genuine grin that caught me off guard. "Look at us, Amelia. Who would've thought we'd make a pretty good team?"

"Don't get too comfortable," I shot back, even as warmth spread through me. "This is a temporary alliance. Once the painting is back, it's back to our usual rivalry."

"Of course." He leaned closer, a spark of mischief in his gaze. "But until then, I think we make quite the duo. Let's catch this thief."

Together, we stepped back into the fray, the vibrant chaos of the gallery no longer just a backdrop, but the stage for our unexpected partnership. The night had transformed from a showcase of art into a high-stakes chase, each moment charged with a blend of tension and excitement. As we moved forward, I could feel the thrill of the unknown electrifying the air around us, and for the first time, the competition felt like an exhilarating game rather than an adversarial battle.

The hum of chatter swirled around us as we made our way through the gallery, adrenaline mingling with the clamor of voices and the pop of champagne corks. With each step, I could feel the thrill of the chase settling in my bones. The paintings loomed like silent sentinels, their vibrant colors now a stark contrast to the dark intentions of the thief lurking among our guests. I caught a glimpse of Liam beside me, his brow furrowed in concentration, and suddenly I was acutely aware of how closely our fates were intertwined.

"Any thoughts on where we should start?" I asked, hoping to keep the focus on our mission and not on the unsettling way my heart quickened every time I glanced at him.

He paused, considering. "Well, if this thief is as clever as you said, he's probably looking for an exit with the least amount of attention. Let's check the back doors and the service areas."

"Brilliant deduction, Sherlock," I replied, unable to resist a playful jab. "Lead the way."

We slipped through the crowd, our movements choreographed like a well-rehearsed dance. With every turn, I caught snippets of conversations laced with anxiety—guests speculating about the thief, discussing the rarity of the stolen piece. The atmosphere had shifted from celebratory to a mixture of fear and uncertainty, a reality I found disconcerting.

As we approached the narrow hallway leading to the service area, I felt the air grow thicker, the sounds of laughter muted to an eerie hush. It was a stark contrast to the vibrant colors of the main gallery, the walls lined with shadowy art that seemed to close in on us. I shivered slightly, pulling my coat tighter around me.

Liam glanced back at me, his expression softening momentarily. "You okay?"

"Just feeling the weight of the night," I admitted, my voice barely above a whisper. "I never imagined opening night would turn into a crime scene."

"Neither did I, but here we are." He offered a lopsided grin that made my heart flutter despite the circumstances. "Let's focus on the mission, partner."

Partner. The word sent a jolt through me, a thrilling mix of camaraderie and something deeper that I was hesitant to explore. Before I could reply, he pushed the door to the service area open, the faint sound of machinery humming inside.

We stepped into the dimly lit space, a stark contrast to the vibrant gallery outside. The fluorescent lights buzzed overhead, illuminating stacks of crates and equipment scattered across the floor. The scent of dust mingled with the faint metallic tang in the air. I felt an uneasy shiver run down my spine.

"Check that corner," Liam said, gesturing toward a pile of crates. "I'll look over here."

I nodded, forcing myself to breathe deeply as I moved toward the shadows. My heart pounded louder than the sound of my footsteps, and I forced myself to concentrate. I rummaged through the boxes, my hands brushing against the rough wood and cold metal.

"What do you think we'll find?" I called over my shoulder, my voice echoing against the walls.

"Maybe some secret stash of stolen art?" he quipped, the playful tone laced with tension. "Or perhaps the thief's evil lair?"

"Maybe they left behind a calling card," I shot back, my fingers finding a dusty cloth that made me recoil for a moment, half-expecting to uncover something sinister. "Or a half-eaten sandwich."

Liam chuckled, the sound warm and reassuring. "Now that's a culinary mystery worth solving."

I was about to respond when I heard it—a faint scuffle just outside the door we had entered. My heart lurched, adrenaline flooding my veins. "Did you hear that?" I whispered, my voice suddenly tense.

Liam nodded, his expression shifting from playful to serious. "Stay here. I'll check it out."

"Wait—" But he was already moving, slipping back into the hallway. My instincts screamed at me to follow, but I hesitated, torn between the safety of staying hidden and the need to support him.

Peering out from behind a stack of crates, I strained to listen. The murmurs from the gallery had returned, but now they were punctuated by something else—urgent whispers and the faint sound of footsteps retreating. I barely had time to process it when Liam reappeared, his eyes wide with intensity.

"It's him!" he said, his voice low but urgent. "I saw the guy in the dark coat—he's moving toward the back exit. We have to follow him!"

"Lead the way," I replied, the thrill of pursuit rekindling my resolve.

We sprinted back through the service area, emerging into the crowd of guests just as panic began to ripple through them. I caught sight of the man in the dark coat slipping through the side door, and without a second thought, I pushed my way through the guests, Liam at my heels.

"Stop!" I shouted, the word bursting from my lips as I caught a glimpse of the thief. He paused, glancing back, his eyes wide with surprise before he bolted down the alleyway behind the gallery.

"Don't let him escape!" Liam yelled, pushing forward with renewed urgency.

The alley was dark and narrow, shadows swallowing the faint glow from the streetlights above. I felt a surge of adrenaline propel me forward, my legs moving faster than I thought possible. Liam was just beside me, his presence both reassuring and invigorating.

We rounded a corner, the thief just ahead, his coat flapping behind him like a dark banner of guilt. "He's gaining distance!" I called out, frustration pooling in my chest.

"Just a little closer!" Liam urged, and I could hear the determination in his voice.

With every step, I felt the cold night air bite at my skin, the thrill of the chase igniting a fierce determination within me. I was ready to catch him, to reclaim what was rightfully ours, but just as we closed the gap, the thief turned sharply into an alley obscured by shadows, vanishing from view.

"Where did he go?" I panted, frustration gnawing at me as I skidded to a halt.

"Right here!" Liam shouted, pointing down another path that branched off the main alley.

Without a moment's hesitation, we barreled down the narrow passage, only to find ourselves standing before a towering wall, a dead end looming ominously in front of us. My heart sank, a mixture of disbelief and anger bubbling inside me.

"This can't be happening," I muttered, scanning the area for any sign of escape.

Liam's eyes darted around, searching for clues. "He must have doubled back. We need to get to the other side of the wall. There might be an exit!"

I nodded, but the moment of urgency shifted as I noticed a figure emerging from the shadows. It was the thief, but not alone. He was flanked by two other men, their faces obscured by the dark. My breath caught in my throat as the realization hit—this was a setup.

"Run!" Liam shouted, his voice slicing through the tension, but it was too late. Before we could react, the men surged forward, surrounding us, their intentions clear and menacing.

My heart pounded, a mix of fear and adrenaline fueling my instincts. In a heartbeat, our world of art and ambition had transformed into something far more sinister, and as the darkness closed in around us, I understood that this chase was far from over.

Chapter 3: The Hidden Canvas

The air was thick with the scent of turpentine and old wood as I stepped into the dimly lit gallery, a world where colors danced and shadows whispered secrets. The flickering lights above seemed to spotlight the chaos of unfinished dreams hanging on the walls, their edges curling like autumn leaves. Each canvas beckoned with stories waiting to be told, but the one that had ensnared my focus was hidden in a back room, obscured behind a thick velvet curtain, as if it were holding its breath, waiting for the right moment to be revealed.

Liam's presence next to me was electric, a current I hadn't anticipated. He moved with a grace that was both confident and cautious, like a lion stalking its prey. I felt my heart thump loudly against my ribcage, a rhythmic reminder of the tension simmering between us. "Do you think it's true?" he asked, his voice a low rumble that vibrated through the silence. "That the artist left behind clues in their work?"

I turned to him, trying to gauge his mood beneath the façade of cool indifference he often wore. His dark hair fell over his forehead, and I resisted the urge to reach out and brush it aside. "I don't know, but if it is true, we need to find out." The words came out sharper than I intended, a reflection of the frustration building inside me.

Liam's expression shifted; the mask cracked just enough for me to catch a glimpse of something softer. "You're quite stubborn, you know that?" he replied, a teasing smile tugging at the corners of his lips. I rolled my eyes, but I could feel the corners of my mouth betraying me, lifting in response to his charm.

As we approached the back room, the sound of our footsteps echoed against the marble floor, mingling with the distant murmur of the city outside. I paused before the heavy curtain, heart racing, feeling like I was about to step into an unknown realm. "Ready?" I whispered, half-excited and half-terrified.

Liam nodded, his gaze steady, and together we parted the fabric, stepping into the dark. The room was filled with the kind of stillness that wrapped around you like a heavy quilt, the kind that makes you think too much. And then, amidst the gloom, I spotted it: the hidden canvas, half-shrouded in shadow, its surface glimmering like a treasure waiting to be unearthed.

"Wow," I breathed, stepping closer. The painting was unlike anything I had ever seen, colors swirling in a tempest of emotions—fiery reds, cool blues, and gentle greens intertwined in an intricate dance. "It's beautiful."

Liam's shoulder brushed against mine as he leaned in, his breath warm against my ear. "What do you see?" he asked, his voice barely above a whisper.

I squinted at the canvas, trying to peel back the layers. "It's chaotic, but there's something... deliberate about it. Like it's trying to tell a story." I looked at him, searching for confirmation. "Do you see it?"

He nodded slowly, and for a moment, the gallery faded away, leaving just the two of us, cocooned in our own world of possibilities. "It's like a puzzle," he said. "Maybe each color represents a different emotion, and the way they intersect could mean something more."

My heart raced at the idea, an electric thrill coursing through me. "If we can figure out the emotions, we might unlock the mystery behind the theft." The thought sent shivers of excitement down my spine. The tension between us was palpable, a mix of ambition and something else I couldn't quite name.

As we examined the painting, our shoulders brushed more frequently, each touch igniting a spark that made it harder to focus. I felt as if I were stepping into uncharted territory, and every brush of his arm sent my mind swirling in directions I hadn't anticipated. It was a dizzying sensation, one that was both thrilling and disconcerting.

"There's something here," I said suddenly, pointing at a particularly vibrant patch of color. "This red looks different from the rest. It's almost as if it's trying to break free." I glanced up at Liam, finding him studying my face with an intensity that made my heart skip a beat.

"Maybe that's the key," he murmured, leaning closer. "What if that represents the artist's pain or passion? Perhaps it was meant to draw attention." His eyes locked onto mine, and for a moment, I lost my train of thought, drowning in the depths of his gaze. The urge to reach out, to touch him, was overwhelming, but I forced myself to pull away.

"Let's not get distracted," I said, shaking my head as if to clear the haze that had enveloped me. "We need to focus on what this painting means."

Liam chuckled softly, a rich sound that reverberated through the silence. "Oh, but it's hard not to get distracted when you're standing this close." The teasing tone in his voice sent a ripple of warmth through me, and I shot him a playful glare, attempting to mask the flutter of my heart.

"Focus," I insisted, trying to suppress a smile. "Let's uncover this mystery before we end up discussing our feelings over a glass of wine."

The moment hung in the air, thick with unspoken words and hidden truths, and as we delved deeper into the meaning of the canvas, I began to realize that this investigation was peeling back layers not only of the art but also of us. With each moment spent together, I was torn between my lingering animosity and an undeniable attraction that twisted my insides. The tension escalated, weaving an intricate web that ensnared us both, drawing us closer to a truth I was both eager and afraid to discover.

A heavy silence enveloped the hidden canvas as we stood, our breaths mingling in the dim light, creating a tension that was almost tangible. I felt as though I were standing on the precipice of something extraordinary, both exhilarating and terrifying. The vibrant colors seemed to pulse with life, each stroke of the brush whispering secrets only we could unlock. I leaned in closer, losing myself in the swirling patterns, while the world outside faded into an indistinct blur.

"Look at this," I said, my voice barely a murmur. I pointed at a delicate swirl of gold that curled through the chaos, its brilliance a stark contrast to the darker hues surrounding it. "This part feels almost like a heartbeat, doesn't it?"

Liam stepped closer, the warmth radiating from him seeping into my skin. "Or a pulse of inspiration," he replied, his eyes narrowing thoughtfully. "It's as if the artist was trying to convey something precious amidst the turmoil." His tone held a reverence that made me glance up, capturing a fleeting moment where I could see his admiration for the art transforming into something more profound—an admiration for the artist themselves.

"Then maybe we should figure out who that artist is," I suggested, the words slipping out before I could rein in my eagerness. The thrill of the chase ignited something deep within me, overshadowing the wariness that usually accompanied my interactions with him.

"Agreed." His smile was conspiratorial, igniting a spark of camaraderie between us. "But if we're going to play detectives, we need a plan."

I raised an eyebrow, unable to suppress the smirk creeping onto my lips. "Are you suggesting I follow your lead? I thought we were supposed to be working together."

"Ah, but you see," he replied, a playful glint in his eyes, "you might be better off letting me take the lead. I have a knack for sniffing out hidden meanings."

"Is that so?" I shot back, crossing my arms in mock defiance. "And here I thought you were just a pretty face."

He laughed, a rich sound that echoed in the intimate space, and the tension between us shifted once more, morphing into something lighter. "I can be both, you know. Don't underestimate the power of a pretty face."

I rolled my eyes, but beneath the banter, I felt an undeniable pull towards him, a warmth that crept into my heart. We were caught in an intriguing dance, where each quip and glance held a deeper meaning, leading us into an unexplored territory laden with unspoken feelings.

As we turned our focus back to the canvas, I couldn't shake the realization that this hidden gem held more than just clues to a theft; it was also a mirror reflecting the complicated layers of our dynamic. I leaned in, letting my fingers graze the edge of the canvas, as if touching it could awaken the artist's spirit and unlock the riddles buried within.

"Do you think the artist intended for us to find this?" I mused, my fingers lingering on the fabric as if it could offer answers. "Or is it just a coincidence?"

"Coincidence seems unlikely," Liam replied, his voice low and thoughtful. "Great art rarely hides without purpose. Maybe it's a breadcrumb leading us somewhere."

My heart raced at the thought. "Then let's follow it."

Liam straightened, a glimmer of mischief lighting his eyes. "Now that's the spirit. But first, we should probably document our findings. If this is connected to the theft, we'll need proof."

As we fumbled for our phones, the atmosphere around us shifted once more. I snapped a few pictures of the canvas, each click of the shutter echoing my growing excitement. This was more than just an investigation; it was a thrilling adventure, a chance to step outside the confines of my usual life.

"Look at you," Liam teased, leaning against the wall with a playful smirk. "You're positively glowing."

"Maybe it's the lighting," I retorted, unable to hide my grin. "Or maybe it's the art."

"Or maybe it's just me," he shot back, a self-assured grin dancing on his lips.

I rolled my eyes again, but inside, I was secretly delighted. We were slipping into a rhythm that felt both exhilarating and terrifying. Beneath the teasing, I sensed the weight of something deeper—a burgeoning connection that shimmered like the gold in the canvas, promising to intertwine our fates.

"Alright, Mr. Detective, what's next?" I asked, tucking my phone away as I faced him, ready for whatever chaos awaited us.

Liam's expression turned serious, his brow furrowing in thought. "We need to research the artist. If there are clues hidden in the work, understanding their background might help us."

"Good idea. But how do we even begin?"

He crossed his arms, an exaggerated pose of contemplation. "Well, we could always start by looking for their previous works or exhibitions. If this piece is significant, it might have been displayed somewhere."

"Let's see if there's an artist registry or maybe a gallery archive," I suggested, my mind racing as I tried to outline our next steps. "There's bound to be something that connects them to this painting."

Liam nodded, his focus sharpening as he pulled out his phone. "Let's split up and meet back here in an hour? That way, we can cover more ground."

"Split up?" I echoed, feigning horror. "Are you sure you can handle being away from my dazzling presence for that long?"

He laughed, his eyes sparkling with mischief. "I might manage, but I'll need a photo of your dazzling presence for motivation."

"Fine, but only if you promise to send me a selfie in return."

"Deal." He grinned, his confidence radiating like the sun, and I couldn't help but feel a thrill at the prospect of delving deeper into this adventure with him.

As we parted ways, the anticipation coursing through me was almost palpable. The gallery, once a mere collection of art pieces, transformed into a labyrinth of mysteries waiting to be unraveled. With every step, I felt the weight of the canvas behind me, its colors pulsing in time with my heart, urging me to discover the truth hidden in the chaos of both art and life.

The thrill of the chase lingered in the air as I stepped into the bright morning sun, leaving behind the musty shadows of the gallery. My heart raced with the adrenaline of our little adventure, and I couldn't shake the feeling that I was on the verge of something extraordinary. The city sprawled before me, a tapestry of life and color, vibrant yet chaotic—much like the canvas we had just uncovered.

With my phone clutched in one hand, I navigated the bustling streets, feeling a renewed sense of purpose. My mind raced with possibilities, all tangled up with thoughts of Liam. His playful banter echoed in my ears, stirring something deep within me that I had tried to ignore. Each word we exchanged seemed to peel back another layer of his guarded persona, revealing glimpses of vulnerability I hadn't expected.

As I approached a quaint café, the aroma of freshly brewed coffee wafted through the air, beckoning me to pause. I stepped inside, the bell above the door jingling softly, and found a cozy nook by the window, the perfect spot for a quick brainstorming session. I ordered a steaming latte and pulled out my laptop, ready to dive into the research that might unravel the mysteries surrounding the hidden canvas.

Between sips of my drink, I typed frantically, scanning through online archives and art databases. The name of the artist remained elusive, like a whisper lost in a crowded room. Frustration bubbled beneath my surface. "Come on, give me something," I muttered to myself, tapping my fingers against the table.

Just as I was about to give up, a link caught my eye—an old interview with an artist who once exhibited alongside the elusive painter. My heart raced as I clicked through, devouring every word. The article revealed the artist's tumultuous history, marred by scandal and passion, but also hinted at a secret series of works inspired by a lost love, a detail that sent shivers down my spine.

"Lost love," I whispered to myself, the words tasting bitter on my tongue. I wondered if this artist had poured their heart into the canvas we discovered, and if that heartbreak was somehow woven into its colors.

Lost in thought, I didn't notice the shadow looming over my table until I looked up. Liam stood there, a half-smirk plastered on his face, his presence commanding the room. "What's the verdict? Have you cracked the case yet?"

I shot him an amused look. "If I could crack the case over coffee, I'd be out of a job. But I think I'm onto something."

"Is that a promise or a threat?" he quipped, sliding into the seat across from me.

"Depends on how you define 'something,'" I replied, trying to keep my tone light while my heart raced. "I found an interview with someone who knew the artist. It seems there was a scandal involving a lost love, which might explain some of the emotions in that painting."

"Scandals and lost loves," he mused, leaning in closer. "Now that's a narrative worth digging into. What else did they say?"

I leaned forward, excited to share the details. "It mentioned a series of secret works, hidden away because the artist didn't want anyone to know about their personal turmoil. If we can find out more about those works, it might lead us to the answers we need."

Liam's eyes sparkled with mischief. "And here I thought you were just a pretty face, but it turns out you're a detective with a nose for scandal. I might need to start taking notes."

I rolled my eyes, but the compliment warmed me. "Well, if you're going to take notes, you should probably write down how charming I am, too."

"Noted," he said with a wink, his gaze lingering on mine, the atmosphere thickening with unspoken tension.

Before I could respond, my phone buzzed, breaking the moment. I glanced at the screen and felt a jolt of excitement. It was an email from a local gallery I had contacted, offering insights into the artist's past. "This could be it," I said, my pulse quickening.

As I opened the email, however, my heart sank. The gallery informed me that they had only a limited amount of information on the artist but suggested I speak to an elderly curator who might know more. "Of course, it's always the elusive person who holds the key," I said, frustration creeping into my voice.

"Sounds like a classic case of needing to shake the tree until the ripe fruit falls," Liam suggested, his tone encouraging. "Where do we find this curator?"

"According to the email, she's at an old gallery downtown," I replied, scanning the message again. "I'll need to call ahead, see if she's available. It could be a shot in the dark, but we don't have much to lose."

"Then let's make the call," Liam said, his confidence infectious.

I dialed the number, the anticipation thickening as the line rang. The sound echoed through the café, mingling with the clatter of cups and chatter of patrons. After a few rings, a voice answered, warm yet slightly crackled with age. I introduced myself and explained the reason for my call, hoping the curator would be as enthusiastic about the artist as I was.

"Ah, the artist you seek," the curator said, her voice soft but firm. "A complex soul, indeed. The lost love you mention is intertwined with his work like shadows in the twilight. You'll want to come by—perhaps today?"

"Yes! That would be incredible," I said, unable to hide my excitement.

"Very well. Just ask for me when you arrive. But be warned, my dear, not all shadows wish to be uncovered," she replied cryptically before hanging up.

I exchanged a wide-eyed glance with Liam. "That was... intriguing," I said, trying to decipher the curator's words.

"Not all shadows wish to be uncovered?" he echoed, a frown creasing his brow. "Sounds like she knows more than she's letting on."

"Or maybe she's just trying to add a bit of drama to our detective story," I said, my heart racing with both excitement and apprehension.

"Either way, we should take it seriously," Liam replied, his tone shifting. "This could lead us closer to the truth—or deeper into the mystery."

As we left the café, the sunlight felt almost electric against my skin, illuminating the path ahead. The city buzzed around us, its pulse quickening in time with my own.

"I can't shake the feeling that we're on the edge of something big," I said, glancing at Liam, whose expression mirrored my thoughts—intensity mixed with a hint of excitement.

"Let's get to this curator," he urged, taking my hand unexpectedly, the warmth of his grip sending a jolt through me. "We'll uncover the truth together."

But as we approached the gallery, the air shifted once more, a weight settling in my stomach. A sense of foreboding crept in, whispering of danger lurking just beyond the bright facade. The doors loomed ahead, inviting yet ominous, and as I reached for the handle, a chilling thought struck me.

What if the secrets hidden in the shadows were not just about the artist? What if they were about us?

Just then, a figure darted past, cloaked in a dark coat, their face obscured. My heart raced as I turned to follow, but the figure vanished around the corner, leaving only a lingering sense of dread.

"Did you see that?" I asked, breathless, my voice trembling.

Liam's grip on my hand tightened. "Yeah, I did. Let's find out what's going on."

But as we stepped inside the gallery, the atmosphere shifted, the air crackling with tension. I couldn't shake the feeling that whatever was waiting for us inside was going to change everything.

Chapter 4: Shadows of the Past

The rain drummed against the windows, a relentless rhythm that echoed the turmoil stirring within me. It had been a week since Liam and I first ventured into the dimly lit library, where dusty tomes whispered secrets of the past. The air was thick with the scent of old paper and leather, a comforting reminder of lives once lived, yet now distant and forgotten. Each turn of the page felt like peeling back layers of a mystery, a puzzle whose pieces were scattered in the recesses of time. But today, there was a heaviness that settled between us, a silent acknowledgment of the weight he carried, one that pressed against my heart like the humid air of a summer storm.

As I shuffled through the worn volumes, my fingers brushed against the spine of a particularly tattered book. Liam stood across from me, arms crossed, his gaze fixed on the window as though the rain held answers he was too afraid to seek. There was a distance in his eyes that tugged at my curiosity and concern alike. I had seen that look before—like a man wrestling with ghosts of a life that no longer existed. The soft glow of the reading lamp illuminated the sharp angles of his face, casting shadows that danced along his cheekbones, revealing the turmoil that swirled beneath the surface.

"Liam," I ventured, my voice barely rising above the rain's symphony. "What are you thinking about?"

He turned to me, and for a moment, I saw something flicker behind his guarded demeanor. A storm brewing beneath the calm surface. "Just... the past," he replied, his voice low and gravelly, like the rumble of thunder in the distance. "You know how it is."

I nodded, although I didn't. My own past was a tapestry of laughter and heartache, stitched together with memories of summer nights and stolen kisses. But Liam's history felt like a gaping chasm, something so profound and dark that I hesitated to peer too deeply.

Yet I couldn't resist the pull, the urge to reach out and hold the fragments of his shattered world.

"I can't help but feel there's more to it," I said, my tone gentle but insistent. "You don't have to share if you're not ready, but... I'm here."

His expression shifted, the walls around him cracking just enough for vulnerability to seep through. He took a breath, a long, measured inhale that seemed to draw in the weight of his memories. "It's about my brother," he confessed, his voice trembling slightly as if the name itself were a fragile thing. "He died in a car accident a few years back. A stupid mistake that cost him everything. And me too."

The revelation hung in the air, heavy and raw, as if the rain outside had turned into a tangible weight pressing against my chest. I wanted to reach out, to comfort him, but I sensed the fragile nature of the moment. The way he spoke, as if each word was laced with the pain of loss, left me yearning to understand the depths of his sorrow.

"I'm so sorry," I said, my heart aching for him. "That must have been devastating."

"It was," he admitted, his gaze now fixed on the floor, as though searching for something lost. "I didn't handle it well. I buried myself in work, pushed everyone away. It felt easier to pretend I was fine."

His honesty disarmed me, and I felt a surge of protectiveness—a desire to shield him from the ghosts that haunted his thoughts. "You're not alone, Liam. I'm here, and I want to help you carry this."

For a moment, our eyes locked, a silent understanding passing between us. I sensed the flicker of hope beneath his guarded exterior, the possibility that he might let someone in, even if just a little. But then the shadows crept back, and I could see the doubt clouding his features.

"I don't know if I can," he murmured, almost to himself, the rain outside intensifying, drowning out our conversation. "It feels like the past is always lurking, waiting to pull me back under."

As he spoke, a shiver ran down my spine. It wasn't just the memory of his brother that loomed large; there was something else—an invisible presence that watched us from the corners of the room, an uninvited guest that felt all too real. I scanned the dimly lit library, the shelves casting elongated shadows that danced like specters in the flickering light. The feeling that someone was watching us gripped me, an instinctual awareness that set my heart racing.

"Do you ever feel like... someone's following you?" I asked, the words tumbling out before I could hold them back.

Liam's eyes darted to the door, then back to me, uncertainty mingling with concern. "You mean like now? I thought it was just me being paranoid."

"No," I said, my pulse quickening. "I feel it too. Something's off. It's like there's a weight in the air, a presence lurking just beyond the edge of our vision."

He straightened, a sudden tension radiating from him. "What do you think it is?"

"I don't know," I admitted, the hair on my arms prickling as I leaned closer. "But I don't think it's just your past we need to worry about. I think it's something darker."

Liam nodded slowly, the shift in the atmosphere palpable. "We should keep our guard up. I don't want to put you in danger."

I held his gaze, my resolve solidifying. "I'm not afraid. I want to face whatever this is—with you."

For the first time, I saw a flicker of something—admiration? Gratitude?—in his eyes, and it warmed me against the chill of uncertainty. The past might have shaped us, but it was the shadows of the present that threatened to consume us both, and together, we would confront whatever lurked in the darkness.

The air crackled with an uneasy tension as we stood in the half-lit library, the rain beating a chaotic rhythm against the windows. The muted sounds outside echoed the turmoil inside me, and for the first time, I felt the weight of our shared vulnerability settle like a mantle over my shoulders. I shifted closer to Liam, wanting to bridge the distance, to assure him that he was not alone in his grief—or in whatever shadow was haunting us now.

"You know," I said, attempting to lighten the mood, "if this were a mystery novel, we'd probably find a secret door behind one of these shelves, leading to a hidden treasure or a cryptic clue." My attempt at humor hung awkwardly between us, but I was determined to coax a smile from him.

He chuckled softly, the sound surprisingly melodic. "Or an angry ghost that just wants to be left alone," he replied, his lips curling into a grin that made the corners of his eyes crinkle in a way I found utterly charming.

"That, too," I said, rolling my eyes in mock exasperation. "Though I must say, I prefer the treasure idea. Ghosts are a bit overrated, don't you think?"

"Depends on the ghost," he shot back, leaning against a nearby bookshelf, the weight of his past momentarily lifted by our banter. "Some are more entertaining than others."

"Like the one that haunts my old high school?" I ventured, diving into a recollection that had lingered in the recesses of my mind. "Legend has it that a jilted prom queen still roams the halls, desperately searching for her lost date."

Liam raised an eyebrow, feigning disbelief. "And how exactly does one become a ghost with unfinished prom business? Is there a haunting manual for that?"

"Absolutely. Chapter One: How to make an unforgettable exit," I said, punctuating my words with a dramatic flourish. "I can lend you my copy if you'd like."

Liam's laughter rang through the dim room, a sound that felt like sunlight breaking through a storm. For a moment, we were just two people in a dusty library, caught in a web of light-hearted teasing, momentarily forgetting the shadows lurking in the corners of our minds.

But that moment of levity was fleeting. As the laughter faded, I noticed the tension return to Liam's shoulders, the shadows creeping back into his eyes. I hesitated, weighing my options. "We can keep talking about ghosts, or we can delve into the depths of what you're feeling. Your choice."

"Let's go with the ghost," he said, but his voice was tinged with reluctance, a faint crack in the bravado he wore so well.

The urge to push him deeper was strong, but I understood that the walls he'd built were not easily torn down. Instead, I leaned back against the shelf beside him, letting the silence stretch comfortably between us.

Time slipped away as we lost ourselves in the ambiance of the library, the soft patter of the rain providing an unexpected soundtrack to our stillness. I could feel the warmth radiating from Liam, and it enveloped me, creating a cocoon that momentarily shielded us from the world outside. But that cocoon was fragile, and it didn't take long for the haunting unease to return.

"What if," I began tentatively, breaking the silence, "we go out for coffee? You know, to escape the shadows of the past? Maybe a little caffeine can drown out the ghosts."

Liam looked at me, the corner of his mouth quirking up, but the weariness in his eyes didn't wane. "You really think a cup of coffee is going to make my past disappear?"

"Not disappear, no," I replied, my voice soft yet playful. "But it could give you the energy to deal with it. And, you know, a bit of caffeine-induced courage can work wonders."

"Courage, huh?" He ran a hand through his hair, the tension in his jaw easing just slightly. "And what if I need more than just courage?"

"Then I'll buy you a second cup. And a pastry, because no one can face their demons on an empty stomach." I nudged him playfully. "Besides, I make an excellent coffee date."

His laughter returned, this time more genuine, and a spark flickered in his eyes. "You might just be right. All right, let's find that coffee. But if the ghosts show up, you're the one who's going to have to deal with them."

"Deal," I agreed, feigning confidence. "Just don't let them talk about their prom dates. It's too painful."

We made our way out of the library, the door creaking ominously as it swung open, as if the shadows were bidding us farewell. The rain had tapered off, leaving behind a crispness in the air that felt invigorating. Stepping into the world beyond the library was like peeling away a layer of dampness that had clung to my skin.

The café down the street was a cozy spot, with rustic wooden tables and the rich aroma of freshly brewed coffee enveloping us like a warm hug. As we entered, the barista greeted us with a bright smile, her energy infectious as she expertly crafted drinks behind the counter.

"What can I get for you two?" she asked, glancing between us.

"Two coffees, please," I replied, then leaned closer to Liam, lowering my voice as if sharing a secret. "And a pastry. Something decadent."

Liam smirked, clearly amused. "You're really committed to this pastry plan, aren't you?"

"Absolutely," I said, my eyes gleaming. "It's part of my strategy to win you over. Nothing says 'trust me' like a chocolate croissant."

"Touché," he conceded, nodding in agreement.

As we settled into a corner booth, I took a moment to observe him. The way he looked at the café's ambiance with a mixture of wonder and caution made my heart ache. He seemed like a man caught between worlds, grappling with the heaviness of the past while longing for the sweetness of the present.

"What's your favorite pastry?" I asked, wanting to steer the conversation back to something lighter.

"Definitely the lemon tarts," he said, his expression softening. "Something about the tanginess balances out the sweetness of life. It reminds me that even the bitter can have its place."

I tilted my head, intrigued by his perspective. "So you're saying we need both the sweet and the sour to make sense of things?"

"Exactly. Without one, the other doesn't stand out." He leaned back, the tension in his posture slowly ebbing away. "It's all about balance."

"Wise words from the ghost of a pastry lover," I teased, raising my coffee cup in a mock toast. "To the lemon tarts of life!"

"To the lemon tarts," he echoed, laughter dancing in his eyes.

As we settled into a comfortable rhythm, the worries of the outside world faded into the background. Our conversations flowed easily, peppered with playful banter and moments of genuine connection. I could see the flicker of light returning to Liam's eyes, a softening of his features that made me ache for him in ways I didn't fully understand.

But even amidst the warmth, a nagging feeling pulled at the edges of my consciousness. We were not just two people seeking refuge in coffee and pastries; we were standing at the precipice of something deeper. And as much as I wanted to forget the shadows lurking in the corners, I knew they would eventually catch up with us, demanding to be faced.

But for now, I would savor this moment, wrapped in the sweetness of our shared laughter and the comforting presence of someone who, despite his shadows, felt increasingly like home.

The café buzzed with the gentle hum of conversation and the clinking of cups, an inviting backdrop that enveloped Liam and me like a warm blanket on a cold day. I could feel the undercurrent of excitement between us, the spark of connection that ignited each time we locked eyes. His laughter was intoxicating, and with every shared smile, I could sense the shadows of his past lifting, if only for a moment.

"Okay, but you can't just say 'lemon tart' and leave it at that," I urged, leaning forward with a conspiratorial glint in my eyes. "What's the story behind your obsession with them? Was there a pivotal lemon tart moment in your life?"

Liam chuckled, his fingers absently tracing the rim of his coffee cup. "It's a long story, and I'm not sure I want to divulge my culinary confessions just yet."

"Come on! It's a perfect opportunity to bond," I pressed, feigning a dramatic pout. "If you tell me, I promise to reveal my secret pastry shame."

He regarded me for a moment, his brows furrowed in thought, then he let out a resigned sigh, as if resigning to a fate he couldn't escape. "Fine. But you better have something good to share in return. It all began at my brother's wedding. I was tasked with making the dessert for the reception. Spoiler alert: I am not a baker."

"Oh, this is going to be good," I said, leaning in, eager for the details.

"I thought I could wing it. How hard could it be? I had seen countless cooking shows. I made the lemon tarts from scratch, and let me tell you, they were the most hideous little things you could imagine. The crust crumbled, the filling was too tart, and somehow, I managed to set the oven on fire."

"No!" I gasped, nearly choking on my sip of coffee. "You're telling me you nearly burned down your brother's wedding?"

"Exactly! But my brother and his fiancée laughed it off, claiming it added character to the event. They dubbed it 'The Great Lemon Tart Disaster,' and it became an inside joke within the family. After that, every time I'd bring lemon tarts to family gatherings, it would turn into a competition of sorts—who could make the best, most outrageous lemon tart. It's ridiculous, really."

I could see a glimmer of nostalgia in his eyes, a rare and beautiful thing that warmed my heart. "That sounds like a wonderful memory. It's the kind of thing that makes family gatherings memorable."

"Yeah, well, they also make for plenty of embarrassment," he admitted, shaking his head with a smile. "But it taught me to laugh at myself and not take life too seriously, you know?"

"Absolutely," I replied, savoring the moment. "Life's too short to be serious all the time. Speaking of which, it's your turn to confess."

Liam's brow arched, and a teasing smile curled on his lips. "Oh, you don't want to hear my shame. Mine involves a very unfortunate run-in with a pie and a school dance."

"Please, enlighten me!" I urged, leaning forward, completely invested.

With mock seriousness, he began, "It was the eighth grade, and I thought I was hot stuff for making a cherry pie. I decided to impress my crush by bringing it to the dance. Naturally, I tripped on my way in, and the pie went flying into the principal's face."

I burst into laughter, imagining the scene, the chaos of cherry filling splattering everywhere. "Oh my god, what did you do?"

"Let's just say my crush didn't go out with me after that, and I was known as 'The Pie Guy' for the rest of the year," he said, shaking his head, clearly amused at the memory. "What about you? What's your pastry shame?"

"Mine is not as glorious, I assure you. My mom decided to have me bake cookies for my sister's birthday party. I took it upon myself to 'innovate' and added way too much baking soda. The cookies were like little rocks. I ended up claiming they were 'crunchy' and sold them to the neighborhood kids as 'gourmet.'"

Liam burst into laughter, the kind that echoed across the café and drew curious glances from nearby tables. "You little entrepreneur! I admire your creativity."

"Hey, a girl's gotta do what a girl's gotta do!" I replied, my cheeks flushed with embarrassment and joy. In that moment, surrounded by the warmth of our shared laughter, I felt an unspoken bond between us solidify, a connection woven through our vulnerabilities and lighthearted confessions.

As the conversation flowed, I glanced out the café window. The sky was beginning to darken, ominous clouds rolling in like a silent threat. The rain had returned, but it was the sudden chill in the air that set off alarm bells in my mind. It felt as if the atmosphere shifted, a prelude to something I couldn't quite grasp.

"Hey, let's grab those pastries to go," I suggested, my unease creeping back. "I think we might need to hightail it out of here before the storm hits."

"Good call," Liam agreed, though his brow creased with concern. "You okay? You seem... off."

"Just feeling a little paranoid," I admitted, forcing a smile to reassure him. "Maybe it's the caffeine or the rain. It can be a little unsettling, can't it?"

"Yeah, it definitely has that effect sometimes," he said, though I could tell he was still searching my face for signs of deeper distress.

We approached the counter, and I ordered a couple of pastries, while Liam insisted on paying. "It's the least I can do after dragging you into my pastry confessions," he insisted with a charming grin.

As we stepped back outside, the rain began to fall heavier, and a sharp wind whipped around us, making me shiver. "Let's hurry," I said, pulling my coat tighter around me. "I'd rather not become drenched like a pair of soggy pastries."

We hurried down the street, the familiar path leading us back toward the library. But as we walked, I couldn't shake the feeling of being watched. It was an itch at the back of my mind, a disquieting awareness that something—or someone—was lurking just beyond my line of sight.

"Do you ever get the feeling that someone's watching you?" I asked, trying to sound casual, but my heart raced in rhythm with my words.

Liam glanced around, his expression shifting from amusement to concern. "Honestly? I've had that feeling since we left the library. It's probably just our imagination, but..."

Before he could finish, a sharp cry pierced the air, followed by a loud crash from a nearby alley. I froze, instinctively grabbing Liam's arm. "Did you hear that?"

His eyes widened, and we shared a glance filled with unspoken dread. Without a word, we moved toward the alley, curiosity battling with instinctive caution. As we approached, the source of the noise came into view—a figure, shrouded in shadows, scrambling to their feet, eyes wide with panic.

"Hey!" I called out, my voice echoing down the alley. "Are you okay?"

The figure spun around, a flash of recognition crossing their face before they turned to flee. I could see it was a woman, her hair wild and matted, her clothes torn as if she had been running for a long time. "No!" she screamed, her voice a frantic wail. "You have to run! He's coming for you!"

My heart thundered in my chest, and I exchanged a look with Liam, a shared understanding igniting between us—this was no longer just about the shadows of his past. Something much darker was closing in on us, and whatever threat this woman spoke of was very real.

Before we could react, a shadow moved behind her, dark and ominous, causing the woman to shriek in terror. I felt every nerve in my body scream for us to run, but instead, I stood frozen, my instincts torn between fear and the urge to help.

"Wait!" Liam shouted, stepping forward, but it was too late. The woman turned and fled into the night, leaving behind a swirling fog of anxiety that clung to the air like a storm cloud, heavy with impending dread.

Then, from the darkness of the alley, the figure stepped into the light, revealing a face I had never expected to see. A face I recognized from my own past—someone who had been a ghost in my life long before I ever met Liam. And with that recognition came a wave of cold fear that threatened to swallow me whole.

Chapter 5: Unearthed Secrets

The dim light of the living room flickered over the worn wooden table, casting long shadows that danced across the scattered newspaper articles and aged sketches. Each fragile page, yellowed with time, whispered secrets of a world long gone, a world entwined with the recent theft of a precious painting that had vanished from the city's most prestigious gallery. My fingers trembled slightly as I traced the headline of one article: "Masterpiece Disappears: Theories Abound." It felt as though the words were beckoning us deeper into the mystery, inviting us to unearth the truth hidden beneath layers of intrigue.

Across from me, Liam was engrossed in a faded sketch that depicted a hauntingly familiar silhouette. The soft glow from the lamp illuminated his furrowed brow, casting an air of determination around him. We had begun this investigation as reluctant partners, each of us driven by a fierce need to prove ourselves. But the more we unraveled the threads of this tangled web, the more I realized that our rivalry had morphed into something altogether different, a tension that crackled like static in the air.

"Look at this," he said, his voice low, filled with an urgency that snapped my attention back to him. He turned the sketch toward me, revealing a meticulous drawing of a warehouse, its edges curling as if the paper itself were reluctant to reveal its hidden depths. "This matches the location mentioned in another article—a hub for art smuggling. It's not just about the painting; it's much bigger than we thought."

I leaned closer, the intoxicating scent of his cologne mingling with the musty odor of old paper and ink. My heart raced, not just from the thrill of discovery but from the awareness of Liam's proximity. "So, we're talking organized crime now?" I asked, trying to keep my tone steady despite the fluttering in my chest.

"Seems that way," he replied, meeting my gaze with an intensity that made my breath hitch. "We need to check it out. Tonight."

"Tonight?" The word slipped from my lips, thick with disbelief. "You can't be serious. We're talking about a potentially dangerous operation. What if—"

"Exactly," he interrupted, leaning forward, his dark hair falling into his eyes, creating an almost boyish charm despite the gravity of the situation. "What if? We need to find out what we're dealing with. If we sit around here, we'll never know."

He had a point. Curiosity mingled with a sense of urgency gnawed at my insides. The painting, once a mere piece of art, had morphed into a symbol of everything I was fighting against—corruption, deception, and a world where the innocent were collateral damage. With a reluctant sigh, I nodded, a mixture of adrenaline and dread coursing through me.

As we gathered our things, the tension hung in the air like a taut wire, ready to snap at any moment. We slipped out into the night, the chill wrapping around us like a shroud. The city, usually bustling with life, felt eerily quiet as we made our way to the warehouse district. Streetlights cast harsh halos against the pavement, illuminating the remnants of a world too consumed by shadows to notice our small, determined figures weaving through the darkness.

When we finally reached the warehouse, a sprawling structure that loomed like a beast against the moonlit sky, I felt a thrill of fear tangle with excitement. The building was unremarkable from the outside, its weather-beaten façade punctuated by broken windows and rusted metal doors, but something whispered to me that within those walls lay answers—or perhaps danger.

"Stay close," Liam murmured, and for the first time, I noticed the tension in his voice, the hint of uncertainty beneath his bravado.

We approached a side door, its surface marred by peeling paint. I pressed my ear against it, listening intently, and could hear muffled voices on the other side, an argument unfolding like a poorly scripted play. The cadence of their voices escalated, punctuated by harsh words that sliced through the air.

"—we need to move it tonight! If they find out we still have it—"

"No! We're not selling it to them. Not after what they did. It's too risky!"

A shiver ran down my spine at the implications of their conversation. I glanced at Liam, his eyes wide with realization. This was it—the connection we had been searching for. We exchanged a quick, charged glance, the heat of the moment igniting something deeper within me, something I had been trying to ignore.

"Are you ready?" he whispered, his breath brushing against my ear, sending a rush of warmth through me.

"Ready as I'll ever be," I replied, forcing a smile, though inside, I felt like a novice adventurer standing at the edge of a cliff, ready to leap into the unknown.

We pushed the door open slightly, just enough to glimpse the interior. The dimly lit space revealed a chaotic scene: crates stacked haphazardly, shadows flitting across the walls, and in the center, two masked figures were locked in a heated argument. The tension was palpable, and I could see the flicker of a painting's edge peeking out from one of the crates, taunting us with its proximity.

Suddenly, the door creaked louder than intended, and their heads snapped toward us. In an instant, the argument was forgotten as chaos erupted.

"Get them!" one shouted, and before I could react, Liam had yanked me back, his body pressing against mine as we ducked behind a crate. My heart raced, adrenaline surging through me as I realized how close we were to being caught.

"Stay down!" he hissed, and I could feel the warmth radiating from him, a stark contrast to the chill of fear coursing through my veins.

Our eyes locked, and in that brief moment, the world faded away. The chaos of the warehouse dissolved into an electric tension, a magnetism that drew us together despite the circumstances. It was as if time had paused, allowing us to explore the uncharted territory between us—a fierce rivalry transformed into something more complex, layered with urgency and desire.

"Liam," I breathed, my voice barely above a whisper, but it was too late. The moment shattered as the masked figures approached, their footsteps echoing ominously against the concrete floor.

With a surge of instinct, Liam pulled me closer, our bodies pressing together as he shielded me from view. The heat of his body against mine ignited an undeniable spark, and in that instant, everything shifted. The danger we faced was real, but so was the connection we were forging—a connection that might just hold the key to our survival.

The chaos swirled around us like a tempest, muffled voices piercing the air with a tense urgency that sent adrenaline surging through my veins. I could feel Liam's breath against my neck, warm and steady, a stark reminder that we were both acutely aware of our predicament. The two masked figures loomed closer, their silhouettes shifting in and out of the flickering shadows. I could barely hear their angry whispers over the rapid thumping of my heart, but I was keenly aware of every heartbeat, every inch of Liam pressed against me.

"We need to move the goods before they find us," one figure snarled, frustration evident in their tone. The other grunted in agreement, scanning the room with an intensity that sent chills down my spine.

I nudged Liam, my voice a frantic whisper. "What do we do? They're going to see us!" The fear in my voice was palpable, laced with an urgency that begged for a plan.

"Just wait," he murmured, his eyes narrowing as he focused on the unfolding scene. "We need to figure out their next move before we make ours."

The masked men were too absorbed in their conversation to notice us. I clung to Liam, and as I did, a strange mixture of fear and excitement ignited something within me, something that twisted and coiled like a spring. Our rivalry had shifted gears, transforming into a partnership steeped in unspoken tension. The idea of us working together was intoxicating, even under the threat of danger.

"What do you think they're planning?" I pressed, inching closer to him as I tried to suppress a shiver that had nothing to do with the chill in the air.

Liam's brow furrowed as he considered the situation. "It sounds like they're about to make a deal—maybe even sell the painting. We can't let that happen."

I nodded, my thoughts racing. The stolen painting had become more than just an object of art; it was a symbol of everything we were fighting against—corruption, greed, and a system that placed profit above integrity. "We have to find a way to stop them," I insisted, a steely resolve hardening in my chest.

Before we could devise a plan, the two figures turned abruptly, their masked faces mere inches from where we crouched. My breath hitched, panic threading through me like a live wire. Just as I thought they would discover us, a loud crash echoed from the far side of the warehouse. The sound reverberated like thunder, momentarily distracting the intruders.

"Go check it out!" one barked, shoving the other in the direction of the noise.

I seized the opportunity. "Now!" I whispered urgently, and without hesitation, I slipped out from our hiding spot. Liam followed closely, moving with a fluidity that belied the danger surrounding us.

We darted toward a row of crates stacked precariously against the far wall, their weathered surfaces providing some cover. I could feel my heart hammering in my chest as I peered over the edge, my breath shallow as I caught sight of the commotion. One of the masked men was fumbling around, clearly shaken, while the other, now alone, was pacing anxiously, glancing back toward us, oblivious to our movements.

"What was that?" he demanded, irritation thick in his voice. "We can't afford to be caught now!"

I exchanged a glance with Liam, my pulse racing at the unspoken plan we both seemed to understand. "We need to create a distraction," he whispered, the corners of his mouth twitching in a smirk that reminded me just how much I loved a good caper.

"Distraction?" I echoed, barely able to suppress a laugh at the audacity of the suggestion. "You mean like throwing a crate or something? Because that's a classic move."

"Yeah, but with a twist," he replied, his eyes glinting mischievously. "On three, we create chaos. Ready?"

"Ready," I affirmed, an exhilarated rush sweeping over me.

"One... two... three!"

As the word left his lips, I flung a nearby crate toward the back of the warehouse. The crash was deafening, a cacophony that echoed like a battle cry. The pacing figure whipped around, confusion etching lines into his masked face.

"Go check it!" he yelled, urgency lacing his voice.

Liam and I seized the moment, darting toward the edge of the room, hearts pounding with a blend of terror and exhilaration. We slipped past the crates, our breaths mingling with the dust that swirled in the air. As we moved further into the warehouse, a nagging thought crept into my mind.

"Do you think we should call the cops?" I asked, a hint of uncertainty creeping into my voice.

"Not yet. We need to know exactly what we're up against first," he replied, his determination unwavering.

Just then, my foot caught on a loose board, and I stumbled, nearly losing my balance. Liam's reflexes were instantaneous; he caught my arm, steadying me with a firm grip that sent a jolt of electricity racing through my body.

"Careful!" he hissed, his eyes wide. "We can't afford to get caught now."

"I know!" I shot back, my voice barely a whisper, but the warmth of his hand on my arm lingered like a brand. "But I didn't sign up for a death wish here, Liam!"

As we inched deeper into the shadows, we found ourselves in a dimly lit room cluttered with art supplies and canvases, their surfaces covered in layers of dust. It was both unsettling and strangely beautiful, an odd juxtaposition of creativity and chaos. The air was heavy with the scent of oil paint and turpentine, a reminder that art was both a passion and a means of crime for these people.

"What if they're storing the painting here?" I murmured, feeling a flicker of hope.

Liam moved closer to a nearby canvas, a larger piece draped with a faded sheet. "Let's find out." With a careful hand, he pulled the sheet aside, revealing a masterpiece that took my breath away.

"This... this isn't the stolen piece," I whispered, marveling at the vibrant colors and meticulous details. It was a breathtaking depiction of a landscape, full of life and emotion, yet it felt oddly out of place amidst the danger surrounding us.

"No, but look at the brushwork," Liam said, his eyes narrowing as he examined the piece. "This artist is renowned for his work with art forgeries. It's possible that they're using this place to create replicas while selling the originals on the black market."

My mind whirled with the implications. "So they're not just stealing; they're creating a whole system around it. It's genius and horrifying all at once."

Just then, a loud crash echoed from outside, the unmistakable sound of metal clanging against concrete. My heart raced as I instinctively moved closer to Liam, who remained calm, assessing the situation with a focused intensity that both soothed and thrilled me.

"We need to get out of here," he said, urgency creeping into his tone.

Before I could respond, the door swung open with a creak, and the two masked figures stumbled into the room, their eyes scanning the shadows with the predatory intensity of wolves on the hunt.

"Where are they?" one demanded, his voice dripping with frustration.

"Damn it!" the other cursed, slamming a fist against the wall. "They can't have gone far. We can't lose that painting!"

With no time to think, I grabbed Liam's arm, my instincts screaming that we needed to move. "This way!" I urged, pulling him toward a narrow side door.

"Wait!" he insisted, but the urgency of the moment propelled us forward. We burst through the door, tumbling into a dimly lit corridor.

As we raced down the hallway, the stakes had never felt higher. I could hear the masked men behind us, their footsteps pounding against the floor like thunder. The thrill of the chase lit a fire within me, blending seamlessly with the electric tension that sparked between us.

"Just a little faster!" Liam urged, glancing back, determination etched into his features.

"Faster?" I gasped, trying to match his pace, my legs burning with exertion. "You make it sound so easy!"

"Just don't look back," he shot back, a playful glint in his eye even amidst the chaos.

And as we tore through the corridor, hearts racing and spirits ignited, it became abundantly clear that this was no ordinary night. Our rivalry, once fraught with tension, had morphed into an exhilarating partnership, filled with unexpected turns and an undeniable chemistry that demanded exploration. In this unpredictable world, where danger lurked at every corner, we were united in our quest—not just for the painting, but for each other.

The narrow corridor twisted ahead of us, dimly lit and filled with an ominous silence that seemed to pulse with every breath. My heart raced not just from the adrenaline of our narrow escape, but also from the electric chemistry crackling between Liam and me. The thrill of being chased mixed with the uncharted territories of our rivalry, leaving me breathless in more ways than one.

"Do you know where you're going?" I panted, struggling to keep pace with him. My mind raced, mapping out every possible route of escape, but the tension clung to the air like a thick fog, clouding my thoughts.

"Not a clue," he admitted with a wry grin, the corner of his mouth twitching as if we were just two kids playing hide-and-seek instead of fleeing potential captors. "But I figure if we keep moving, we'll eventually find a way out."

"Brilliant strategy, Mr. Genius," I replied, trying to keep the panic at bay with sarcasm. "Next time, maybe we'll consult a map before diving headfirst into an art smuggling ring."

He chuckled, a sound that felt like sunlight breaking through the clouds, even in our dire situation. "Maps are overrated. You just have to trust your instincts."

Trusting instincts had landed us in a world of trouble, but I couldn't deny that every moment spent with him sparked something exciting. We turned a corner, and the corridor opened into a larger room, dimly illuminated by the faint glow of flickering lights.

"Okay, this looks promising," Liam whispered, scanning the area. The room was cluttered with canvases, many partially completed or damaged, but they all radiated an aura of creativity—one that clashed starkly with the criminal dealings we were caught up in.

Before we could take a step inside, a loud crash resonated from behind us, followed by the sound of hurried footsteps. "They're right on our tails!" I exclaimed, urgency replacing my earlier bravado.

"Quick! We need to hide!" He gestured toward a stack of crates at the far end of the room, and we sprinted towards them, ducking behind the stacked wood just as the door swung open.

A moment later, two masked figures entered, their body language tense as they scanned the space. I peered through a gap between the crates, my breath hitching in my throat as I caught a glimpse of one of them. His eyes darted around, restless, as if searching for any sign of us.

"Did you hear that noise? They can't have gone far," one of the men muttered, his voice gravelly and low.

"Check the other side," the other snapped, his tone impatient. "I'll cover this area."

Liam shifted beside me, the warmth of his body a reassuring presence in the dark. "We can't stay here forever," he murmured, his breath hot against my ear, igniting that same spark that had ignited moments before. "We need a distraction."

I felt a rush of adrenaline as a wicked idea formed in my mind. "How about we make it seem like the painting is over there?" I pointed toward an abandoned canvas draped carelessly across a nearby easel. "If we can throw them off, we might just make it out of here."

"Alright, but we'll have to be quick." Liam's eyes sparkled with mischief as he grasped my hand, the connection sending a jolt of electricity through me. "On three."

"One... two... three!"

In one swift motion, we both bolted from our hiding spot, dashing toward the easel. I yanked the canvas from its stand and hurled it across the room. It landed with a loud crash, the sound echoing through the vast space like a gunshot.

"What the—" one of the masked men shouted, and we took our chance, sprinting toward the back exit, our footsteps pounding against the concrete floor.

"Go, go, go!" I urged, my heart pounding louder than the chaos we left behind. We burst through a door, stumbling into a narrow alleyway that reeked of mildew and despair. The night air was thick, but it felt like freedom wrapped in darkness.

We pressed our backs against the cold brick wall, catching our breaths, the thrill of escape mingling with an exhilarating sense of danger. "I can't believe that worked!" I laughed, the sound breaking through the tension that hung between us.

"Sometimes you just have to wing it," Liam replied, a smirk dancing on his lips. "Though I'm sure the real criminals would have a few choice words about our method."

I took a moment to relish the relief, my pulse finally beginning to slow. "Yeah, well, at least we're not just sitting ducks waiting to be caught."

Liam leaned closer, his expression turning serious. "We need to find out what they're planning next. We can't just let them get away with this."

I nodded, the weight of his words settling over me. "But how? They've got the advantage now. They know we're onto them."

"Then we need to turn the tables," he said, a fierce determination igniting in his gaze. "We need to gather more intel. Find out who's behind this operation and what they're really after."

"And then what?" I shot back, a hint of skepticism lacing my voice. "Play the role of art detectives while dodging bullets?"

"Why not? We're already halfway there," he replied, his voice light yet serious, the sparkle in his eyes making it hard to resist his enthusiasm.

I hesitated, knowing he was right. "Okay, but we need a plan. We can't just rush in without knowing what we're up against."

"Right," he agreed, his tone shifting back to one of focus. "Let's head to the local art community. If there's an underground ring, someone there will have information. We might even find a lead on the stolen painting."

"Sounds like a plan, but I hope you don't expect me to charm the art crowd," I said, rolling my eyes. "They can be a bit... pretentious."

"Come on," he teased, nudging me playfully. "You have that special something. Just flash that charming smile, and you'll have them eating out of your hand."

"Charming smile?" I laughed, shaking my head. "More like my not-so-subtle eye roll when they start rambling about 'the essence of art.'"

"Essence, shmessence," he replied, chuckling. "You're more than capable of holding your own. I'll just be your sidekick."

The moment felt like a breath of fresh air, despite the peril that loomed just outside our temporary refuge. "Alright, then. Sidekick it is. But remember, if things get hairy, I'm not taking the fall for you."

"Deal," he said, extending his hand for a shake. "Now, let's find out what secrets this city is hiding."

We turned to leave the alleyway, the weight of the night pressing upon us, but just as we stepped into the light, a low growl echoed from the shadows behind us.

The air shifted, and without warning, two figures emerged from the darkness, their expressions concealed by the shadows, but the glint of something sharp in one of their hands left no room for doubt.

"Going somewhere?" one of them asked, his voice smooth yet threatening.

My heart sank as dread pooled in my stomach. The night had shifted again, and the danger was suddenly all too real.

Liam's grip tightened around my wrist, and in that moment, I realized that whatever lay ahead, we were in it together. But the stakes had just risen, and I could only hope our combined instincts were enough to see us through the looming threat. The air crackled with tension as we faced our pursuers, the path ahead fraught with uncertainty.

Chapter 6: The Fire Within

The world around us bursts into chaos as we sprint from the warehouse, the heavy scent of damp wood and rust lingering in the air, mingling with the sharp, acrid smell of smoke. Each step I take sends a jolt of exhilaration through me, my heart pounding like a drum echoing in the vastness of the night. Moonlight casts silver shadows on the cracked pavement, illuminating Liam's features just enough for me to glimpse the fierce determination etched across his brow. He glances at me, his blue eyes flashing with a mixture of urgency and something else—something that ignites a flame deep within my chest.

"Keep moving!" he shouts, his voice slicing through the cacophony of distant sirens and the distant roar of flames. I nod, breathless, and push myself harder, my legs responding to the thrill of the chase. The adrenaline surges, transforming every mundane thought into a tapestry of vivid colors, each more vibrant than the last. I can feel it in the pit of my stomach, an intoxicating mix of fear and exhilaration that I can't quite shake off.

We duck into an alley, shadows wrapping around us like a comforting blanket. The bricks are cold beneath my palms as I lean against the wall, panting, the world narrowing to just the two of us in this fleeting moment. There's a rawness in the air, a crackling energy that feels alive, thrumming through the silence of the alley. It's then, in this cocoon of darkness and desperation, that I see Liam anew. He's not just a rival; he's a man fighting against the odds, against whatever monster lies within that damned warehouse.

"Are you okay?" His voice, low and husky, pulls me from my thoughts. I nod, though my heart flutters with uncertainty. Am I really okay? The danger still lingers, but in his gaze, there's a warmth that thaws the ice around my heart, one that I had tightly encased in layers of resentment and distrust. The walls I built to keep him out begin to tremble, and I fight the urge to let them fall.

"Yeah, I'm fine. Just a little out of breath." My words come out breathless, and I can't help but offer him a teasing smile, trying to mask the whirlwind of emotions swirling inside me. "Maybe I should run more often."

He chuckles, the sound rich and melodic, and for a moment, the weight of the world feels lighter. "Running from bad guys is good cardio," he quips, his lips curving into a smirk that makes my heart race for reasons I can't quite articulate. There's a magnetism between us, a connection forged in the fires of chaos. It's both exhilarating and terrifying, and I find myself drawn to him in a way I never expected.

But the moment is shattered like glass as a piercing alarm blares in the distance, a stark reminder that our reprieve is temporary. Reality crashes in like a rogue wave, washing away the stolen joy. "We need to go," I say, the urgency piercing through the haze of newfound feelings.

"Right." Liam's eyes dart to the mouth of the alley, assessing our options. "We can't head back toward the warehouse; they'll be searching that area."

"Then where?" I glance around, desperate for a plan, for an escape route. I can't let myself get distracted by the chemistry between us, not now.

"Follow me." He takes off down the alley, and I'm quick to follow, the chase igniting a spark within me that makes me feel more alive than ever. We weave through the maze of streets, my heart racing not just from the chase but from the thrill of being so close to him, the air between us crackling like a live wire.

As we turn a corner, I spot a flicker of movement—a shadow darting into an open doorway. "Did you see that?" I gasp, my instinct urging caution. Liam halts, his body tense as he scans the street.

"Stay behind me," he commands, and I can't help but feel a surge of irritation mixed with something else—appreciation? He moves forward, and I reluctantly follow, every fiber of my being screaming for me to take charge, to not let him be the hero.

But he doesn't need to play the knight in shining armor; he's already captivating enough as the flawed, dangerous man I've been trying so hard to resist.

The door creaks open, and I catch a glimpse of a dark interior filled with shadows. "We should check it out," I whisper, my curiosity piqued despite the nagging voice in my head.

"Are you insane?" He looks at me incredulously, the spark of fear in his eyes battling with his protective instincts.

"Maybe a little," I admit, a grin breaking through my apprehension. "But what if they're in there? We can't just run away."

Liam hesitates, weighing the risk against the possibilities. "Fine. But stay close."

I nod, excitement coursing through my veins as we step into the darkness. The moment we cross the threshold, the atmosphere shifts, thickening with tension and uncertainty. I can't shake the feeling that we've entered a new realm of danger—one where our fears might not be the only thing lurking in the shadows. The walls close in, and I can feel the heat of his body next to mine, the unspoken connection intensifying with each passing second.

"What if they know we're here?" I whisper, my voice barely a breath, but it hangs in the air between us, palpable and charged.

"They don't," he replies confidently, but there's a flicker of uncertainty behind his bravado. "At least, not yet."

We venture deeper, my heart racing as I sense the heartbeat of the place—a strange, pulsing rhythm that mirrors my own. Each creak of the floorboards sends shivers up my spine, heightening my senses. I can hear Liam breathing next to me, steady and calming, and despite the darkness enveloping us, I feel a flicker of hope.

Perhaps in this moment, amidst the chaos and danger, I could find more than just a way out; perhaps I could find a way into Liam's guarded heart.

The darkness envelops us as we step into the old building, the air thick with dust and the scent of forgotten memories. A solitary beam of moonlight pierces through a broken window, illuminating fragments of scattered debris and long-abandoned furniture that groans under the weight of time. I can almost hear the echoes of laughter and footsteps that once filled this space, now replaced by a suffocating silence that amplifies the sound of our breaths.

"Welcome to my personal haunted house," Liam murmurs, his voice low and playful, breaking the tension that clings to us like a second skin. "I hope you don't mind the ambiance."

"I've seen worse," I reply, trying to match his light-heartedness with a grin. It's a feeble attempt, but I can't let the shadows envelop me completely. As the walls seem to close in, I feel a flicker of unease creep up my spine, but Liam's presence offers a sliver of reassurance.

We move further inside, our footsteps muffled by layers of dust. The floorboards creak under our weight, a symphony of groans that hints at the building's frailty. It's as if the structure itself is a living entity, breathing in the stories of its past while holding its secrets close. Each step sends a shiver of anticipation through me, electrifying the air between us.

"Do you think anyone else is here?" I whisper, scanning the dark corners, half-expecting a figure to emerge, a specter from the past.

"Only the ghosts of bad decisions," he replies with a wry smile, but his eyes flicker with concern. "We should keep moving. I'd rather not be surprised by anything living."

My heart races at the thought, an odd mix of fear and exhilaration. "Right, because 'living' sounds much worse than 'dead,'" I retort, trying to inject humor into the tension. But beneath the jest lies an undercurrent of truth. There's something sinister lurking in the shadows—an awareness that makes my skin prickle.

Liam gestures toward a doorway at the end of the hall, where shadows dance on the walls like restless spirits. "Let's check that room. If there's anyone in here, I'd prefer to find them on our terms."

I nod, my heart pounding as we approach. The door hangs slightly ajar, creaking ominously as we push it open. Inside, the air is stale, heavy with secrets that cling like cobwebs to the corners. The room is bare, save for a solitary table and a couple of mismatched chairs that seem to mock our presence. A single light bulb dangles from the ceiling, flickering like a heartbeat on its last leg.

"Charming place for a clandestine meeting," I quip, glancing around. "Very rustic."

Liam chuckles, but his eyes are sharp, scanning for any signs of life—or danger. "I think I'd prefer a coffee shop with free Wi-Fi and pastries."

"Only if I get a double chocolate muffin," I shoot back, and for a moment, we both share a laugh, the absurdity of the situation slicing through the tension like a knife. But the sound of our laughter dies down, replaced by the weight of uncertainty hanging in the air.

Suddenly, a noise from behind a nearby wall—a crash followed by the unmistakable sound of voices—snaps us back to reality. My heart sinks. "Did you hear that?"

"Yeah, and it didn't sound like the ghosts of bad decisions," he murmurs, his face turning serious. The mirth fades, replaced by a palpable tension that coils between us.

"We should go." I pull on his arm, but he shakes his head, his expression resolute.

"We can't just run without knowing what we're dealing with. I'd rather face them here than out in the open."

His words strike a chord within me, igniting a spark of bravery I didn't know I possessed. "Okay, but if we do this, let's do it smart. I'll distract them while you find a way out, right?"

"Uh, no. That's not how this works," he replies, a mix of incredulity and concern furrowing his brow. "I'm not letting you put yourself in danger."

"I think we're already in danger, Liam. The only question is how we handle it," I retort, my voice firm.

He studies me, and for a moment, I wonder if he can see through my bravado to the quivering nerves beneath. "Fine. But you stay behind me, got it?"

"Whatever you say, Captain Braveheart."

We both chuckle softly, but the laughter fades as we brace ourselves for what lies ahead. Together, we inch toward the door, our movements synchronized, as if we're dancing to an unspoken rhythm. The voices grow clearer, the harsh tones unmistakable.

"I told you they'd come this way," one voice hisses, laced with contempt.

"Shut up. We need to get out before they find us," another replies, panic threading through their tone.

I glance at Liam, who nods slightly, his eyes narrowing in focus. "We need to get a better look. Let's peek through the door."

I hold my breath as we press our faces against the cracked wood, the darkness outside swallowing us whole. A group of men huddles together, their silhouettes barely visible in the low light. They seem anxious, glancing over their shoulders as if the shadows themselves are watching.

"What do you think they're up to?" I murmur, my pulse quickening.

"Something illegal, I bet," Liam replies, his voice barely above a whisper. "We should slip out and call for help."

I nod, heart racing, but before we can make a move, one of the men suddenly straightens, eyes darting in our direction. "Did you hear that?"

Panic surges through me, and I take a step back, but Liam grips my wrist, holding me in place. "Stay still," he whispers.

The seconds stretch like elastic, each heartbeat echoing in the silence. Just as I think we might escape, the door bursts open, slamming against the wall with a force that sends a jolt through me. I gasp, stumbling back as the group of men spills into the room, their faces twisted with anger and confusion.

"There they are!" one of them shouts, pointing straight at us.

I turn to run, but Liam's hand tightens around mine, anchoring me to him. "We can't split up!"

"Right, because that always ends well," I shoot back, adrenaline fueling my resolve.

"Trust me," he insists, pulling me toward the opposite exit, urgency driving his every move.

Together, we dart past the startled men, who scramble to regain their composure, a mix of surprise and fury contorting their features. The path behind us is chaotic, their shouts echoing in the confined space, but I don't dare look back. With each step, I feel the tension crackling like static electricity, the danger igniting a fire within me that demands to be unleashed.

We burst through another doorway, emerging into the cool night air, the world outside a stark contrast to the darkness we left behind. The thrill of escape surges through my veins, but as I glance at Liam, the reality of our situation settles heavily upon us both. The chase isn't over; it's just begun.

We tumble into the cool night air, the chaos of the warehouse fading into a haunting memory behind us. The city stretches before us, a web of shadows and neon lights flickering like distant stars, and for a moment, I'm disoriented by the contrast. The cacophony of sirens and shouting from behind reminds me of the urgency pressing against my chest. But it's the way Liam's hand still grips mine that brings me back to reality, grounding me amidst the chaos.

"We can't just stand here," he says, glancing over his shoulder, his eyes wide with a mix of adrenaline and determination. "They'll be right on our heels."

"Yeah, I'm aware," I reply, forcing a laugh that sounds more like a gasp. "What's our escape plan? You know, aside from running into the night like a pair of headless chickens?"

His mouth quirks up at the corner, and for a split second, the fear dissipates, replaced by that spark of humor I've come to enjoy. "Let's find somewhere safe to regroup. There's a café a few blocks away that stays open late. We can blend in and figure out our next move."

"Great, because nothing says 'let's plot our escape' like overpriced coffee and stale pastries," I quip, but I follow his lead, our footsteps echoing against the pavement.

As we hurry through the streets, the adrenaline still courses through my veins, lending each of my movements an exhilarating edge. My thoughts swirl like autumn leaves caught in a gust of wind. How did I end up here, running for my life with the very person I've spent so long trying to outsmart? The past feels like a different world, and the lines between ally and enemy blur with every passing moment.

We arrive at the café, its neon sign buzzing in the night. It feels both familiar and foreign, a cozy haven amidst the chaos swirling outside. The rich aroma of coffee fills the air, grounding me as we step inside. It's warm and inviting, a stark contrast to the chill of the night. I glance at the barista, who barely looks up from his phone as we approach the counter, lost in the flickering glow of the screen.

"Two coffees, please," Liam orders, his voice steady despite the tension radiating off him. I lean against the counter, trying to steady my breathing, while my mind races to process everything that just happened.

As we wait, I glance around, my senses heightened. The other patrons seem blissfully unaware of the storm brewing outside, their laughter and chatter a soothing backdrop to our urgency. I catch my reflection in the glass, hair tousled, cheeks flushed from the chase, and my heart sinks. I look like a mess, but it's a mess filled with adrenaline and a strange kind of exhilaration.

"Here you go," Liam says, sliding a steaming cup toward me. The warmth seeps into my hands, and I close my eyes, savoring the moment of normalcy, even as my heart races with the knowledge that danger lurks just outside.

We find a secluded table in the corner, a perfect spot to keep an eye on the door while allowing us a moment to breathe. As we sit down, the weight of our situation sinks in, and I can no longer ignore the tension crackling between us. "So," I begin, my voice lighter than I feel, "what's the plan, Captain? We just sit here sipping coffee until the bad guys find us?"

Liam smirks, but his eyes darken with seriousness. "First, we lay low. Then we need to figure out who those guys were and what they want."

"Right, because nothing says 'let's do some detective work' like overpriced coffee and a side of anxiety," I respond, taking a tentative sip of the steaming brew. The rich flavor bursts across my tongue, momentarily distracting me from the mess of emotions swirling inside.

"Hey, I'm all for a nice cappuccino, but we might be better off heading to the police," he suggests, though I can see the reluctance in his eyes.

"Right. And then what? Explain that we were in a warehouse, doing whatever it is we were doing? They'll want to know what we were looking for, and honestly, I'm still trying to figure that out." I set my cup down with a decisive clink, the sound echoing in the quiet booth.

Liam leans forward, his intensity palpable. "We have to consider the possibility that whoever those men were, they're not just after us. They could be part of something much larger, and we've stumbled into it."

The words hang in the air between us, laden with implications that send chills racing down my spine. "And if we're not careful, we could end up in over our heads," I whisper, the reality of our situation sinking in deeper.

His gaze softens for a moment, a flicker of vulnerability surfacing before he masks it with determination. "We'll figure it out. Together."

"Together," I echo, though the word feels heavy on my tongue, laden with unspoken promises and complexities. The spark that ignited between us moments ago flickers again, but now it carries a weight that could tip the scales in either direction.

Just as I open my mouth to respond, the door swings open, and a gust of cool air rushes in, bringing with it a wave of tension. A group of men, the same ones we'd encountered at the warehouse, strides into the café, their presence imposing and filled with intent. My heart drops, and I instinctively shrink back in my seat, pressing myself into the shadowy corner.

"Did you see who went in here?" one of them barks, scanning the café with sharp, predatory eyes.

Liam's hand finds mine beneath the table, squeezing tightly. "Stay calm," he murmurs, but I can hear the underlying tension in his voice.

"Why would they come in here?" I ask, panic fluttering in my chest. "What do we do?"

"Act normal," he urges, though I can feel the heat radiating from his body, his pulse racing like mine.

I take a breath, steeling myself as they move deeper into the café, their eyes darting from table to table. I can't shake the feeling that they're searching for us. The barista, oblivious to the danger, continues to fumble with his phone, blissfully unaware of the tension escalating in the room.

"Can we help you?" the barista finally asks, looking up, confusion etched on his face.

One of the men sneers, leaning closer. "We're looking for someone. Did you see a pair of idiots run in here? Maybe wearing slightly disheveled clothes?"

I hold my breath, glancing at Liam, who appears unflappable despite the storm brewing around us. But I can see the tension in his jaw, the flicker of danger in his eyes.

"Look, I haven't seen anyone like that," the barista replies, clearly unnerved.

As the men begin to move toward our table, dread settles in the pit of my stomach. This was it. They would discover us, and we'd be trapped. I could almost hear the sound of my own heartbeat, echoing in the silence that enveloped us.

"Time to go," Liam whispers, but before we can make a move, the lead man locks eyes with me. Recognition washes over his face, a predatory gleam igniting in his gaze.

"There they are!" he shouts, pointing directly at us.

Instinct kicks in, and we both leap from the table, adrenaline surging as we bolt toward the exit. The world blurs around me, the scent of coffee and sweat mingling as I push through the door. I can hear shouts behind us, the unmistakable sound of footsteps pounding against the pavement as we race into the night, the darkness swallowing us whole.

But as we dart down the street, I can't shake the feeling that we're being hunted, and with each breath, I feel the net tightening around us. Just ahead, an alleyway beckons, a dark promise of concealment, and without a second thought, we dive into its shadows, hearts racing, breaths quickening, as we disappear into the night—into the unknown.

Chapter 7: Tangled Hearts

Sunlight poured through the dusty attic window, casting a warm golden hue on the forgotten treasures that had accumulated over the years. Each object whispered stories of the past, but today I was on a mission, driven by an insatiable curiosity and the need to unearth more than just old family relics. The attic smelled of aged wood and a hint of lavender, remnants of my grandmother's attempts to ward off the musty air. As I maneuvered around boxes and trunks, my heart raced with a mix of excitement and apprehension.

The attic felt like a time capsule, and as I pushed aside a tattered quilt, my fingers brushed against something cold and smooth. I pulled back to reveal a canvas, its surface obscured by years of neglect. With a few gentle tugs, I freed it from its resting place and carefully leaned it against a nearby trunk. The painting was vibrant, a swirl of colors capturing a wild, romantic landscape. But it wasn't just the artistry that struck me—it was the signature, neatly inscribed in the bottom corner, that made my heart stop.

"R. Sinclair," I read aloud, the name echoing through the attic. My breath caught in my throat as the realization hit me. Liam's family, my family—the tangled roots of our histories intertwined more deeply than I ever imagined. We had spent weeks ensnared in a rivalry fueled by misunderstandings and ancient grudges, yet here lay a testament to something more profound, something that bridged the chasm between us. I could almost hear the laughter of children playing, the echoes of family gatherings, and the bonds that had frayed with time.

As I settled onto the floor, the cool wooden planks beneath me grounding my racing thoughts, I couldn't help but wonder how this discovery would affect our fragile connection. Each encounter with Liam had unraveled a thread of tension I hadn't even recognized was there, revealing a tapestry of emotions I struggled to navigate. I thought of his sly grin and the way his eyes sparkled when he spoke passionately about his dreams, and I felt a tug in my chest—a blend of longing and fear. Affection was one thing, but vulnerability was another beast entirely.

Just then, a light knock broke my reverie. I looked up to see Liam standing at the attic door, his dark hair tousled and a curious glint in his eye. "Are you hiding from the world up here, or have you uncovered a treasure?" His voice was teasing, yet there was a hint of concern threading through his words.

With a deep breath, I gestured for him to come closer. "I might have found something that could change everything." The weight of the painting rested in my hands, and I turned it so he could see.

His expression shifted from playful to serious as he stepped forward, his brows knitting together in concentration. "Is that...?" he started, then trailed off, words catching in his throat. The revelation hung in the air like a delicate thread, and I could sense the shift in his demeanor.

"It's signed by your ancestor," I stated, my voice steady despite the turmoil inside. "Your family and mine—they were connected."

For a moment, the silence enveloped us, thick and heavy. I could see the cogs turning in his mind as he processed the information. "Connected how?"

I felt a mix of exhilaration and dread as I responded, "It seems our families have a shared history. This painting must have been passed down through generations. It could be a symbol of a bond that was once strong."

His eyes narrowed, an intriguing blend of skepticism and intrigue flickering across his face. "Or it could just be an old piece of art that has no real significance."

"Maybe," I conceded, "but what if it's not? What if this means our families weren't always at odds? That there's more to our story than rivalry?"

Liam stepped back, crossing his arms as he weighed my words. "And if we dive into this, what happens to the rivalry? What happens to us?"

The question hung heavy in the air, demanding an answer I wasn't sure I could provide. I had built walls around my heart, fortified by years of conflict and disdain, but with each passing moment in his presence, those walls were crumbling. "I don't know," I admitted, my voice softer than before. "But I can't ignore how I feel about you. It terrifies me."

The vulnerability of my confession caught me off guard, and I braced for his response, the air electric with unspoken words. He stepped closer, his expression shifting from uncertainty to a kind of understanding that sent a thrill through me.

"You're not the only one feeling that," he said, his voice low, almost conspiratorial. "Every time we spar or exchange barbs, I can't help but feel like we're dancing around something more."

My heart raced, the pulse of possibility thrumming in my ears. "Then why do we keep doing this? Why don't we just admit that there's something between us?"

"Because," he began, a grin tugging at the corners of his mouth, "the banter is too fun. But..." He hesitated, his eyes searching mine. "I think I'd rather explore this connection than pretend it doesn't exist."

The air crackled with a newfound energy as the painting leaned against the trunk, a silent witness to our shifting dynamic. I could feel the weight of history, both familial and personal, pressing down on us, urging us to choose between the safety of our established roles and the thrill of something unknown.

"What do we do now?" I asked, my voice barely a whisper, as if the question itself might shatter the fragile moment we were building.

His grin widened, a spark igniting in his eyes. "I think we find out together."

In that moment, the attic faded away, the dusty relics of the past overshadowed by the brightness of possibilities unfolding before us. The path ahead might be fraught with complications, but for the first time, I felt a glimmer of hope—a promise of something deeper that had the power to transcend the tangled histories of our families.

The thrill of discovery had woven itself into the fabric of our days, a vibrant tapestry of revelations that shimmered with possibility. Yet, just as quickly as the excitement swelled, an ominous shadow loomed over us, dimming the light of our newfound knowledge. It started subtly—a fleeting glance caught in the corner of my eye, a hushed whisper in the gallery where we were poring over documents. But soon enough, it morphed into a tangible presence, a figure lurking in the periphery of our lives like a dark cloud threatening a summer's day.

"Do you ever feel like we're being watched?" I asked Liam one afternoon as we sifted through a mountain of papers in the dimly lit library of his family estate. The scent of old books mingled with the faintest hint of leather, a comforting aroma that belied the tension in the air. I looked up from a brittle manuscript that detailed the history of a painting long thought lost, my heart pounding as I sensed something—someone—just beyond our reach.

Liam paused, his brow furrowing as he considered my words. "If I did, I'd like to think I'd have the good sense to turn tail and run," he replied, a half-smirk playing at the corners of his mouth. "But seriously, why would anyone care about us? We're just a couple of nosy people chasing shadows."

"Those shadows are starting to feel a bit too solid for comfort," I retorted, scanning the room as if the air itself might betray our secret.

The sound of the clock ticking in the background felt ominous, a reminder that time was slipping away, and with it, our chance to unravel the truth.

Chapter 8: Truth or Dare

As days turned into a blur of late-night research and whispered conversations, my instincts tightened into a knot of dread. We were closing in on something monumental—the identity of the mastermind behind the recent art thefts—but with every step forward, the threat of exposure loomed larger. We were two reluctant detectives, stumbling through the dark with nothing but our wit and determination to guide us.

That determination came crashing down one stormy night when the culmination of our efforts culminated in a breakthrough. A name had emerged from the depths of obscurity: Julian Voss, a disgraced former associate of Liam's family. Rumor had it he had a score to settle—a vendetta simmering just beneath the surface. The revelation felt like a slap across the face, sending shockwaves through the fragile air of our investigation.

"Voss?" Liam echoed, the name tasting bitter on his tongue. "I should have known he'd surface eventually. He's always been lurking in the shadows, waiting for the right moment to strike." His fists clenched, a storm brewing behind those familiar green eyes.

"You say that like you know him," I said, my voice low. "What's his deal? Why now?"

"It's complicated," he muttered, pacing the small space like a caged animal. "He's always been obsessed with our family's legacy. When my father cut ties with him, it was like throwing a lit match into a powder keg. He thinks he's owed something. Revenge is his art form, and we're his canvas."

A chill ran down my spine as I realized the extent of the danger we had stumbled into. This wasn't just about stolen paintings; this was personal. Voss's motives ran deeper than I had anticipated, intertwining with the very fabric of Liam's life. My heart raced—not only from fear but also from the growing complexity of my feelings for him. Each revelation about Liam's past only drew me closer, binding us together in a web of love, fear, and unyielding desire that pulsed with the intensity of a live wire.

"Then we need to act fast," I insisted, the resolve in my voice surprising even myself. "We can't let him get the upper hand. We need to figure out where he's hiding and stop him before he makes his next move."

"Stop him?" Liam's incredulity was palpable. "What do you suggest we do, exactly? Storm his lair with a squirt gun and a pocketful of glitter?"

"Do you have a better idea?" I shot back, not bothering to mask my irritation. "You can't just wait for him to come to you. We need to be proactive."

He paused, a flicker of admiration crossing his features. "You're right. We need to gather more information. But I won't let you put yourself in danger. You're too important to me." His words hung in the air, thick and sweet, weaving into the tapestry of our complex bond.

"Important? Or just convenient?" I teased, my attempt at levity landing heavier than I intended. The vulnerability in his eyes caught me off guard, a revelation that tugged at the edges of my heart.

"More than you know," he said softly, and just like that, the moment shifted, laden with an unspoken understanding that crackled like electricity between us. The tension was palpable, a delicate thread stretched taut, ready to snap at any moment.

The next morning, we set out to track down Voss, piecing together a patchwork of clues that led us to a rundown warehouse on the outskirts of town. The sky above was a sullen gray, mirroring the apprehension knotting in my stomach. As we approached the dilapidated structure, a sense of foreboding wrapped itself around us like a shroud.

"Are you sure this is the right place?" I asked, squinting at the broken windows that stared back at us like empty eyes.

"According to the intel, yes. He's been using it as a hideout." Liam's voice was steady, but I could see the tension coiling in his shoulders.

"Great. So we're breaking into a fortress of solitude. Just another Tuesday in the life of a would-be detective," I said, attempting to mask my unease with sarcasm.

As we crept through the shadows, adrenaline surged through my veins, urging me onward. Each creak of the floorboards beneath our feet echoed like a warning bell, and I couldn't shake the feeling that we were not alone. Every instinct screamed at me to turn back, but the thought of Voss slipping through our fingers pushed me forward, deeper into the darkness of the unknown.

And then, just as we reached the heart of the warehouse, we stumbled upon the truth, a revelation that would change everything. The stark reality of our situation hit me like a freight train, and suddenly, it was no longer just about art theft—it was about survival.

The atmosphere inside the warehouse was thick with tension, each breath a reminder of the peril we faced. Dust particles danced in the weak shafts of light filtering through the cracked windows, creating a surreal ambiance that belied the danger lurking within. The silence was deafening, interrupted only by the distant sound of dripping water echoing through the empty space.

Liam and I exchanged a glance that spoke volumes; in that fleeting moment, we were allies in this chaos, bound by a shared mission that felt as much about our survival as it was about justice. My heart raced as we crept further into the belly of the beast, our footsteps muffled against the grimy floor.

"Do you think he's here?" I whispered, my voice barely more than a breath.

"Let's hope he's as scared of us as we are of him," Liam replied, attempting to inject a note of bravado into the situation. His attempt to lighten the mood fell flat, but I appreciated the effort.

As we rounded a corner, a flicker of movement caught my eye. I instinctively reached for Liam's arm, grounding myself in the connection between us. "Did you see that?" I asked, my voice barely above a whisper, tinged with both fear and excitement.

"Just shadows and dust, I'm sure," he reassured, though I could see the steely resolve hardening in his features. "But we need to keep moving."

We slipped further into the heart of the warehouse, adrenaline pumping through our veins like a wild river. I mentally cataloged our surroundings—every rusted beam and every shattered crate might hold the key to finding Voss. With each step, I could feel the web tightening around us, the stakes escalating with every fleeting second.

"Here, over here!" Liam suddenly exclaimed, gesturing toward an open doorway at the far end of the room. It was a dark tunnel leading into an unknown space, an unsettling promise of what lay ahead. My stomach fluttered with a mix of dread and determination.

As we approached, the shadows thickened, shrouding everything in an eerie cloak of uncertainty. "After you, fearless leader," I quipped, forcing a smile despite the rising tension. Liam shot me a look that was half-amused, half-worried.

"Let's not get too cocky. That's usually when things go south," he replied, his voice low and serious. The banter was a fragile lifeline, tethering us to a sense of normalcy in a world that had turned upside down.

We stepped through the doorway, and the atmosphere shifted drastically. The air was damp and cool, the scent of mildew wrapping around us like a wet blanket. I scanned the walls, which were lined with forgotten crates and debris. It was a makeshift gallery of sorts, filled with art that had clearly been acquired through less-than-savory means. Each piece seemed to whisper tales of betrayal and loss, an echo of the lives entwined with the art we sought to recover.

"Look at this," I said, my fingers brushing against a painting partially obscured by a tattered sheet. It was an exquisite landscape, vibrant and alive, yet somehow melancholic. "This shouldn't be here; it belongs to someone who has been searching for it."

"Yeah, and it's a little too pristine for a dump like this," Liam observed, his brow furrowing in thought. "Voss wouldn't stash anything here unless it was important to him. We need to figure out what he's planning."

Just as I nodded, a low chuckle reverberated through the dim space, a sound that froze the blood in my veins. We turned, and there he was—Julian Voss, leaning against a column, his arms crossed and a smirk playing on his lips.

"Well, well, if it isn't the dynamic duo. I must admit, I was starting to think you'd lost your nerve," he drawled, the mocking tone dripping with disdain.

"Funny, I was just thinking the same about you," I shot back, summoning courage from the depths of my being. "What are you doing here, Voss? We know about your plans."

His smirk widened, a wolfish grin that sent chills down my spine. "Do you? Or do you just think you do? You're playing a dangerous game, and I'm afraid you're not very good at it."

Liam stepped in front of me, a protective stance that sent my heart racing, both with admiration and fear. "You don't scare us, Voss. We're here to put an end to whatever you're plotting."

"Such bravado," Voss replied, his eyes glinting with malice. "But you have no idea what you're up against. This isn't just about art anymore; it's about legacy, power, and revenge. I'm just getting started."

With a swift motion, he gestured behind him, and suddenly, the dim light illuminated several figures emerging from the shadows. My stomach dropped as I realized we were not alone. A group of men, hardened and determined, stepped forward, surrounding us with predatory intent.

"Liam, we need to—" I began, but Voss cut me off with a chilling laugh.

"Too late for that, darling. You've walked right into my trap. I hope you're comfortable, because you're about to become part of a very intricate masterpiece."

The walls of the warehouse seemed to close in around us, the weight of his words pressing down like a suffocating fog. My heart thundered in my chest, each beat echoing a desperate prayer for escape. I glanced at Liam, our eyes locking in a moment of unspoken understanding—this wasn't just a fight for justice anymore; it was a fight for our lives.

And then, without warning, Voss took a step closer, his expression darkening as he raised a gloved hand, signaling his men to move. My breath caught in my throat, the realization hitting me with brutal clarity: we were trapped, ensnared in a web spun from the very shadows we had sought to confront.

Just as chaos erupted around us, a loud crash resonated through the warehouse, shaking the very foundations of our nightmare. The sudden cacophony sent a rush of adrenaline coursing through me, igniting a spark of hope amidst the chaos.

"What was that?" Liam shouted, his voice a beacon in the turmoil.

But before I could respond, a figure burst into the room—an unexpected savior, perhaps—but with the element of surprise came uncertainty. The masked stranger charged forward, disrupting Voss's carefully laid plans, and in that split second, the game changed dramatically.

"What the hell is going on?" I cried, my heart racing as the warehouse descended into a whirlwind of confusion and clashing bodies.

But as I turned to follow the chaos, the stranger caught my eye, and the mask slipped just enough for me to glimpse the unexpected truth—this was someone from our past, someone I never thought I'd see again, and they were here, standing at the precipice of a reckoning that would forever alter the course of our lives.

With a heavy heart and a mind racing against time, I realized that we were about to plunge headfirst into a fight that would test our strength, loyalty, and the very fabric of our relationship. As the dust settled, I knew one thing for sure: the web was tightening, and our next move could very well determine our fates.

Chapter 9: Whispers in the Dark

The air in the gallery was thick with the scent of linseed oil and old wood, a fragrant reminder of the countless hours my grandmother had poured into her craft. Each painting hung like a whisper of her soul, vivid hues and bold strokes revealing her passions, while the shadows of the room seemed to quiver in response to the stories they held. It was within this sacred space that I found solace, yet today, unease snaked its way through my thoughts like an insistent vine.

I ran my fingers along the frames, tracing the delicate patterns carved into the wood, each groove and flourish a testament to my grandmother's meticulous nature. Her artistry had always captivated me, a blend of realism and whimsy that pulled you into another world. But it wasn't just the artwork that fascinated me; it was the life behind it, the woman who had shaped my family's legacy with each brushstroke. As I stood surrounded by her creations, I felt a deep yearning to understand her better, to peel back the layers that had concealed her truths from me.

Tucked away in the far corner of the room, I noticed a painting half-hidden behind a large canvas, its edges frayed and colors dulled with time. Curious, I leaned closer, brushing away the dust that had settled like a soft blanket. The image was hauntingly beautiful—an ethereal landscape that seemed to pulse with energy, a riot of greens and blues that promised mystery. But it was the journal propped against the easel beside it that caught my eye. Bound in faded leather and embossed with a symbol I couldn't quite decipher, it beckoned me with an inexplicable urgency.

With a quick glance over my shoulder, I reached for the journal, feeling the cool leather beneath my fingertips. I opened it cautiously, the pages crackling softly as they surrendered to the air. Each entry was a jumble of sketches and notes, fragments of thoughts interspersed with wild doodles that hinted at the chaos of a creative mind. But as I flipped through, something shifted—a nagging sense that I was trespassing on private revelations.

One sketch in particular caught my attention: a map dotted with strange symbols and annotations that appeared to lead to a place I'd never heard of. My heart raced as I traced the lines with my finger, an unfamiliar thrill coursing through me. "What on earth were you up to, Grandma?" I murmured, glancing around the gallery, half-expecting her spirit to materialize and enlighten me.

The shadows deepened as the afternoon light waned, and I sank into the worn armchair nestled in the corner. My heart thrummed in my chest, a rhythmic echo of the tension that had begun to fester in my life since that fateful encounter. Liam's presence was a constant reminder of the dangers lurking just beyond our doorstep. His dark, brooding gaze seemed to follow me wherever I went, igniting a complex whirlwind of emotions. Was he my protector or my captor? Each time he stepped into the room, the air thickened with unspoken words and desires that twisted my insides into knots.

I had never been one to shy away from feelings, but with Liam, everything felt amplified. The way he brushed past me, the heat of his body mingling with the coolness of the room, sent shivers down my spine. There was a magnetic pull that drew us together, yet the tension crackled between us like static electricity—thrilling yet unnerving. I had seen glimpses of vulnerability beneath his rough exterior, flashes of a man wrestling with his own demons. But in those moments, it was easy to forget about the darkness that loomed outside, the dangers that could threaten to tear us apart.

In the midst of this chaotic swirl of emotions, I returned to the journal. I couldn't shake the feeling that these pages held the key to understanding my family's secrets—and perhaps, my own. I flipped to a more recent entry, the ink fresh and bold, and the words struck me like a thunderclap:

"The past is a tempest, and we are the ships navigating its treacherous waters. Beware the whispers in the dark; they carry truths you may not be ready to face."

I felt a shiver race down my spine, the warning echoing in my mind. What truths lay hidden within these pages? Was my grandmother trying to shield me from something? I flipped through more entries, piecing together fragments of her life—an affair that ended in heartbreak, a secret pact with a figure obscured by shadows, a legacy of artistry that intertwined with darker undertones.

The light dimmed further, shadows curling around the edges of the room as dusk enveloped the world outside. The tension in my chest tightened. Was it merely the weight of my discoveries, or did it have something to do with Liam? I glanced toward the door, half-expecting him to appear, his presence a balm and a burden all at once.

As if summoned by my thoughts, the door creaked open, and Liam stepped into the gallery, his silhouette a dark contrast against the soft glow of the hanging lights. He paused, his gaze sweeping over the paintings, and then settled on me, the tension in the air shifting palpably. "What are you hiding?" he asked, his voice low and gravelly, cutting through the stillness.

I closed the journal instinctively, hiding its secrets behind the facade of casual interest. "Just admiring Grandma's collection," I replied, forcing a smile that felt more like a mask than a genuine expression. But I could see the flicker of curiosity in his eyes, the way they darkened with the weight of unsaid words.

"Admiring or searching?" His tone held an edge, one I recognized from our earlier conversations—sharp, incisive, as if he were peeling back my layers, one by one. The connection between us felt electric, a tension that simmered just beneath the surface, threatening to bubble over.

"Maybe a little of both," I admitted, my pulse quickening as I met his gaze. "There are things in this family I didn't know existed, things that might change everything." The journal sat between us, a silent witness to the unfolding drama, and for a moment, the world outside faded into the background, leaving only the weight of our unspoken truths hanging in the air.

Liam stepped further into the gallery, his presence amplifying the already charged atmosphere. "Things that might change everything?" He arched an eyebrow, his expression a mix of skepticism and intrigue, as if challenging me to peel back my own layers. I could feel the weight of his scrutiny, and it only served to heighten the urgency buzzing beneath my skin.

I took a deep breath, feeling the tension twist in my chest like a tightly wound coil. "There are mysteries here, Liam—hidden stories that could explain so much about our family." The truth felt heavy on my tongue, a weight I was only beginning to comprehend. As I spoke, the vivid colors of the paintings danced around us, each brushstroke a reminder of the vibrancy of life that felt like it was teetering on the edge of chaos.

"Like the one where your grandmother was an artistic genius and your family was a parade of secrets?" he said, a hint of sarcasm lacing his words. But I caught the glimmer of interest in his eyes, the way they flickered with the same curiosity that had sparked my own.

"Yes, exactly! But it's more than that." I glanced back at the journal, the pages begging for attention like restless spirits. "There are connections here, patterns in the chaos. It's like she was trying to tell me something through her art, through this journal." My voice grew fervent, each word spilling forth with the passion of someone determined to unearth the truth.

He stepped closer, the shadows deepening around us as he leaned against the wall, arms crossed. "So, what's stopping you from diving in? Isn't that what you're good at—digging until you hit bedrock?"

His challenge hung in the air, teasing and daring, but it also felt like a lifeline thrown into my tumultuous sea of uncertainty.

"I'm not sure I'm ready for what's buried beneath the surface," I admitted, vulnerability creeping into my voice. "What if the truth is more than I can handle?" My heart raced at the thought, images of shattered illusions flashing through my mind.

"Trust me, sweetheart," he said, his tone shifting to one of sincerity. "You're tougher than you think. And whatever this is, it won't swallow you whole." He reached for my hand, his grip warm and steady, a tether in the midst of my spiraling thoughts. The spark between us was undeniable, and I could feel the magnetic pull drawing us closer, urging me to share my fears.

I opened my mouth to respond, but just then, a loud crash echoed from the back of the gallery, shattering the moment. We both jumped, hearts pounding in our chests. I released Liam's hand instinctively, the warmth dissipating as adrenaline surged through my veins.

"What was that?" I whispered, my voice barely audible over the thudding pulse in my ears.

"Stay here," Liam ordered, the commanding tone in his voice leaving little room for argument. He moved toward the source of the noise, a figure of strength and resolve, and I couldn't help but follow, my curiosity piqued and anxiety buzzing like a swarm of bees.

We crept through the narrow hallway leading to the back of the gallery, the shadows swallowing us whole. The air was thick, laden with the scent of paint and varnish, each breath a reminder of the artistry surrounding us. As we rounded the corner, I spotted a shadowy figure hunched over a fallen sculpture, its fragile form shattered on the ground.

"Who are you?" Liam barked, stepping protectively in front of me, muscles tensed like a coiled spring. The figure froze, glancing up, and the dim light revealed a familiar face, one that sent a jolt of recognition racing through me.

"Mia?" I exclaimed, my voice a mix of disbelief and relief. My childhood friend, once inseparable from my world, stood before us, her hair wild and eyes wide with panic. "What are you doing here?"

"I didn't mean to scare you!" Mia stammered, scrambling to her feet, brushing the debris off her jeans. "I thought I'd find you here. I... I had to see you." Her breath came in quick bursts, as if she had run a marathon to reach me.

Liam's stance relaxed slightly, but the protectiveness in his posture remained, like a lion guarding its territory. "Why were you sneaking around in the dark?" he asked, suspicion lacing his words.

"I wasn't sneaking!" she insisted, her voice rising with indignation. "I came to talk to you, but the door was locked, and I thought maybe I could find a way in without bothering anyone. I just..." She trailed off, glancing at me, and the panic in her eyes shifted to something softer, a glimmer of nostalgia. "I missed you."

I stepped forward, my heart warming at her words. "I missed you too, Mia. But what's going on? Why now?" The urgency in my voice must have mirrored the concern in my chest. The gallery, once a refuge, now felt like a stage set for revelations, and I was acutely aware of Liam's presence beside me, a silent witness to our reconnection.

Mia took a deep breath, her gaze darting between Liam and me. "I know things have changed, but I have to tell you something important." She hesitated, the weight of her words hanging in the air, her resolve seeming to waver. "I've been hearing whispers—things about your family, things that might explain... well, everything."

My heart raced at her revelation, an unsettling mix of excitement and dread curling in my stomach. "What kind of whispers?" I pressed, leaning closer, desperate for clarity.

"There are rumors, and I don't know how much is true, but there's talk of a hidden legacy—something about your grandmother's art and the people she associated with." Her voice dropped to a whisper, as if the walls themselves were eavesdropping. "I think it goes deeper than just art; it's about power and influence, secrets that could change your life."

Liam's expression shifted, a flicker of concern crossing his features as he moved closer, drawing the three of us into a tight circle of urgency. "What exactly are you saying, Mia?" His voice was calm but firm, as if trying to anchor the storm brewing within us.

"I can't say much without evidence, but you need to be careful. There are people who don't want those secrets to come out." Her eyes darted to the shadows that clung to the corners of the gallery, and I could almost feel the ghosts of our past brushing against us, whispering their warnings.

As the implications of her words settled in the air, I exchanged a glance with Liam, his steady gaze grounding me amidst the whirlwind of emotions. A part of me felt the thrill of discovery, but another part, the more cautious side, recoiled at the thought of stepping into the unknown. "What do we do?" I asked, my voice barely more than a breath, the weight of the decision looming like an impending storm.

"I'm not saying we have to plunge into the deep end without a life vest," Mia said, a note of desperation lacing her voice. "But I think you need to find out what's going on. Whatever it is, it's tied to your grandmother's legacy—and to you."

Her words stirred something restless within me. The thought of uncovering buried family secrets was exhilarating, but the risks felt overwhelming. "What if we open a Pandora's box we can't close?" I replied, the uncertainty twisting like a snake in my gut. "What if the people who want these secrets buried come after us?"

Liam's brow furrowed, his jaw set in determination. "Then we prepare. But sitting here in the dark won't help." He turned to Mia, his intensity unyielding. "What do you know about these whispers? Who's behind them?"

Mia glanced nervously at the scattered pieces of the fallen sculpture, as if hoping they might offer her a way out of the mounting pressure. "I don't have names, just rumors. I heard them from people at the gallery, collectors who speak in hushed tones when they think no one's listening. There's talk about your grandmother's paintings being more than art—some believe they're keys to something valuable. Something powerful."

"Powerful?" I echoed, the word hanging in the air, heavy with implications. "You mean like…money? Influence?"

"More like something that could change the course of history," she replied, her voice dropping to a near whisper. "People are desperate for it. And that desperation can make them dangerous."

Liam stepped closer, his gaze unwavering. "We can't ignore this. If there's something out there that could threaten you, we need to figure out what it is before it's too late."

"Right, because that sounds like a brilliant plan," I quipped, trying to mask my rising anxiety with sarcasm. "I can't wait to dive into a world filled with shadowy figures and family feuds."

He shot me a smirk, a hint of amusement breaking through the tension. "You've already got a taste of it, and look how well you handled yourself."

I couldn't help but roll my eyes. "Yes, I'm a champion at wrestling with danger and existential dread."

"Good. Then you're halfway prepared," he said with a teasing glint in his eyes, but the seriousness of the situation lurked just beneath the surface.

"Let's not forget we're standing in a gallery filled with art and a lot of uncertainty," Mia interjected, her expression growing grave again. "We need to act fast. If there are people watching you, we can't afford to let them know we're onto them."

Liam turned to me, his voice dropping to a conspiratorial tone. "So, what's our first move? We can't just sit here and wait for someone to come knocking on the door."

My mind raced, thoughts colliding in a chaotic dance. "We should investigate the gallery's history, see if there's any mention of this 'key' Mia talked about. Maybe we can find clues in the art itself, or in your grandmother's notes."

"Agreed. But we need to be discreet," Mia added, glancing nervously toward the door as if expecting someone to burst in at any moment. "If anyone sees us digging around, it could draw unwanted attention."

"Perfect. Just what I wanted to hear," I said dryly, but beneath my sarcasm, a sense of determination began to solidify. "We can start with that old storage room in the back. I remember Grandma used to keep her older works there, and maybe some records, too."

Liam nodded, his expression serious yet encouraging. "Let's move before we're interrupted again."

As we made our way to the storage room, the gallery felt alive with whispers, each painting watching us like a thousand unblinking eyes. The echoes of the past seemed to swirl around us, a ghostly chorus urging us forward. I felt a thrill of fear and excitement, the thrill of stepping into the unknown.

The storage room door creaked as we pushed it open, revealing a dimly lit space crammed with canvases stacked against the walls and boxes overflowing with art supplies. Dust motes danced in the fading light, swirling like secrets waiting to be uncovered. I stepped inside, the musty smell of old paint and varnish washing over me, a comforting yet eerie embrace.

"Start looking for anything unusual," Liam instructed, his eyes scanning the room. "We'll divide and conquer."

Mia and I nodded, and we began rifling through boxes and shifting canvases. The room felt both familiar and foreign, a treasure trove of memories mixed with the promise of revelation. I could almost hear my grandmother's laughter echoing in the corners, a reminder of the artist who had shaped not just her life but mine as well.

"Here!" Mia exclaimed, her voice cutting through the silence. She held up a folder filled with loose sheets of paper. "I think this might be what we're looking for."

My heart raced as I approached, leaning over her shoulder to glimpse the contents. The pages were filled with sketches, intricate designs and notes that seemed to spiral into chaos. A series of symbols repeated across the sheets, each more complex than the last.

"What do you make of these?" I asked, my pulse quickening as I felt the weight of significance in the air.

"I don't know," she said, biting her lip. "But they look like they could be connected to the whispers."

Liam leaned in closer, his brow furrowed. "These aren't just doodles. They look like...like a cipher or a code."

"Great, just what we need," I muttered. "A secret language to decode while we're being hunted by shadowy figures."

"Maybe we can find the key to unlock it," Mia suggested, her excitement palpable despite the gravity of the situation.

But as we pored over the sketches, the tension in the room shifted abruptly. A noise echoed outside, heavy footsteps approaching with purpose. My heart sank, fear coiling around my chest.

"Someone's coming," I whispered, my voice trembling. "We need to hide!"

Without waiting for a response, I grabbed Mia's hand and pulled her behind a stack of canvases, Liam close at our heels. We crouched low, hearts racing as we strained to listen. The footsteps grew louder, echoing in the confined space, accompanied by murmurs that sent chills down my spine.

"Stay quiet," Liam whispered, his voice a low growl.

The door creaked open, and a figure stepped into the room. My breath hitched as I caught a glimpse of a familiar silhouette. The world spun, and for a moment, I couldn't tell if I was imagining things. "No, it can't be..." I breathed, the realization hitting me like a thunderclap.

As the figure turned, their features illuminated by the dim light, I felt a surge of disbelief and fear. It was someone I never expected to see here, someone whose presence threatened to unravel everything we had uncovered. The shadows deepened, cloaking our hiding place in uncertainty, as the door creaked shut behind them, leaving us shrouded in silence and dread.

Chapter 10: The Unraveling Thread

The air in downtown Boston crackled with a charged electricity, a kind of energy that thrummed beneath the skin and pulled me toward the center of the lavish art auction that glittered like a jewel in the heart of the city. I stood outside the grand building, a stately affair adorned with polished marble and framed by glowing street lamps that cast an otherworldly glow. The sound of clinking glasses and laughter floated through the open doors, mingling with the low hum of classical music that seeped into the chilly evening air. The world around me felt as though it had transformed into a playground of wealth and privilege, where the elite flitted like fireflies from one expensive piece of art to the next, each one a glimmering thread in the tapestry of their extravagant lives.

I glanced at Liam beside me, his presence both a comfort and a reminder of the whirlwind that had led us here. The tension in his jaw betrayed the apprehension he felt, and I could sense his reluctance to peel back the layers of our families' entangled histories. "Are you sure about this?" he asked, his voice low and laced with concern. It was a reasonable question, one I had wrestled with for days. The journal's revelations had dug deep into the soil of my mind, sprouting doubts and questions I could no longer ignore. I thought about the secrets nestled within its pages, the hidden truths about our parents that tied us together in a way that felt both intimate and invasive.

"We need to know, Liam," I replied, my determination hardening into resolve. "This is more than just about us now. It's about understanding who we are and the choices our families made." I took a deep breath, inhaling the faint scent of jasmine from the potted plants lining the entrance. The evening was ripe with possibility, and I could feel my pulse quicken, both from excitement and the underlying fear that had been my companion since the journal fell into my hands.

As we stepped inside, the atmosphere enveloped me like a warm embrace, rich and intoxicating. Golden chandeliers hung from the ceiling, casting a soft light over the polished floor, where guests wandered, their designer heels clicking against the marble in a rhythm that seemed almost choreographed. I caught snippets of conversations about art, investments, and scandalous rumors that made me feel like I was peering into a world far removed from my own. The walls were adorned with breathtaking paintings and sculptures, each piece telling a story I desperately wanted to hear, yet I could sense the unspoken tensions lurking just beneath the surface of the polished veneer.

"Look at that one," Liam murmured, nodding toward a large canvas that dominated the far wall, splashed with colors that danced and swirled like the chaos of my thoughts. "It's mesmerizing, but also... unsettling."

I followed his gaze, intrigued by the way the artwork seemed to pulsate with life, echoing the turmoil of my own heart. "Just like us," I said with a wry smile, attempting to lighten the moment. His lips twitched in response, but the shadow of seriousness clung to him like a cloak.

"Let's find some answers," he suggested, and together we navigated the crowd, weaving through elegantly dressed patrons who seemed too absorbed in their own worlds to notice us. Each step felt weighted, as though we were crossing invisible thresholds into realms of hidden truths.

As we moved deeper into the auction, the buzz of excitement intensified. Bidders raised their paddles with fervor, eager to secure their pieces of artistry as if they were also claiming parts of their identities. My eyes roamed the room, seeking something—a whisper of connection, perhaps, or a glimmer of recognition. I could feel it in the pit of my stomach; someone was watching us, hidden in the shadows, their gaze a tangible force that sent a shiver down my spine.

"Do you feel that?" I asked, my voice barely above a whisper. Liam's brow furrowed in confusion as he scanned the room. "It's like there's a storm brewing beneath all this glamour."

"Maybe it's just your imagination," he replied, but I caught the unease flickering in his eyes.

"Or maybe it's something more." I turned my attention back to the art, hoping to shake off the feeling. A painting caught my eye, a serene landscape that contrasted sharply with the chaos around us. I stepped closer, losing myself in the details—the brush strokes, the subtle blending of colors, the way light danced across the canvas.

"Beautiful, isn't it?" a voice beside me remarked. I turned to see a woman with dark, cascading hair and piercing green eyes that sparkled with mischief. "But it hides a secret, just like all the best pieces do."

"Secrets?" I echoed, intrigued. "What do you mean?"

"The history behind that one is tangled," she said, a knowing smile curving her lips. "A family affair, just like the ones you're unraveling, I suspect." Her gaze shifted to Liam, lingering for a moment too long before returning to me. "Be careful where you tread. The past has a way of reaching out when you least expect it."

I glanced at Liam, whose expression mirrored my own confusion and curiosity. "Do you know something?" I pressed, my heart racing. The room around us faded into a blur as the woman leaned in closer, her voice dropping to a conspiratorial whisper.

"Trust your instincts," she said, her tone a mix of warning and intrigue. "The truth can be both a blessing and a curse." With that cryptic message hanging in the air, she turned and vanished into the throng of bidders, leaving me with a head full of questions and a heart pounding with the thrill of the unknown.

The auction continued around us, yet I felt detached, a mere spectator in a play that was spiraling out of control. The laughter and chatter swirled like a distant echo, but beneath the surface, the tension thickened like a storm cloud ready to burst. I exchanged a glance with Liam, and in that fleeting moment, we both understood—this was more than an art auction. It was a chess game, and we were stepping into the arena, unaware of the dangers that lay ahead.

The auction hall pulsed with an unrelenting rhythm, a heartbeat that echoed through the crowd, merging with the hum of anticipation and whispered secrets. Each art piece seemed to glisten under the golden light, its beauty both captivating and oppressive, much like the emotions swirling within me. I could almost feel the air crackle with unspoken words, as if the very walls held their breath, waiting for a revelation.

Liam stood beside me, his posture tense, eyes darting around the room like a hawk surveying its domain. "You really think we'll find something here?" His voice was a mix of hope and skepticism, a cocktail of emotions that mirrored my own.

"I have to believe we will," I replied, forcing a smile that felt more like a mask than a genuine expression. "The journal mentioned connections to art, and this auction is overflowing with history. It's bound to hold some clues." I stepped closer to a nearby painting—a surreal piece with twisted figures and vibrant colors that seemed to reach out for attention, pulling me deeper into its chaotic world. It resonated with the turmoil I felt inside, a reflection of the confusion that had been my constant companion since I discovered the truth about our families.

"Or it could just be an overpriced mess," Liam quipped, but the faint smile tugging at his lips suggested he was warming to the idea.

"Beauty is in the eye of the beholder, or so they say," I shot back, elbowing him gently. "Besides, if it's a mess, at least we'll have something to laugh about later."

We wandered further into the room, drawn by the whispers of possibility and the glimmers of hope that danced just out of reach. Guests flitted past us, their laughter ringing like chimes, yet there was an undercurrent of tension threading through the air. I caught snippets of conversation—"inheritance," "betrayal," and "lost treasures"—words that flickered like shadows, hinting at the deeper mysteries tangled in the fabric of this event.

A sudden burst of applause drew my attention, and I turned to see a well-dressed auctioneer gesturing flamboyantly as he introduced the next piece—a grand portrait that commanded attention, its frame adorned with intricate gold leaf. As the crowd leaned forward, eager to bid, I felt a tingle run down my spine. Something about the painting felt eerily familiar, as if it had been a part of my life long before this moment.

"Doesn't it remind you of something?" I murmured to Liam, who stood beside me, his brow furrowed in concentration.

"Like what?" he asked, glancing from the painting to me, clearly unsure.

"I don't know yet, but it feels like a memory just out of reach," I replied, my voice barely a whisper as I allowed my thoughts to roam. "Perhaps it's tied to the journal, or maybe even our families."

His eyes narrowed as he studied the painting, a look of determination crossing his features. "Let's find out."

With renewed purpose, we made our way closer to the front, weaving through the elegantly dressed patrons and their clinking champagne glasses. The closer we got, the more I could sense a tension building in the air, a subtle shift that made the hair on my arms stand at attention. I leaned in toward Liam, lowering my voice to a conspiratorial whisper. "What if we aren't the only ones searching for answers tonight?"

"Could be," he replied, his expression growing serious. "We might have competition."

Before I could respond, the auctioneer's voice boomed through the room, cutting through the murmurs and laughter like a knife. "Ladies and gentlemen, we have a truly extraordinary piece coming up next! This portrait is not only a stunning example of craftsmanship but is also rumored to have ties to one of Boston's most influential families."

A ripple of interest coursed through the crowd, and I exchanged a glance with Liam. "What if this is it?" I whispered, excitement bubbling within me.

"Let's hope we can get a good look before it's auctioned off," he said, and with that, we edged closer, our focus sharpening as the room fell into a hush. The painting was unveiled, revealing a striking figure in elegant attire, eyes piercing and alive, as if they were watching us even now. It was a masterful work, capturing not just a likeness but the very essence of the subject.

"Who is that?" I breathed, captivated by the intensity of the gaze fixed on me.

"Looks like a Hawthorne," Liam murmured, the name rolling off his tongue like a secret he wasn't entirely comfortable sharing. "I think the family has a long history with art collecting."

"Exactly what we need," I said, my heart racing with the thrill of discovery. "We need to dig deeper into this connection."

The auctioneer's voice rose again, encouraging bids that flew through the air like confetti. As the numbers climbed, my focus shifted to a figure lurking at the edge of the crowd. A man with a sharp jaw and a predatory gaze was watching us, his presence palpable, as if he were part of the shadows that danced around the room. My instincts screamed at me, an alarm ringing in my head. Who was he, and what was his interest in us?

"Liam," I whispered, my heart thudding loudly against my ribs. "I think we might have a problem."

"What?" He turned to follow my gaze, and I felt the tension between us heighten.

"Look at that guy over there," I said, nodding discreetly toward the stranger, whose eyes bore into us with unsettling intensity.

"Do you think he's following us?" Liam asked, scanning the crowd as if looking for a ghost that only I could see.

"I don't know, but something's off. He's been watching us since we walked in," I replied, my stomach knotting with unease.

Just then, the auctioneer called for the final bid, and the energy in the room shifted. The man stepped forward, his presence commanding attention as he raised his paddle high, a confident smirk playing on his lips. The auctioneer paused, acknowledging him with a nod that felt almost conspiratorial.

I turned to Liam, my voice barely more than a breath. "What do we do?"

"We keep our distance," he said firmly. "But we need to find out who he is."

As the final bid was struck, and the painting was sold to the man with the smirk, I felt a strange mix of victory and dread. There was a story here, an unravelling thread that wove through our lives and into this art auction. I could feel it tugging at my consciousness, leading me deeper into a mystery that felt bigger than either of us.

"Let's stick close," Liam said, his tone resolute. "We'll follow him."

With determination ignited, we slipped into the crowd, shadows among shadows, fueled by a shared sense of purpose and the tantalizing promise of unraveling the secrets that bound our families together.

As we maneuvered through the sea of well-heeled patrons, I kept my gaze trained on the man who had caught my attention, my heart pounding with a mixture of fear and exhilaration. He had blended into the crowd with an effortless grace, but now his dark suit and polished shoes made him stand out like a raven in a flock of doves. His confident swagger was unsettling, a predator among prey.

"Do you think he knows we're onto him?" I whispered to Liam, my voice barely cutting through the soft strains of music that filled the air. I felt a sudden rush of adrenaline, the kind that thrummed in my veins like an electric current.

"Let's hope not," he replied, his expression a mix of caution and determination. "Stay close to me, and keep your eyes peeled. If he's connected to our families, then he could be the key to everything."

Just as I was about to nod, the crowd surged forward, drawn by the allure of another artwork being unveiled. I lost sight of the man, a fleeting shadow amidst the glittering tableau of luxury and desire. Panic surged through me, and I felt an inexplicable sense of urgency. "We have to find him," I urged, my voice rising above the din of the room. "I have a feeling he knows something."

Liam squeezed my hand, a reassuring gesture that did little to quell the storm brewing in my chest. "Let's cut through the crowd. We can circle around the display area."

Together, we made our way toward the edge of the room, navigating through clusters of guests engrossed in animated discussions about art and fortune. I could feel my pulse thrumming in my ears, a constant reminder of the danger that lurked beneath the surface of this glamorous façade. Each clink of a glass, each burst of laughter, felt like a mask concealing the deeper, darker truths that were begging to be unearthed.

Finally, we reached a quieter corridor lined with more paintings, a sanctuary away from the fray. I paused to catch my breath, scanning the area for any sign of the man who had piqued my curiosity.

"Where could he have gone?" I muttered, frustration tinging my words.

"Let's check the next room," Liam suggested, motioning to a set of double doors at the end of the hall. He pushed them open, revealing an intimate gathering—a smaller group of collectors discussing art in hushed tones, the atmosphere thick with intrigue. The walls were lined with exquisite pieces, their beauty underscored by the soft glow of strategically placed lights.

I stepped in cautiously, my eyes darting around, searching for a familiar silhouette. My gut twisted as I scanned the faces, each one a mask hiding stories that had yet to be told. Just then, I spotted him—a flash of that dark suit, leaning casually against the wall, his attention seemingly on the conversation happening beside him. But there was something in his posture, a tension that belied the ease of his stance.

"There he is," I whispered, urgency seeping into my tone. "What's our move?"

Liam's expression hardened as he observed the man. "We need to be careful. Let's blend in, act like we belong here. I'll initiate a conversation. You keep an eye on him."

Nodding, I straightened my posture, summoning every ounce of confidence I could muster. We approached a group engaged in lively debate over an abstract piece that appeared to challenge the very fabric of reality. "What do you think?" I asked, feigning casual interest as I drew closer to the man. "Is art meant to provoke thought or simply to be admired?"

He turned, surprise flickering in his eyes before a charming smile broke through. "Both, I suppose. But isn't the real magic found in the stories behind the art?" His gaze slid to the side, subtly indicating his awareness of my ulterior motive.

I leaned in slightly, intrigued. "You sound like someone who knows quite a bit about it. Any recommendations for a novice like me?"

"Ah, a fellow seeker of truths," he replied, his smile widening. "My name is Victor Hawthorne." He extended a hand, which I took reluctantly, my instincts prickling with recognition.

"Hawthorne?" I repeated, trying to mask the unease that twisted in my stomach. "As in the family connected to—"

"Art and secrets, yes. We're known for both." His tone shifted, becoming more serious, as though the weight of his lineage pressed down on him. "And you are?"

"Just a curious admirer," I replied, keeping my tone light while internally wrestling with the implications of his name.

Liam stepped closer, an eyebrow raised in caution. "I'm Liam. We're here to learn about the art world, like anyone else, right?" His voice had that charming lilt, a practiced ease that always seemed to win people over.

Victor's eyes narrowed slightly, assessing us with a calculated gaze. "And what exactly are you hoping to learn? The history behind the art? Or perhaps the connections that bind us all?" There was a hint of challenge in his tone, as if he could sense the underlying quest driving us.

"Both," I replied, my heart racing as the conversation took a sharper turn. "History is often more fascinating than the present."

"Indeed," he mused, his gaze lingering on me as if sizing up my resolve. "But be careful. The past can sometimes be a double-edged sword."

"Isn't that the truth?" Liam chimed in, his voice laced with an easy charm that belied the tension simmering beneath the surface. "What would you say is the most valuable lesson you've learned from your family's legacy?"

Victor chuckled softly, a sound devoid of warmth. "Trust no one. Especially not in a room full of art collectors. Everyone has an agenda." His words hung between us like a challenge, igniting an unspoken tension.

Before either of us could respond, a sudden commotion erupted from the auction floor, voices rising in alarm. The door swung open, and a group of security personnel rushed past us, their expressions grim. The atmosphere shifted palpably, a ripple of concern washing over the guests.

"What's happening?" I asked, my heart racing as I turned back to Victor.

His expression morphed into one of annoyance. "Looks like the night is about to take a turn for the worse. Stay close, and whatever you do, don't get involved." With that, he began to back away, disappearing into the throng of attendees, leaving me with an unsettling sense of foreboding.

Liam grabbed my arm, pulling me closer as we watched the chaos unfold. "We should go," he urged, his eyes scanning the room. "This doesn't feel right."

But as we turned to leave, the lights flickered, plunging the room into brief darkness before the emergency lights kicked in, casting eerie shadows across the gallery. Gasps filled the air, and I felt a surge of panic rise within me.

Then came the unmistakable sound of shattering glass, followed by a commotion that rattled through the crowd like an electric shock. I felt my pulse quicken, a primal instinct urging me to flee, but my feet felt rooted to the spot.

"Stay close!" Liam shouted over the noise, but even as he spoke, chaos erupted, people screaming and scrambling for the exits.

Suddenly, amidst the confusion, I caught a glimpse of a figure slipping out through a side door—a dark silhouette, familiar yet fleeting. My heart raced, and before I could process my own thoughts, I broke away from Liam, chasing after the shadow that felt like a tether to the answers I craved.

"Wait!" Liam shouted, but I was already lost in the crowd, driven by an instinct I couldn't fully grasp. I pushed through the chaos, the world around me a blur of movement and sound, my mind racing with the implications of what was unfolding.

As I reached the door, I paused just long enough to look back at the chaos I was leaving behind, a swirling maelstrom of fear and uncertainty. My heart hammered in my chest as I pushed through, stepping into the dimly lit hallway beyond.

And then, silence enveloped me. I stood there, breathless, my pulse echoing in my ears as I strained to hear any hint of movement. The darkness felt heavy, pressing down on me like a weight, and as I took a step forward, something sharp caught my eye—a glimmer of light reflecting off a polished surface.

I turned slowly, my heart racing as I drew closer, only to find the unmistakable outline of a familiar object—an ornate dagger embedded in the wall, the blade gleaming wickedly, its hilt adorned with intricate carvings that spoke of a history long forgotten.

"What the—" I began, but before I could finish, a chilling laugh echoed down the corridor, cold and mocking. My skin prickled, and I felt the hairs on the back of my neck stand on end.

"Did you really think you could uncover the truth so easily?" The voice dripped with disdain, wrapping around me like a serpent ready to strike.

I spun around, adrenaline surging through my veins, ready to confront the darkness that threatened to engulf me. But as I turned, the corridor lay empty, save for the dagger glinting in the low light—a sinister invitation to unravel the secrets that lay hidden just beneath the surface.

With every instinct screaming at me to run, I realized I was standing at the precipice of something far more dangerous than I had ever imagined, the threads of fate twisting around me like a noose, drawing me deeper into a web of deception and intrigue. I took a deep breath, clenching my fists as I prepared to face

Chapter 11: Shadows of Deceit

The gallery thrummed with energy, a potent blend of soft laughter and clinking glasses, each note weaving into a tapestry of sophistication and wealth. I could feel the palpable excitement vibrating through the air as I stood beside Liam, his presence a comforting anchor amidst the swirling chaos of the art auction. The walls, adorned with masterpieces that whispered stories of their creators, closed in around us, but the vivid colors and intricate details painted a world far removed from the tension brewing beneath the surface.

Liam leaned closer, his breath a warm tickle against my ear. "You see that one?" He pointed discreetly toward a vibrant abstract piece, its swirls of red and blue almost pulsating with life. "The artist is notorious for hiding clues within his work. They say if you look closely enough, you might find a treasure map." His eyes sparkled with mischief, and I couldn't help but chuckle, a sound that mingled with the crowd's murmur.

"Only you would think about treasure maps in an art gallery," I teased, feeling a warm flush creep up my neck. "I'm more concerned about the prices on those pieces. They could buy a small island."

He laughed softly, the sound rich and genuine. "True, but wouldn't it be worth it if we found a way to make our fortune?"

The banter flowed easily between us, each playful jab wrapped in the warmth of camaraderie. Just then, a flicker of movement caught my eye—a man in a tailored suit slipped past us, his demeanor slightly off, like a key that didn't quite fit in the lock. I narrowed my eyes, a spark of intuition igniting in the pit of my stomach.

Suddenly, chaos erupted, shattering our moment of levity. A high-pitched scream cut through the ambient noise, drawing every eye toward the center of the gallery. The commotion centered around a massive canvas, its vibrant colors reduced to a blur as people surged forward, desperate to get a glimpse. My heart raced as I pushed through the throng, adrenaline coursing through my veins. I needed to know what was happening.

"Stay close!" Liam shouted, his voice barely audible above the growing panic. But as I turned to respond, the crowd shifted, a wave pulling us apart like a riptide dragging me away from safety. Panic tightened its grip on my chest as I searched for him, but the sea of faces was unyielding, a throng of confusion and chaos.

In that moment, I was utterly alone.

I stumbled back, my breath hitching in my throat as I watched in horror. A figure darted from the crowd, a glimmering object clutched tightly in his hand. It was a small sculpture, worth more than my entire year's salary—a masterpiece that had only moments ago been displayed on a pedestal for eager buyers. I moved instinctively, following the thief as he slipped through the side door, the scent of desperation and expensive cologne trailing in his wake.

The dimly lit hallways of the gallery enveloped me, shadows creeping along the walls like ghosts. My heart thudded in my chest as I navigated the narrow corridors, each step echoing ominously in the silence. The whispers began, curling around me like smoke, weaving through the darkness. They spoke of deceit and danger, tales of a game far more sinister than I had imagined.

"You shouldn't be here," a voice hissed, low and menacing, from the shadows.

I froze, my breath catching. "Who's there?" I called, the bravado in my voice barely masking the fear clawing at my insides.

No response, just the soft rustle of fabric as the figure shifted. My instincts screamed at me to run, to turn back to the safety of the main room and Liam's reassuring presence. But I was drawn to the darkness, curiosity mingling with dread, urging me to uncover the truth hidden in these shadowy corners.

I crept forward, the air thick with tension, each footfall a challenge against the silence. The walls were adorned with smaller, less impressive artworks—pieces that seemed to fade into the background, unnoticed in the flurry of the auction. My fingertips brushed against the cold surface of a frame, and I stumbled back as a loud crash resonated from further down the hall, the sound ricocheting off the walls like a gunshot.

"Where are you?" I whispered into the void, my voice trembling. I pressed on, heart racing, each shadow flickering with the potential for danger. My mind swirled with a myriad of thoughts: Was this all part of the auction? A diversion for something larger? I had to know, but at what cost?

Suddenly, a door creaked open just ahead, light spilling out into the darkness like a beacon. I felt drawn to it, a moth to a flame. I approached cautiously, peering inside. The room was sparsely decorated, a single lightbulb dangling from the ceiling, illuminating a table littered with papers and—oh my God—a map. My breath quickened as I recognized the symbols scattered across the page, their meaning elusive yet oddly familiar.

A voice broke through my reverie, smooth and unsettling. "Looking for something?"

I spun around, meeting the gaze of the man who had stolen the sculpture, his smirk disarming yet laced with danger. He stepped into the light, revealing an enigmatic aura that set my nerves on edge. "You've wandered into something you don't understand, darling."

A chill slithered down my spine. "What do you want?" I managed, the defiance in my tone struggling against the instinct to flee.

"Information," he said, his tone silky smooth. "And perhaps, if you're clever enough, a way out of this tangled web."

His grin was disconcertingly charming, as if the thief had perfected the art of disarming anyone with a flash of white teeth.

"Information is a currency of its own," he continued, leaning casually against the doorframe, arms crossed as if we were simply having a friendly chat about the weather. "You see, darling, you're standing in the middle of a heist, and I'd rather not have a little bird like you chirping to the authorities."

I squared my shoulders, unwilling to show him the shivers of unease racing down my spine. "And what if I refuse? Am I your hostage now?" I shot back, trying to keep my voice steady despite the quivering trepidation clawing at my throat.

"Hostage is such a strong word." He chuckled, a low, melodious sound that felt wrong in the situation. "Think of it as... a collaborative effort. You can either help me, or I'll have to silence you." His eyes glinted, and the way he spoke suggested that he relished the power he held.

"Silence me? With what? A stolen sculpture?" I countered, forcing a laugh that came out a little shaky. I knew I needed to buy time—every second counted, and I had to figure out how to escape this precarious situation.

"You're sharper than I expected." He stepped closer, and I instinctively took a step back, the cold wall pressing against my back reminding me of my isolation. "But you still don't quite understand the game being played here. What you're dealing with is bigger than a mere artwork. This is about control, power, and secrets that could bring down empires."

The weight of his words settled heavily in the air, and I felt an unsettling mix of fear and intrigue. "What secrets?" I managed to ask, trying to sound more curious than terrified.

"Oh, I can't share all the details just yet. But let's just say this gallery holds more than art—it harbors connections that could either save or damn us all." He extended a hand toward the map spread across the table, his demeanor shifting from playful to deadly serious. "And I need someone with your... tenacity to help me retrieve what's been lost. It's a matter of time before those involved realize that pieces are missing."

"Lost? Or stolen?" I replied, unable to keep the skepticism from my voice. "And why should I trust you? You just stole a piece of art right in front of everyone!"

"Because, my dear," he said, his tone softening just enough to be disarming, "if you're caught here alone, you'll be implicated as an accomplice. They'll never believe that you simply stumbled into this mess."

His words echoed in my mind, a strange mixture of fear and curiosity blooming within me. I hated the way he seemed to be reading me so easily, as if my internal struggle was written plainly across my face. "And what's in it for me?" I asked, challenging his authority, fighting to keep control over this bizarre conversation.

He chuckled again, but there was something darker lurking beneath the laughter. "Besides your freedom? Well, how about a chance to become a player in a game that could change everything?"

The prospect danced tantalizingly close, but danger lurked like a shadow behind him, whispering warnings in my ear. "You must think I'm naive if you believe I'd step into your trap without knowing the stakes."

"Oh, I have no doubt you're anything but naïve," he replied, the amusement in his voice swirling into something more sinister. "But think carefully. You could walk away and bury your head in the sand, or you could step into the light and help me retrieve what was stolen—before it's too late."

Before I could respond, a sound from behind him startled us both. The door swung open, revealing a figure cloaked in darkness, silhouetted against the dim light spilling into the room. I squinted, heart racing, unsure if my luck had turned or if danger had come calling once again.

"Are you both going to stand around chatting, or are we actually going to get this done?" The newcomer stepped forward, revealing a tall woman with striking features—her hair a cascade of dark curls, eyes sharp and assessing. She had the air of someone who was used to getting what she wanted, and it sent a shiver of recognition through me.

"Who are you?" I demanded, my voice breaking the tension that crackled in the air like static.

"Just a friend," she said, her tone casual, as if we weren't standing in the midst of a heist gone awry. "But I'm much more useful than he is." She gestured toward the thief, a smirk playing on her lips. "After all, I know where the real treasure lies."

"Treasure? Are we still talking about art, or have we crossed over into pirate territory?" I shot back, a flicker of sarcasm slipping through the rising tension.

"Art is merely the surface, darling," she replied, unfazed. "What we're after is much more valuable."

I glanced between the two of them, the enormity of the situation starting to crystallize. "And what makes you think I'd want to get involved in your little treasure hunt?"

"Because you have something we need," the woman said matter-of-factly, eyes narrowing slightly. "Your connection to the auction. You're not just a bystander; you're a piece of this puzzle."

I couldn't help but laugh, though the sound was laced with a hint of nervousness. "And what if I refuse?"

"Then we'll have to make it very unpleasant for you," the thief chimed in, his tone shifting back to that predatory edge. "And we wouldn't want that, now would we?"

My heart pounded in my chest, each beat urging me to reconsider my options. I had stumbled into a game that I didn't fully understand, yet the stakes were higher than I ever imagined. I could feel the weight of their gazes, calculating and waiting for my response.

"Fine," I said, drawing in a deep breath, the resolve forming in my chest like steel. "But if I'm going to do this, I want to know everything. No more secrets."

The two exchanged glances, a silent conversation passing between them, before the woman nodded. "Very well. But trust is a fragile thing, and you'll need to tread carefully."

"Trust is earned, not given," I countered, my voice firm. "So let's see if you can earn mine."

As I stepped further into the room, the thrill of danger laced with the pulse of uncertainty surged within me, awakening something that had lain dormant for too long. This was my chance to not only reclaim my autonomy but to uncover the layers of deception hidden beneath the artful exterior of the gallery. The game had just begun, and I was determined to play my part—whatever it took.

The air crackled with tension as I stood there, caught in the web of intrigue spun by two enigmatic figures. The woman's gaze bore into me, a mix of challenge and curiosity, while the thief leaned back against the wall, arms crossed in that annoyingly confident way that made me want to punch him and ask him for the details at the same time.

"Let's get one thing straight," I said, trying to project authority I didn't entirely feel. "I'm not here to play your little game. I want to know exactly what's going on and why you think I'm the right person for this... adventure."

"Adventure? Is that what we're calling it?" the thief said, his tone light and mocking. "I prefer to think of it as a thrilling escapade, filled with danger and deceit. It has a nicer ring to it, don't you think?"

"Danger and deceit? Sounds like a Tuesday for me," I replied, crossing my arms defiantly. "But that doesn't mean I'm signing up for your circus without knowing the show."

The woman chuckled, her dark curls bouncing slightly. "Fair enough. My name is Cassia, and the charming thief over there is Kade." She gestured toward him with an exaggerated flourish. "We're looking for a particular piece that went missing during tonight's auction. One that has a certain... historical significance. If it falls into the wrong hands, it could create chaos."

"Chaos? That sounds dramatic," I remarked, feigning nonchalance while my pulse quickened. "What's so special about this piece? Is it a stolen relic? A cursed painting? Or just another overpriced canvas with delusions of grandeur?"

Kade's grin faded as he stepped forward, the playful tone replaced by something more serious. "It's not just any painting, sweetheart. It's rumored to hold the key to a hidden collection of artifacts—things that could change the power dynamics in the art world forever. Not to mention that several powerful people are after it. They're willing to do whatever it takes to get their hands on that painting."

A chill slid down my spine as I considered the implications. "And you want me to help you find it?"

"Precisely," Cassia interjected, her voice smooth and persuasive. "You have connections here. You know the ins and outs of the gallery and its patrons. You're our best chance at recovering it without raising too much suspicion."

"And if I refuse?" I asked, testing the waters, wanting to see how far I could push.

"Then we have a little problem," Kade said, his voice dropping to a conspiratorial whisper. "We're not the only ones hunting for it. If you walk away now, you'll be putting yourself in danger. You'll have to look over your shoulder everywhere you go."

I narrowed my eyes, weighing my options. "And if I help? What's in it for me?"

Cassia stepped closer, her expression earnest. "We can offer protection, and if we succeed, you'll gain access to information and connections you've only dreamed of. This could be your entry into a world you've always been on the outskirts of. Plus, there's a hefty reward for the painting."

The thought of freedom, power, and prestige danced tantalizingly in my mind, but the sense of foreboding loomed large. "And how do I know I can trust you?"

Kade shrugged, a gesture that felt almost too casual for the gravity of the situation. "You don't. But trust is a luxury we can't afford right now. All you have is this moment. Are you in or out?"

I hesitated, caught between the allure of adventure and the instincts urging me to retreat. With a deep breath, I made my decision. "Fine. I'll help. But I want full transparency. No more secrets."

"Deal," Cassia said, extending her hand, and I grasped it firmly, feeling the electric tension between us. Kade followed suit, and with a reluctant smile, he sealed our unholy alliance.

"Now, where do we start?" I asked, crossing my arms and adopting my best investigative stance.

"The auction house has a basement," Cassia explained, her voice low as if revealing a long-held secret. "Rumor has it that they store some of the more controversial pieces down there. We might find a lead. And if we're lucky, the painting itself."

A sudden crash echoed down the hall, reverberating through the gallery and cutting our conversation short. My heart jumped into my throat, and Cassia's expression hardened, eyes narrowing as she strained to listen.

"Sounds like the party is getting out of hand," Kade said, his demeanor shifting from playful to alert. "We need to move, now."

With Kade in the lead and Cassia following closely, we made our way through the labyrinthine corridors, each corner feeling like a potential trap. I was hyper-aware of every sound—the creak of floorboards, the distant murmur of voices, and the growing din from the main auction area.

As we approached a heavy door marked with the words "Authorized Personnel Only," Kade paused, glancing back at us. "This is it. We'll split up once we're in. I'll check the storage room on the left; you two take the right."

"Wait," I interjected, a rush of concern threading through me. "We should stick together. This isn't a picnic; it's a heist."

Kade smirked, leaning casually against the wall. "Believe me, sweetheart, the less you see of me, the better for you. Trust me on this."

Before I could protest further, he pushed the door open, revealing a dimly lit corridor. Cassia and I stepped inside, the musty air heavy with the scent of dust and forgotten treasures.

As we made our way down the narrow passage, my senses heightened. Every shadow seemed to shift, and I felt like prey in a predator's lair. "What exactly are we looking for?" I whispered, trying to keep my voice steady.

"Anything that looks out of place," Cassia replied, her eyes scanning the shelves lined with crates and art pieces draped in cloth. "We're looking for any signs of the painting or anything that could lead us to it."

Just then, a low growl resonated from the darkness ahead, freezing us in our tracks. I exchanged a wary glance with Cassia, heart pounding as I strained to see what lay ahead.

"Did you hear that?" I asked, my voice barely above a whisper.

Cassia nodded, her eyes wide. "I think we should—"

Before she could finish, the growling grew louder, morphing into a rumble that echoed through the corridor. In an instant, a figure lunged out of the shadows—an imposing man, his face obscured by a mask, brandishing a crowbar like a weapon.

"Stop right there!" he roared, and in that moment, the air thickened with danger.

My mind raced. This was no longer just a search for a stolen painting. We were in over our heads, and the stakes were higher than I had ever imagined.

"Run!" I shouted, adrenaline propelling me forward, and as we darted back down the corridor, I couldn't shake the feeling that we had crossed a line from which there was no turning back. The growl of the shadows behind us deepened, promising that the game was just beginning.

Chapter 12: The Chase

The narrow streets of Boston twisted like a labyrinth, each corner revealing an unexpected scene that seemed to pulse with life and possibility. I felt the energy of the city vibrate beneath my feet, the ancient cobblestones echoing tales of a thousand footsteps before mine. With every stride, my heart raced in rhythm with Liam's, the thrill of the chase propelling us forward. I could smell the sharp tang of salt from the harbor, a briny reminder of the mysteries that lingered just out of reach, and the sweet scent of fresh pastries wafting from a nearby café momentarily distracted me from our purpose.

Liam moved beside me, his presence a steadying force amidst the chaos. His tousled hair caught the morning sun, framing his face with an effortless charm that made my stomach flutter. "If we don't catch this guy soon, I might need to invest in a new pair of running shoes," he quipped, shooting me a playful grin. The warmth in his eyes sparked something deeper than mere camaraderie, igniting a heat that flared between us like a secret shared under the cover of night.

"Or I could lend you mine," I shot back, a teasing lilt in my voice. "I hear pink is your color." My laughter rang out, bright against the backdrop of city sounds: a distant siren, the chatter of pedestrians, the rhythmic clanging of the harbor bells. The banter felt like a lifeline, a momentary reprieve from the whirlwind of danger that nipped at our heels.

Our latest lead—a scrap of paper with an address scrawled in hurried handwriting—had sent us into the heart of the city. Each step we took seemed to pull us deeper into a world of shadows and secrets, a place where the familiar became strange, and danger lurked just beyond the corners. The streets were alive, the summer air thick with the scent of roasted chestnuts and the mingling voices of people enjoying their day. Yet beneath that vibrant surface lay an undercurrent of tension, an awareness that we weren't just hunters; we were also the hunted.

We turned a corner onto Newbury Street, the upscale boutiques a stark contrast to the urgency of our mission. "Why do I feel like we're running in circles?" I muttered, glancing at the pedestrians who glided past us, blissfully unaware of the chaos swirling in our world. Each one wore a facade of normalcy, oblivious to the underbelly of deception we had stumbled into.

Liam leaned closer, his breath warm against my ear. "Because we're not just chasing a thief; we're chasing shadows. But we'll find him." The confidence in his voice sent a shiver down my spine, both reassuring and thrilling. I could feel the weight of his determination like a tangible force, binding us together in this moment.

I was about to reply when my instincts kicked in. I felt it—the prickle at the back of my neck, the sensation that something was off. My gaze swept the street, catching sight of a figure lingering just beyond the throng, their eyes trained on us. My heart leaped into my throat, an alarm bell ringing in my mind.

"Liam," I whispered, tugging at his sleeve. "Look over there." My finger pointed to the shadowy figure that seemed too still, too intent on our every move.

His brow furrowed, and the playful glint in his eyes vanished, replaced by a sharp focus. "I see him. Let's move." The urgency in his tone urged me forward, our playful exchange giving way to a primal need to survive. We navigated through the crowd, weaving between shoppers and tourists, our hearts pounding in sync, the thrill of the chase morphing into a desperate need to escape.

With every stride, I felt the adrenaline coursing through my veins, a fire igniting within me. The city became a blur of colors and sounds, each moment unfolding in a vivid tapestry of danger and desire. I could hear Liam's steady breaths, the cadence of his footfalls matching mine. As we pushed past a street vendor selling flowers, the aroma of fresh blooms mingled with the salty air, creating an intoxicating blend that sent my senses into overdrive.

"Keep going," he urged, his voice low and fierce, guiding me deeper into the maze of Boston's streets. My heart raced, but not just from fear; the electric charge between us was undeniable, each glance we exchanged crackling with an intensity that set my skin alight.

We ducked into an alleyway, the cool shade a brief sanctuary from the sun's relentless heat. The world outside faded for a moment, and in the hush of the narrow passage, our breaths mingled, quick and sharp. I could see the muscles in Liam's jaw tense, the flicker of determination in his eyes. There was an intensity about him that drew me closer, as if the chaos of the chase had stripped away any pretense, leaving raw emotion exposed.

"Are we safe here?" I asked, my voice barely above a whisper, yet it felt like a declaration in the charged silence.

"For now," he replied, the space between us narrowing as he leaned closer. I could feel the warmth radiating from his body, a stark contrast to the chill of fear that had seeped into my bones.

And then, in that fleeting moment where time hung suspended, our lips met, a collision of breath and warmth that electrified the air around us. The kiss was tentative yet fervent, a promise amid the uncertainty. My heart soared, but just as quickly, reality crashed back in. The echo of footsteps reverberated outside the alley, pulling us from our moment of bliss.

"Back to the chase," I murmured, breaking away reluctantly, the thrill of danger mingling with the pulse of something deeper—a connection that transcended the chaos of our pursuit.

"Let's go," Liam said, his eyes sparkling with determination, and as we stepped back into the fray, I knew that the hunt was far from over. But amid the danger, something new had ignited between us, a fire that would not easily be extinguished.

We plunged back into the chaos of Boston's streets, where the din of honking horns and the laughter of café patrons created a dizzying backdrop to our frantic escape. Liam's hand found mine, fingers lacing together like they were meant to be entwined. In that moment, it felt less like we were two people running from danger and more like we were two adventurers lost in a world of our own making, ready to face whatever came next.

I darted a glance at him, trying to gauge the expression behind his steely resolve. "You know," I teased, "if I survive this, I might just need you to promise to take me to dinner. This whole 'running for our lives' thing has made me rather hungry."

He chuckled, a rich sound that mixed with the bustle around us. "Only if you promise not to order something that comes with an extensive list of side effects. I have enough problems without adding your culinary choices to the mix."

His laughter was infectious, a spark that lit up the growing tension inside me. Yet, I felt the weight of the unknown pressing in, a reminder that our playful banter was merely a thin veil over the danger lurking just out of sight. We navigated through the crowded streets, where sunlight danced through the gaps between buildings, illuminating the world around us in patches. I caught snippets of conversations, snippets of lives that seemed so blissfully unaware of the darkness we were entangled in.

"There!" I suddenly shouted, my heart racing as I spotted a flash of movement down the alley. "He's heading toward the waterfront!"

Liam's grip tightened around my hand as we sprinted after the shadow. The scent of the harbor, a mix of sea salt and engine oil, filled my lungs as we rounded the corner. We pushed past a vendor selling colorful kites, their bright hues a stark contrast to the grays and blues of the impending storm clouding my mind.

"Think he'll try to escape by boat?" Liam questioned, his breath coming in quick bursts.

"Let's hope not," I replied, my heart pounding with a mix of excitement and dread. "I'm not quite ready to start swimming."

The chase led us closer to the water, where the air grew thick with humidity, the clouds overhead roiling in dark anticipation. I could hear the low hum of engines and the occasional shout of dock workers preparing for the day's haul. Every step felt like a countdown, and with each second, the tension coiled tighter within me.

Then I saw him—a figure darting between the boats, a glimpse of a gray jacket vanishing behind a yacht. "This way!" I called out, pulling Liam along as we followed the trail. The docks creaked underfoot, wooden planks shifting with our weight. The clanging of metal against metal reverberated in the air, the rhythmic sounds echoing the urgency of our pursuit.

"Do you think he knows we're onto him?" Liam asked, his voice edged with urgency.

"Let's hope he's too focused on escaping to worry about us," I panted. The realization that we were indeed the prey sent a shiver down my spine. We had started as hunters, but with every step, it felt like the hunter had become the hunted.

A sudden loud shout pierced the air, slicing through the ambient noise. "Hey! Stop!"

We froze momentarily, eyes darting to the source of the voice. Two uniformed officers, badges glinting in the gray light, stood at the edge of the docks. Panic surged through me. If they caught us, if they thought we were involved in something shady, our pursuit would come to an abrupt halt.

Liam caught my gaze and nodded slightly. "We can't let them see us."

With a quick glance back at the officers, I sprinted towards the nearest boat, a sleek motor vessel docked haphazardly. "This way!" I whispered urgently, climbing aboard, the boat rocking gently beneath us.

He followed, leaping onto the deck with surprising agility. We crouched low, hidden behind the cabin, our breaths mingling with the salt and sweat that lingered in the air.

"Do you think they saw us?" I whispered, my heart thumping loudly enough that I feared it would give us away.

"Doubtful," Liam replied, scanning the area. "But we can't stay here for long. We need a plan." His eyes flickered to the harbor, where boats bobbed like corks, each one a potential escape route.

I felt the pulse of adrenaline surge again, an intoxicating blend of fear and exhilaration. "What if we grab one of those smaller boats?" I suggested, my mind racing. "It could be fast enough to get us out of here, and we'd be off the radar."

"Smart thinking," he replied, a sly grin breaking through the tension. "As long as you promise to steer clear of the ocean's culinary delights."

A laugh escaped my lips, momentarily easing the tightness in my chest. But the sound quickly faded as the reality of our situation crashed back.

Suddenly, the thief emerged from the shadows, his gray jacket unmistakable. My breath caught as he looked around, eyes narrowed, clearly searching for any signs of us. "He's here!" I hissed.

Liam's hand shot out, grabbing my arm. "We have to move. Now."

We scrambled from our hiding place, ducking low as we crept toward the edge of the dock. The thief was only a few boats away, and I could see the frantic way he scanned the harbor, his every move a testament to the pressure of his own desperation.

"Look!" Liam pointed. "There's a smaller vessel just down the line. If we can reach it first, we might be able to cut him off."

I nodded, heart pounding as we set off, every nerve in my body on high alert. The stakes had never felt higher, the thrill of the chase palpable in the salty air. As we darted between boats, I felt a surge of determination. We weren't just chasing a thief; we were chasing a future—one that flickered with the possibility of adventure, danger, and perhaps, a little romance.

"Just one more push," Liam murmured as we neared the boat. "On three, we make a run for it."

My heart raced in sync with his, each beat echoing a promise: we would not back down, no matter the cost.

We surged forward, adrenaline coursing through us as we neared the small boat. The sun glinted off its polished hull, a beacon of hope amid the swirling chaos of the docks. Liam and I exchanged a determined glance, the unspoken pact between us solidified in that brief moment—a shared understanding that whatever lay ahead, we would face it together.

"One, two, three!" Liam urged, and we launched ourselves toward the boat, limbs pumping like the pistons of a well-oiled machine. I felt the wind whip through my hair as we leaped aboard, the deck vibrating under our weight. With a quick look over my shoulder, I saw the thief glancing our way, a flash of panic etched on his features. It was all the motivation we needed.

"Get the engine started!" I shouted, my voice barely rising above the clamor of the harbor. I rushed to the control panel, fumbling for the ignition. My fingers trembled slightly, not just from fear but from the thrill of it all. I was steering my fate, along with Liam's, into uncharted waters.

Liam was right beside me, the lines of his jaw set with fierce determination. "I'll handle the lines," he replied, darting to the back of the boat. He untied the ropes with a practiced ease that both amazed and reassured me. "Just make sure we're ready to move as soon as we're free!"

With a flick of a switch, the engine roared to life, shaking the entire vessel as I wrestled with the throttle. My heart raced, mirroring the engine's growl, every beat echoing the urgency of our situation. "Come on, come on," I whispered to the boat, willing it to respond.

The thief was no longer just a shadow in the distance; he was bolting toward us, panic fueling his movements. "We've got company!" I yelled, eyes wide as I shifted my focus to the horizon, scanning for any possible escape route. The open water gleamed like an inviting promise, but the docks were a maze that could easily swallow us whole.

"Just keep the boat steady!" Liam's voice sliced through the haze of my concentration, and I locked eyes with him. He had a fire in his gaze, a fervor that urged me on. I nodded, determined to match his intensity.

With a quick tug, the ropes fell away, and I shoved the throttle forward. The boat lurched, tearing away from the dock with a sudden rush. The water sprayed up around us, glistening like diamonds in the sunlight. My heart raced, not just from the exhilaration of speed but from the thrill of freedom, a taste of adrenaline-soaked escape.

"Hold on!" I called out as we hit the waves, the boat bucking and pitching. The harbor unfolded before us, and I steered toward the open water, leaving behind the safety of the docks and the lingering threat of our pursuer.

Liam steadied himself against the side, eyes locked on the thief now frantically running along the dock, shouting to the officers. "He's getting help!" he shouted, his voice laced with urgency.

"Then we need to be faster," I replied, feeling the weight of the moment pressing down on me. "We need to lose him before he gets on a boat of his own."

I pushed the throttle further, the boat responding with a fierce growl. The shoreline began to blur into a colorful streak as we cut through the water, the wind whipping against our faces, a raw reminder of the danger still trailing behind us.

"Where are we headed?" Liam shouted over the wind, urgency clear in his tone.

"Anywhere but here!" I laughed, exhilaration bubbling up inside me. "The farther we get from the docks, the better!"

The laughter faded as I glanced back and saw the gray jacket once more, the thief now scrambling to commandeer a nearby fishing boat, its motor sputtering to life. "Oh no," I gasped, my stomach sinking. "He's coming after us."

"Can he outrun us?" Liam asked, his voice steady, though I could sense the tension coiling between us.

I tightened my grip on the wheel, heart pounding with a mix of dread and adrenaline. "Not if I can help it." The horizon stretched endlessly before us, promising freedom, yet I felt the pressure of time slipping through my fingers like sand.

"Let's zigzag! It'll make it harder for him to get a clean shot," Liam suggested, adrenaline fueling his words.

"Good idea!" I executed a sharp turn, the boat skimming the surface as it tilted slightly, the salty spray splashing against us. The thief's boat followed, its engine roaring to life as he closed the gap, determination etched on his face. I couldn't let fear grip me; I had to believe we could outsmart him.

"Keep an eye on him," I instructed, glancing at Liam. "I'll maneuver us around the buoy!"

"I see him!" Liam shouted, pointing. "He's right behind us, and he's gaining!"

A surge of frustration bubbled within me. We couldn't afford to be caught now, not when we were so close to unraveling the mystery that had ensnared us. "Hold tight!" I barked, shifting course again, the boat slicing through the water as I danced with the waves.

The thief's boat roared closer, and I felt the tension in the air shift. "We need a plan," I muttered, scanning the waters for any possible escape routes. "What if we can get him to chase us into the shallows? He might run aground!"

"Or we could use the wind to our advantage," Liam suggested, his eyes darting around, taking in our surroundings. "We could swing around that rocky outcrop up ahead and let him crash into the rocks."

The idea sparked a flicker of hope. "Let's do it!" I veered toward the rocky outcrop, praying the boat would respond as we dipped into the wind. The thief was hot on our tail, his boat nearly neck-and-neck with us, the desperation in his eyes unmistakable.

"Now, let's see if you can keep up!" I shouted, revving the engine as we rocketed forward. The wind whipped through my hair, and the shoreline began to blur, a rush of color and sound as we veered sharply around the rocks.

"Cut the engine!" Liam yelled, the urgency in his voice cutting through the wind.

I hesitated for a heartbeat, then complied. The engine sputtered to silence, and the boat drifted quietly, the only sound the gentle lapping of the waves against the hull. We were hidden behind the outcrop, waiting with bated breath.

"Where is he?" I whispered, peering around the rocks. My heart pounded as I scanned the horizon, the silence thick and suffocating. Just as I thought we might have outsmarted him, the roar of an engine shattered the stillness.

"He's right there!" Liam hissed, and my breath caught in my throat as I spotted the thief's boat swinging around the rocks, its engine howling as it surged toward us.

"He's coming!" I gasped, scrambling for the throttle, heart racing as the realization hit me like a slap. There would be no hiding now.

The thief's gaze locked onto ours, a look of pure determination fueling his pursuit. My heart raced, caught between the rush of adrenaline and the chilling knowledge that the chase was far from over.

"Start the engine!" Liam urged, the urgency in his voice matching the pounding in my chest.

I turned to him, panic flaring in my chest as the thief closed the distance. "What if we can't get away?"

"Then we fight," Liam replied, determination etched into every line of his face.

Before I could respond, a flash of something shiny caught my eye, and I realized with dawning horror that the thief wasn't just aiming to catch us; he was aiming to stop us—by any means necessary.

"Liam—" I began, but the words fell short as I saw the gun in the thief's hand, glinting menacingly in the sunlight. The realization hit me with an icy grip, and as the world spiraled into chaos around us, I knew that the chase had transformed into something far more dangerous than either of us had anticipated.

Chapter 13: Ghosts of the Past

The mansion loomed before us like a specter of its former self, shrouded in a tangle of ivy and shadows. A dilapidated sign creaked on its hinges, the letters long faded, but I could still make out the name: Hawthorne House. It had been a lavish estate once, a beacon of grandeur perched atop the hill, but now it sat abandoned, its glory long forgotten. The evening sky, smeared with the bruised colors of dusk, cast an eerie glow on the crumbling façade, and a chill crept up my spine as we crossed the threshold.

Liam moved beside me, his usual confident stride faltering slightly as we stepped into the darkened foyer. The air was thick with the scent of damp wood and something metallic, like rusting dreams. Dust motes danced in the fading light, swirling around us like whispers from a bygone era. I could hear the sound of our footsteps echoing against the walls, each step a reminder of the lives that had once filled this space, laughter that had long since faded into silence.

"Just think of the parties they must have thrown," I said, trying to lighten the heavy atmosphere. "Ball gowns, champagne, and maybe even a scandal or two."

Liam smirked, but it was shadowed by something deeper. "Or perhaps a family torn apart by secrets," he replied, his voice low and tinged with a sorrow I couldn't quite decipher. I glanced at him, catching the flicker of pain in his eyes. This place held more than just dust and decay; it held the weight of his past, a past that we were about to confront in more ways than one.

As we moved further into the mansion, the peeling wallpaper revealed ghostly patterns, remnants of beauty fading like the memories of those who had once inhabited the space. The grand staircase spiraled upward, its balustrade twisted and warped, but I was drawn to a door at the end of the hallway, half-hidden behind a collapsed beam. There was an undeniable pull, a whispering curiosity that urged me forward.

"Hey, look at this," I called out, pushing the door open with a reluctant creak. The hinges protested, but the room inside seemed to exhale a breath of nostalgia. Sunlight streamed through a dusty window, illuminating a small chamber cluttered with forgotten treasures: a cracked mirror, moth-eaten drapes, and stacked canvases, each one whispering tales of the past.

But it was what lay at the center of the room that caught my breath. Against the far wall stood an array of stolen artworks, each canvas a portal to another world, vibrant colors trapped within the confines of this forgotten room. A chill slithered down my spine as I recognized one of the pieces: a painting that had once hung in Liam's brother's studio. The colors sang, and yet, they seemed to weep.

I turned to Liam, who had entered the room behind me. His expression shifted, muscles tensing as he scanned the artwork. The floodgates of his memories opened wide, and I could see it—the pain, the loss, the rage boiling just beneath the surface. "How could they?" he whispered, his voice raw, and I reached for him instinctively.

"Liam, I—"

"They took everything from him," he interrupted, his eyes glistening with unshed tears. "Everything."

The weight of his words hung in the air, heavy and unyielding. I stepped closer, my heart aching for him. "But we can find out who did this. We can make it right."

His gaze flicked to mine, a storm brewing within the depths of his dark eyes. "I don't know if I want to make it right," he admitted, the honesty of his confession slicing through the tension like a knife. "What if I don't want to confront my past?"

The atmosphere thickened, the room seemingly closing in around us as the truth of his words settled. I understood all too well the fear of reopening wounds long thought healed. "Liam," I began, feeling the urgency of the moment, "you're not alone in this. We're in this together."

He turned his body toward mine, the distance between us narrowing, and I felt the warmth radiating off him like a beacon in the darkness. "Together, huh?" His voice was almost playful, a tentative smile forming on his lips that momentarily banished the shadows. "You realize that means you have to deal with my delightful family history, right?"

I grinned, trying to lighten the mood. "And you'll have to endure my charming quirk of talking to inanimate objects. It's a deal."

A soft chuckle escaped him, the tension easing ever so slightly. "Deal." But as quickly as the moment of levity arrived, it was swept away by the weight of the revelation.

"Look," I said, gesturing to the paintings. "If we find the source of these stolen artworks, we can shed light on what happened to your brother. Maybe even discover who's behind the smuggling ring. It's time to stop running from the past."

Liam took a deep breath, his resolve hardening as he stepped closer to the artwork, examining each piece with newfound determination. "You're right," he said, the tremor in his voice replaced by a fierce intensity. "This is more than just my brother's legacy; it's about justice. I won't let his memory be tarnished by cowards."

We began to sift through the canvases, each stroke of paint sparking forgotten memories within Liam. As he spoke, fragments of his brother's life unfurled like petals, revealing a man who had been vibrant, passionate, and full of dreams—dreams now shattered by betrayal and greed.

My heart raced as we uncovered clues, piecing together the tapestry of their shared history, but I could feel the shadows of our own feelings lurking just beneath the surface. With each shared memory, I became acutely aware of how intertwined our lives had become. The air crackled with an energy that was both thrilling and terrifying, a taut line between friendship and something deeper.

As we stood in that hidden room, surrounded by ghosts both personal and collective, I knew we were on the precipice of something monumental. The past may have its claws in us, but together, we would unravel the threads of deception, exposing the truth that lay dormant within the walls of Hawthorne House.

The atmosphere inside Hawthorne House was a paradox, a blend of nostalgia and sorrow that hung thick in the air, like the lingering scent of a long-extinguished fire. As I stepped deeper into the hidden room, I felt a strange kinship with the forgotten artworks around us, each piece a fragment of a life that had once pulsed with color and vibrancy. In the shadow of decay, the canvases still seemed to breathe, their stories begging to be heard, and as Liam stood next to me, I could almost see the echoes of his brother's spirit swirling around him, intertwining with his own.

"Do you think he would've wanted this?" Liam murmured, running his fingers over the edge of a framed piece, its glass cracked but the painting still remarkably intact. "To be remembered like this, in a place that feels more graveyard than gallery?"

I leaned against the wall, contemplating his words. "I think he would have wanted to be remembered, period. Whether it's in a grand gallery or a hidden room, what matters is the heart behind the art." I paused, trying to gauge his reaction. "Besides, every masterpiece has its shadows. Maybe these paintings just found their way back home."

Liam's gaze softened, the storm in his eyes easing slightly. "Home, huh? This place doesn't feel like home to me. It feels like a tomb."

The honesty of his confession hung between us, a fragile thread connecting our vulnerabilities. "Tombs can hold beauty, too," I said, a hint of teasing in my voice. "Like those ancient Egyptian sarcophagi that were filled with gold. They were about more than just death; they were about the journey."

A slight smile tugged at the corners of his mouth, and for a fleeting moment, the weight of the past seemed to lift. "I never took you for a history buff. Is that the best you've got? Sarcophagi?"

"Hey, I have layers!" I protested, throwing my hands up in mock indignation. "There's a whole world of facts in this head of mine—art history, ancient cultures, and random trivia about fruit flies. Impressive, right?"

He chuckled, a sound that was both a relief and a balm. "Very impressive. What's next? A lecture on the mating habits of fruit flies?"

"Only if you're interested," I shot back, my grin widening. But beneath our light banter, I could feel the gravity of the situation pressing down on us again. The stolen art loomed large, a silent accusation in the air. "We should keep looking. There must be something here that can lead us to who did this."

Liam nodded, his expression shifting back to focus. "Right. Let's find some clues before the ghosts start asking for a reunion tour."

We began our investigation in earnest, sifting through the layers of dust and neglect. Each piece of art we unearthed seemed to hold its own narrative, some vibrant enough to pull at the strings of emotion buried deep in my heart. A series of landscapes, filled with vivid sunsets and rolling hills, caught my eye. I stepped closer, mesmerized by the delicate brushstrokes. "This one is stunning," I said, reaching out to touch the edge of the frame.

"Yeah, my brother loved landscapes," Liam replied, his voice quieter now, tinged with an undercurrent of pride. "He said they reminded him of freedom."

"Freedom is a beautiful thing," I said softly, trying to lighten the mood. "And something tells me your brother had a wild side."

He laughed, the sound breaking through the tension once more. "Oh, you have no idea. He once tried to convince me that painting a mural on the side of the school would boost morale. Spoiler alert: it didn't go over well."

I smirked. "I can picture it now—his rebellious teenage phase, armed with a paintbrush and a dream."

Just as the atmosphere began to shift again, something caught my eye—a wooden box, half-hidden beneath a pile of canvases. I knelt down to retrieve it, brushing away cobwebs and dust. The box was ornate, with intricate carvings of twisting vines, the craftsmanship exquisite despite the years of neglect.

"What's that?" Liam asked, his curiosity piqued.

"Only one way to find out," I replied, lifting the lid. Inside lay a collection of photographs, faded but still vivid enough to evoke emotions. The images depicted a younger Liam with his brother, their smiles bright and carefree against the backdrop of a summer's day.

I picked one up, my heart squeezing at the sight. "Look at you two. So much happiness."

Liam's breath hitched as he leaned closer, his fingers brushing against the edges of the photographs. "We were inseparable back then," he said, a wistful smile creeping across his face. "Every day was an adventure. I used to think we were invincible."

"Invincible," I echoed, the weight of that word resonating between us. "What happened?"

His expression darkened, the lightness fading as he took the photo from my hand and traced the outline of his brother's face with his finger. "Life happened, I guess. We grew up, and things changed. The dreams we had… they didn't always survive reality."

The silence that followed was thick, each of us lost in our thoughts, the laughter of the past overshadowed by the sorrow of the present. Then, as if the universe were conspiring against our moment of introspection, the floorboards creaked ominously beneath us, sending a shiver through the air.

"What was that?" I asked, instinctively taking a step closer to Liam.

"Probably just the house settling," he said, though the uncertainty in his voice belied his bravado.

"Right. Just the house. Or it could be ghosts complaining about us rummaging through their stuff."

Liam shot me a look, half amused, half apprehensive. "You're really trying to lighten the mood here, aren't you?"

"Hey, someone has to keep the fear at bay. Besides, if there are ghosts, I bet they're just wondering what we're doing in their old haunt."

Before he could respond, the sound came again—louder this time, a distinct shuffle of footsteps echoing from somewhere deeper within the mansion. My heart raced, adrenaline kicking in. "Okay, that definitely wasn't the house."

"Maybe we should go?" Liam suggested, a mix of urgency and concern in his eyes.

I shook my head, unwilling to back down. "We can't just leave now. Whatever—or whoever—that is could be tied to the smuggling ring."

"Great. So we're about to have an unexpected encounter with an art thief?" he asked, his voice laced with sarcasm but a flicker of fear danced in his gaze.

"Maybe it'll be a ghost who knows the answers," I quipped, trying to mask my own apprehension. But the tension crackled like static, and I could see it in Liam's eyes—our adventure had taken a sharp turn, plunging us into a dark unknown where the past refused to be buried.

We exchanged a glance, a silent agreement forged between us, a mixture of curiosity and dread urging us forward. The footsteps echoed again, the sound drawing us deeper into the heart of the mansion, where shadows twisted and the past intertwined with the present. Whatever awaited us in the depths of Hawthorne House, we were ready to confront it—together.

The footsteps echoed once more, a rhythmic thud that reverberated through the decrepit walls of Hawthorne House, each beat amplifying the tension coiling between us. My heart raced, a wild drumbeat in my chest, as I glanced at Liam. The warmth of our earlier laughter faded, replaced by a palpable anticipation. "So, how do you want to play this?" I asked, attempting to sound casual even as I felt the edges of my bravado fray.

"Play it cool?" Liam suggested, raising an eyebrow as if that would be enough to diffuse the mounting pressure. "Or we could barge in like we're on a scavenger hunt for mischief. Both options have their merits."

"Why not mix them? A little stealth, a little chaos. That's the spirit of adventure, right?" I replied, my voice barely above a whisper as I took a cautious step toward the source of the noise.

"Sure. Stealth and chaos: the classic combination for any successful investigation," he quipped, smirking at me despite the situation. The flicker of humor was a welcome distraction, but the reality of our predicament was never far behind.

With each tentative step, I could feel the old wood beneath my feet creak in protest, as if the house itself were warning us against our intrusion. I turned toward a narrow hallway leading deeper into the mansion, shadows clinging to the corners, a curtain of darkness waiting to swallow us whole. "This way?" I ventured, my voice barely a murmur, almost swallowed by the oppressive silence that followed.

Liam nodded, his expression shifting from playful to resolute as he stepped closer, his hand brushing against mine. The warmth of his touch sent a jolt through me, a grounding force in a house that felt increasingly unwelcoming. "Lead the way, fearless explorer," he said, his tone lightening the air but tinged with a seriousness that was hard to ignore.

We slipped into the hallway, the shadows stretching out like fingers grasping for something long lost. The floor was a patchwork of dust and debris, each step disturbing a history that was better left undisturbed. Just ahead, a door stood slightly ajar, an inviting sliver of darkness beckoning us closer.

"Should we knock?" I asked, half-joking, knowing full well that the notion was absurd.

"Only if you want to announce our presence to whatever might be lurking inside," he replied, his voice low and conspiratorial. "I'd rather sneak in like ninjas. Or, you know, something less dramatic."

I pushed the door open, the hinges creaking ominously as we stepped into the dimly lit room. The air was stale, heavy with the scent of mildew and forgotten memories. A single light bulb flickered above, casting long shadows that danced along the walls. In the center of the room sat an old table, its surface cluttered with an assortment of items—papers, bottles, and a few more paintings.

"Looks like a hoarder's paradise," I remarked, stepping further inside. I picked up a crumpled piece of paper, its ink faded but still legible. "Wait, this looks like a ledger," I said, my eyes narrowing as I studied the scrawled handwriting. "It might detail the stolen artworks."

Liam leaned over my shoulder, his breath warm against my ear. "What does it say?"

I scanned the document, the letters blurring slightly under the flickering light. "It mentions specific pieces, along with prices and names—wait, there's an address here," I said, my pulse quickening. "This could lead us to the mastermind behind the smuggling ring!"

"Let's take it with us," he said, excitement sparking in his eyes.

Just as I tucked the ledger into my pocket, a sudden crash resonated from the far side of the room, shattering the fragile moment. We both turned, hearts pounding in our chests, and I saw a shadow flit across the far wall—a dark figure darting out of view.

"Did you see that?" I whispered, a lump forming in my throat.

Liam nodded, his expression grim. "We should check it out. Just... be careful."

I moved forward cautiously, every instinct screaming at me to retreat, but curiosity propelled me onward. The hallway led to a narrow staircase, spiraling down into a darkness that seemed to breathe. I hesitated for a moment, glancing back at Liam. "Do you think it's safe?"

"Safe is relative, isn't it? We could find a treasure trove of art or an angry ghost. Either way, I'm all in," he said with a teasing grin that did little to assuage my nerves.

"Great, nothing like a potential ghost encounter to really get the heart racing." I stepped onto the staircase, feeling the chill wrap around me like a cloak. Each step seemed to take us further into the depths of the house, the air growing colder, the atmosphere heavy with secrets.

As we reached the bottom, a faint light flickered ahead, illuminating what looked like a storage room crammed with even more art—pieces covered in dust but still bearing the unmistakable mark of beauty. It was as if we had stumbled upon a hidden treasure.

"Wow," I breathed, stepping inside. "This is incredible."

But before I could take in the full scope of the room, a loud bang erupted from behind us, the door slamming shut with a force that rattled the walls.

"What the—" Liam began, turning sharply, his expression shifting from awe to alarm.

I rushed to the door, twisting the knob in a frantic effort to escape. "It won't budge!" I shouted, panic rising in my chest.

"Step back!" Liam ordered, stepping beside me. He shoved against the door with all his strength, but it held firm, as if some unseen force had sealed us inside.

"Is this a horror movie now?" I asked, my voice tight with fear.

"Don't worry; I'm pretty sure we're not the first people to be trapped in an old mansion," he said, trying to inject a bit of levity into the situation. But I could hear the strain in his voice, a hint of desperation that matched my own.

We exchanged frantic glances, the tension building like a coiled spring. "What if whoever was here before us comes back?" I said, biting my lip.

Liam's gaze sharpened, his body rigid with focus. "We need to find another way out. Stay close."

Before I could respond, a shadow flickered at the edge of the room, darting behind a large canvas leaning against the wall. My heart raced as I followed the movement, dread pooling in my stomach.

"Did you see that?" I whispered, barely able to catch my breath.

"Yeah," he replied, his eyes narrowing. "We're not alone."

Just as the words left his lips, a figure emerged from behind the canvas, silhouetted against the dim light—a tall, hooded figure with an aura of menace that sent a chill coursing through my veins.

"Welcome," the figure said, voice smooth yet chilling, echoing in the small room. "I've been expecting you."

Before I could process what was happening, I felt a surge of fear that rooted me to the spot, the weight of what lay ahead pressing down as the figure took a step closer. The air crackled with tension, and in that moment, I realized that we were caught in a web spun by more than just ghosts; we were entangled in a dangerous game, where the past was about to collide violently with the present.

Chapter 14: The Mask of Betrayal

The sun dipped low on the horizon, casting long shadows that danced across the cobblestone streets of Harrow's End. I stood at the edge of the market square, the scent of spiced apples and roasted chestnuts wafting through the air, tinged with a hint of impending rain. My fingers toyed absently with the locket around my neck, a relic from simpler times. The weight of it felt heavier than usual, a reminder of the innocence that had been swiftly stripped away. Just yesterday, I had believed that trust could be easily given and that friendship was forged in loyalty. Today, the ground beneath my feet felt as unstable as a ship at sea.

My heart raced as I spotted Nora across the bustling square, her fiery hair a beacon amidst the crowd. She moved with purpose, dodging children chasing after stray dogs and merchants hawking their wares. When she finally caught my eye, her expression shifted, mirroring the tumult within me. It was the kind of look that spoke volumes—shadows of worry danced in the depths of her emerald eyes. I couldn't shake the unease that had settled in my stomach, an insistent reminder that things were not as they seemed.

"Juliet!" she called, her voice slicing through the chatter. I stepped forward, the sound of my boots echoing off the stone walls. "You have to see this." There was a tremor in her voice that set my teeth on edge. "It's about Marcus."

Marcus. My heart sank at the mention of his name. Our friendship had blossomed under the warm light of camaraderie, built on shared secrets and laughter that rang through the quiet nights. But with each whispered plan and conspiratorial glance, a tension had woven its way between us, a fraying thread in an otherwise sturdy fabric.

"What is it?" I asked, the urgency of her tone pushing me forward.

"Meet me at the old mill. It's... it's urgent," she said, glancing around as if the very air had ears. I felt the world narrowing around me, the vibrant colors of the market fading into a muted palette of fear and suspicion. I nodded, my resolve firming as I turned to make my way through the throng of people. Each step felt weighted, my mind racing with possibilities—both good and disastrous.

The old mill stood at the outskirts of town, its weathered wooden frame a sentinel of countless secrets. As I approached, the familiar creak of the door sent a shiver down my spine. Inside, the air was thick with the scent of damp wood and the memories of yesteryears. Nora waited for me in the dim light, her face pale, the confidence I'd come to rely on now replaced with a haunting uncertainty.

"Juliet," she began, her voice a whisper, "I overheard something." The way her words hung in the air felt like a spell, one that could unravel the very fabric of our world. I stepped closer, the tension palpable between us. "It's about the council. There are whispers—dark whispers about a traitor among us."

I frowned, my stomach churning as the implications sank in. "What do you mean?"

"I heard Marcus talking to someone," she confessed, her gaze dropping to the floor. "He was sharing details about our plans. The upcoming meeting, our strategies. It was like he was feeding information directly to the enemy."

A cold shiver crawled down my spine, and I felt as though the ground had shifted beneath my feet. The world spun, each revelation tightening the noose of betrayal around my heart. Marcus, my confidant, my ally—how could he? I had trusted him with everything, my secrets, my fears. "Are you sure?" I asked, desperate for the truth to be anything but what it seemed.

"I wish I weren't," Nora replied, her voice trembling. "But I can't shake the feeling that he's not who we thought he was. We need to confront him, to find out where his loyalty truly lies."

"Confront him?" I echoed, disbelief coloring my words. "What if he denies it? What if he—"

"—what if he's a liar?" Nora interrupted, her eyes narrowing with resolve. "We don't have the luxury of doubt, Juliet. We need to act. Now."

The resolve in her voice ignited a spark within me, a flame that had flickered and threatened to extinguish. With every heartbeat, the realization of my own vulnerability became clearer. I was a player in a game I didn't fully understand, and the rules had changed without warning. "Fine," I said, my voice steadier than I felt. "Let's find him. We'll get to the bottom of this."

As we made our way back toward town, the weight of our mission pressed heavily on my chest. I couldn't shake the image of Marcus's smile, the way his laughter had always made me feel safe. Now it felt like a mask, one that concealed treachery and deceit. I was unearthing a truth I wished I could ignore, but it loomed like a dark cloud overhead, threatening to pour down and drench me in despair.

When we reached the tavern, a sense of foreboding hung in the air. The door creaked open, and I felt the warmth of the room wash over me, yet it did nothing to quell the chill that had settled in my bones. There, amidst the lively chatter and clinking of mugs, sat Marcus, a familiar figure surrounded by laughter and camaraderie, blissfully unaware of the storm brewing just beyond his reach.

With a quick glance at Nora, I steeled myself and approached him, every step an exercise in courage. As I drew closer, I could hear snippets of conversation—hollow laughter and camaraderie that felt tainted by the shadows of betrayal. I inhaled deeply, the weight of my resolve pushing me forward, each heartbeat echoing with a question that needed answering. "Marcus," I said, forcing a smile that felt more like a grimace. "Can we talk?"

Marcus turned, his expression morphing from joviality to confusion as he recognized me. The laughter around him ebbed, replaced by a tension that vibrated through the room like the strum of a plucked string. I could almost hear the thoughts of those nearby as they realized that this was not just an innocent meeting; the air crackled with anticipation, and I felt like a tightrope walker teetering between two worlds—friendship and betrayal.

"Juliet! What's the matter?" He gestured to the empty seat beside him, his brow creasing in genuine concern. "Join us for a drink! We were just discussing the upcoming festival." His attempt at casual camaraderie was too polished, too rehearsed, as if he were trying to play a part in a script where I had no lines.

I shook my head, my heart thumping against my ribs like a wild animal seeking escape. "We need to talk, Marcus. It's important."

His expression shifted, the light in his eyes dimming slightly, like a candle flickering in a sudden draft. "Can't it wait? The others are waiting for you to join." He motioned vaguely at our shared friends, but I could sense the fraying edges of his confidence.

"No, it can't," I insisted, my voice a touch sharper than I intended. Nora stood behind me, her presence a grounding force, yet I could feel her uncertainty radiating through the air. The once warm atmosphere felt as chill as the winter wind.

"Alright," he finally relented, and I could see the gears turning in his mind, calculating risk and reward. "Let's step outside."

As we made our way to the back of the tavern, the cacophony of laughter faded into a dull murmur, leaving only the sound of our footsteps crunching against the gravel path. The moonlight spilled over the alley, illuminating his face, which I had come to know so well, now cloaked in an air of guardedness.

"What's going on?" he asked, leaning against the rough stone wall, arms crossed defensively.

"Nora overheard something. Something that implicates you," I began, my heart racing. "You were speaking to someone about our plans. You were giving away our strategies."

His reaction was immediate—a tightening of his jaw and a flash of something unreadable in his eyes. "That's absurd. I would never betray you like that."

"Then explain it to me! Because right now, it sounds like you're trying to protect someone, and I need to know who." I took a step closer, my voice lowering as though we were in a confessional. "Because if it's true, Marcus, if you're feeding information to the enemy, I can't just stand by and watch."

"I'm not feeding anyone anything!" His voice rose, echoing against the walls, and I felt the weight of other eyes pressing in. "You're being paranoid, Juliet. The pressure is getting to you. This fight is wearing on all of us."

"No, it's not paranoia if it's based on facts!" I shot back, desperation creeping into my tone. "Nora heard you. There's something happening, and I need you to tell me the truth."

For a moment, silence reigned. The air hung heavy between us, charged with unsaid words and the possibility of all we once held dear unraveling in an instant. I watched as his expression shifted, a mixture of emotions flickering across his face—fear, anger, guilt.

"Fine," he said at last, exhaling sharply. "I did meet with someone, but it wasn't what you think. I was trying to gather information, to protect us."

"Protect us?" I echoed, incredulity coloring my tone. "By putting us at risk? Who were you meeting?"

"Lydia," he admitted, the name hanging in the air like a curse. "She's a council member, but she's been asking questions, and I thought... I thought if I could get close to her, we could learn her true intentions."

Nora stepped forward, her brows knitted in concern. "Lydia? She's always been a bit too ambitious for her own good. Are you sure she's not playing you?"

Marcus ran a hand through his hair, frustration palpable. "I know how it looks, but I swear I wasn't betraying anyone. I was trying to stay ahead of the game!"

"By meeting with someone who could be a potential threat?" I shot back, incredulity turning to anger. "You can't be serious, Marcus. This isn't just about you anymore. You're risking all of us."

He pushed off the wall, pacing as if he could outrun the truth. "I didn't think it would come to this! I just wanted to make sure we had the upper hand. You know what it's like out there! We can't trust anyone!"

A flicker of understanding broke through my anger. He was right; trust was a commodity in short supply, especially in our world. But even so, the knife of betrayal cut deep. "You need to tell us everything, Marcus. We can't afford any more secrets."

He stopped pacing and faced me, eyes aflame with conviction. "I promise I'll be transparent from now on. But we need to act quickly. If there's a traitor among us, they'll try to silence us."

"What do you suggest?" Nora asked, her voice steady despite the chaos around us.

"We confront Lydia together," Marcus replied, determination hardening his features. "If she's playing both sides, we need to expose her before it's too late."

As we made our way back to the main hall of the tavern, the atmosphere felt even more charged. I could almost hear the ticking clock of fate counting down, each second pushing us closer to a reckoning that would change everything. My heart raced not just with fear, but with a sense of resolve. I was tired of playing the victim in this twisted game. We would shine a light on the shadows lurking around us, no matter the cost.

The tavern door swung open, and the raucous laughter hit us like a wave. It felt surreal, a bizarre contrast to the storm brewing within our trio. We slipped back into the heart of the gathering, where friends sat unaware, sipping their drinks and sharing stories. I caught Marcus's eye, a silent agreement passing between us—this was far from over.

With each step toward our friends, I felt the weight of my choices bearing down on me. Would we be able to uncover the truth? Or would our bond shatter like glass, leaving us vulnerable in a world that thrived on deception? The stakes had never been higher, and as I locked eyes with Nora, I knew we would fight tooth and nail to protect what little trust remained. Because in this game of shadows, loyalty was as fragile as a flickering candle in the wind.

The tavern's atmosphere buzzed with the hum of unsuspecting revelry, laughter and cheers mingling with the clinking of glasses, oblivious to the undercurrents swirling around us. I moved through the throng, heart pounding in time with the pulse of the evening. Nora followed closely, her expression one of fierce determination mixed with a hint of fear, while Marcus seemed to grapple with a storm of his own emotions, caught somewhere between guilt and resolve.

We reached a small table in the corner, one that provided a sliver of privacy but left us exposed to the wider world. "Act normal," I whispered, sliding into my seat, as if the tension radiating from us didn't scream of the storm brewing just beneath the surface. Nora glanced at Marcus, who had assumed a facade of nonchalance, and then leaned in, her voice low but urgent.

"Okay, what's the plan?"

Marcus cleared his throat, looking at both of us as if he were trying to muster the courage to plunge into a cold pool. "We need to approach Lydia without raising any alarms. If she's working against us, we can't give her a reason to suspect that we know."

Nora scoffed, the sound sharp and incredulous. "Sure, because walking in with all the subtlety of a bull in a china shop is our best bet."

"Thanks for the vote of confidence," Marcus shot back, a hint of a smile breaking through the tension. "We're in this together, remember? Besides, we can't let our nerves get the better of us. We need to appear calm."

"Calm, right," I said, taking a deep breath to steady myself. The sheer absurdity of our situation twisted my stomach. "Let's hope we can convince her that we're here for a friendly chat and not because we suspect her of treason."

"I can put on my charming face," Marcus said, feigning a suave demeanor that made Nora chuckle despite the gravity of the situation. "You know, the one that got me this far."

"Charming, huh?" I shot back, arching an eyebrow. "I was thinking more along the lines of a well-timed joke to distract her."

"I do have a few up my sleeve," he replied, leaning back with a mock air of confidence. "But this isn't the time for comedy, Juliet."

"I know, I know." My smile faded, replaced by the seriousness of our mission. The laughter around us faded into the background, replaced by the weight of our conversation. "Let's just find her."

Just then, a figure appeared at the edge of the tavern, drawing the eye of every patron. Lydia stood there, draped in a deep green cloak that shimmered under the flickering lanterns. Her presence commanded attention; she had a way of gliding through a room that made her seem both alluring and dangerous. The moment her gaze landed on our table, I felt a chill race up my spine.

"Speak of the devil," Nora murmured under her breath.

"Remember," Marcus said, lowering his voice, "act natural."

As she approached, her lips curved into a smile that didn't quite reach her eyes, those sharp, piercing orbs that seemed to scrutinize everything and everyone. "Well, well, if it isn't my favorite trio," she purred, settling down across from us as though she had a right to be there. "What a lovely surprise."

"Lydia," I said, forcing a smile. "We thought we'd check in on you. It's been too long since we've all gotten together." The words tasted like ash in my mouth.

She leaned back, assessing us with a critical eye. "Oh, has it? I must say, it seems like the tension in the air could cut through steel. What's on your minds?"

I glanced at Nora, who nodded ever so slightly, urging me to keep it light. "You know, the usual—talk of the festival, the food, the decorations. There's so much to do, we thought we'd get your insights," I replied, my voice laced with feigned nonchalance.

Lydia's lips twisted into a knowing smile. "Insights? Oh, darling, I have plenty of those. But tell me, are you really here for small talk, or is there something more pressing on your minds?"

"Just curious," Marcus interjected, his tone light but his gaze steady. "We hear you've been busy with council matters. Thought you might have some insider tips."

Her laughter tinkled like glass, both sweet and dangerous. "Insider tips? What an interesting phrase. You know, I've always believed that knowledge is power, but only if you know how to use it."

The subtext hung heavily between us, each of us dancing around the truth while knowing that the game had begun. I felt the urge to press, to find the cracks in her facade, but something held me back.

"Of course, we all want to wield our knowledge wisely," I replied, forcing my tone to remain light, though my heart raced. "What's your take on the current state of things? We've heard whispers that things are shifting within the council."

Her eyes sparkled with mischief, and I wondered if I'd stepped into a trap of my own making. "Whispers, you say? How delightful. You know, those who listen closely often hear more than they should."

"Sounds like a warning," Nora interjected, her tone teasing but her gaze unwavering. "Should we be concerned?"

"Concern is a matter of perspective," Lydia replied, tilting her head, a finger tapping against her chin. "What you perceive as a threat could just as easily be an opportunity."

Marcus's brow furrowed slightly. "Is that your way of saying we should keep our friends close but our enemies closer?"

"Oh, sweet boy," she said, leaning in, her voice dropping to a conspiratorial whisper. "It's always wise to be wary of everyone. The ones you trust the most can easily become your greatest adversaries."

The weight of her words crashed down around us, and I felt the walls of the tavern begin to close in. "What do you mean by that?" I pressed, feeling the urgency build within me.

"Simple," she replied, her smile widening. "Trust is a fragile thing, isn't it? And betrayal? Well, it often comes from the most unexpected places."

Before I could respond, a loud crash echoed from the far side of the tavern. The raucous laughter faded into stunned silence as a group of cloaked figures burst through the door, their faces obscured, but their intent clear. They moved with purpose, scanning the room like wolves on the hunt.

My breath hitched in my throat as I exchanged glances with Marcus and Nora, the gravity of our situation crashing over us like a tidal wave. Lydia's smile remained fixed, but her eyes flickered with something—was it fear or amusement?

"What is this?" I demanded, rising to my feet, adrenaline flooding my veins.

"Oh, you'll find out soon enough," she replied, her voice dripping with irony as the cloaked figures began to separate, closing in around us.

With a sudden, jarring realization, I understood that we were standing on the precipice of a revelation that could tear our world apart. Trust had become a luxury we could no longer afford, and as the shadows converged around us, I braced myself for the storm that was about to break.

"Marcus, we need to—"

But the words never left my mouth as the cloaked figures moved in, their intentions veiled beneath layers of secrecy. I could feel the walls closing in, the air thick with tension as I prepared for the inevitable confrontation, unaware that the moment would shift everything I thought I knew about loyalty and betrayal.

Chapter 15: The Heart's Descent

The evening light cascaded through the tall windows, casting golden shards of sunlight that danced upon the old oak floor, illuminating the dust motes swirling lazily in the air. It was a small, quaint house, nestled at the end of a quiet street lined with cherry blossom trees, their petals scattering like confetti in the gentle breeze. This place, filled with the scents of fresh lavender and baking bread, once felt like a sanctuary. Now, standing in the living room, it seemed a bittersweet reminder of all I stood to lose. The family portrait hung crookedly on the wall, its faded colors whispering tales of laughter, love, and the unyielding grip of time.

My grandmother had always said that photographs captured a moment, but they also imprisoned the memories within their frames. I traced the outline of our faces with a trembling finger, my heart a tumultuous mix of nostalgia and grief. The vibrant smiles of my childhood self and the loving gaze of my grandmother seemed like a different world—one that had evaporated in the wake of the storm we found ourselves in. I had been so naive back then, blissfully unaware of how the cracks in our lives would deepen, pulling us into the abyss of uncertainty.

Just then, I felt a warm presence behind me. Liam stepped into the light, his silhouette framed by the soft glow, his brow furrowed in concern. "You okay?" His voice was a gentle rumble, a comforting anchor in a sea of chaotic emotions.

I turned to him, my heart swelling with gratitude. "Just... looking at this old thing." I gestured toward the portrait, hoping to disguise the welling tears that threatened to spill. "It's funny how much can change."

He moved closer, his shoulder brushing against mine, a quiet solidarity in the shared silence. "I get it. Sometimes it feels like you're standing on a cliff, looking down into the unknown." His eyes held a depth of understanding that made me feel seen, and in that moment, I realized how much I relied on him.

"I don't know how we're going to get through this," I admitted, the vulnerability of my confession spilling out like a fragile whisper. "Every step we take feels like we're just digging ourselves deeper."

Liam's expression hardened for a moment, as if he were weighing his words carefully, but then softened. "You're not alone, you know. I've got scars of my own." He paused, the shadows of his past flickering in his eyes. "It's okay to be scared. I think we all are. But we're in this together."

The air grew thick with unspoken truths. His admission caught me off guard, and I found myself craving to know more. "What do you mean?" I pressed gently, intrigued.

He ran a hand through his tousled hair, a nervous habit I'd come to recognize. "When I was younger, I lost my brother. It was… sudden. Just like that, he was gone." His voice cracked slightly, a fissure in the carefully constructed walls he had built. "It left a mark, you know? Made me wary of everything, of getting close to anyone. I didn't want to feel that pain again."

The weight of his words hung in the air between us, heavy and raw. It struck me like a lightning bolt, illuminating the darkness that had settled in my heart. I reached out, finding his hand and squeezing it tight. "I can't imagine that. I'm so sorry."

He nodded, his gaze unwavering as he looked down at our intertwined fingers. "But here we are, right? Facing down our own monsters together."

The softness in his voice wrapped around me like a comforting blanket, and I felt the trembling edge of my fears begin to thaw. Perhaps the bond we were forming was forged in shared pain, but it was also laced with the hope of healing. "I'm not great at this," I confessed, letting out a shaky laugh. "Emotional stuff has never been my forte."

"Join the club," he chuckled, the sound warm and inviting. "But sometimes, it's the messy bits that make life worth living. We just have to embrace the chaos."

I smiled, the tension in my chest easing a little. "Chaos? I might be a professional at that." I gestured to the portrait once more, feeling the ghosts of my past swirling around us. "It's just... hard to let go, to move on when everything feels so tangled."

"Maybe moving on doesn't mean forgetting," he suggested softly. "It could mean carrying those memories with us, using them to fuel our fight instead of holding us back."

His insight cut through the fog of my despair, illuminating a path I hadn't considered. "I like that," I admitted, feeling a flicker of determination ignite within me. "It's just... I want to keep my family safe. I want to protect them, and I'm terrified of what might happen next."

His expression shifted, turning earnest as he held my gaze. "We'll protect each other. I promise. Whatever comes our way, we'll face it together."

In that moment, I felt a spark ignite, a powerful connection forged from our shared vulnerabilities. It was a bond that tangled our hearts, complicating the already precarious situation we found ourselves in. Yet, beneath the weight of our confessions, there was a sense of resilience blooming—a promise that together we could navigate the storm that lay ahead, no matter how daunting it seemed.

As the last rays of sunlight slipped away, darkness began to envelop the room, but it felt different now. It was no longer a cloak of despair, but a canvas waiting to be painted with our stories—our fears, our hopes, our intertwined destinies. Together, we would rewrite the narrative, turning the heart's descent into an ascent toward something greater, something more profound.

The quiet intimacy of that moment lingered between us, almost tangible, as if the very air was charged with unspoken promises. The world outside faded into a hushed background, the rustling leaves and distant laughter blending into a soothing symphony. As I stood there, holding Liam's gaze, the portrait became a mere backdrop to the deeper connection that had just unfurled. It was one thing to share fears; it was another to weave them into a tapestry of understanding.

"I was just thinking," I said, breaking the silence with a lightness that contrasted the heaviness of the conversation. "If you can handle my family drama, I can handle yours." I attempted a playful grin, but my heart raced with an undercurrent of sincerity. "I mean, you're right; maybe chaos does make life interesting."

Liam chuckled softly, the sound a balm for my frayed nerves. "You have no idea what you're signing up for. My family is like a reality show waiting to happen. They put the 'fun' in dysfunctional."

"Great! I'll bring popcorn." I leaned against the wall, feeling the weight of the world lift just a little. "In that case, what's the latest episode about?"

He grinned, the tension easing from his shoulders. "Oh, let me see. Last I checked, my sister was engaged in a fierce debate with my mother about whether or not cats are better than dogs. It's escalated to the point of cat pictures being displayed like war trophies."

"Sounds riveting," I replied, laughing. "Does your mom have a fighting chance?"

"Only if she can prove that dogs have more Instagram followers," he said with a wink. "But honestly, it's all just noise. They love each other fiercely, even if they sometimes forget it in the heat of the moment."

I felt a flicker of something warm in my chest, an appreciation for the chaos he described. "Love is funny like that, isn't it? It can make people act a little... insane."

"Right? And we're all just trying to navigate it without drowning in the madness." His eyes locked onto mine, and I could see a hint of admiration swirling in the depths. "But we'll find our way through, right?"

"Together," I echoed, sealing the promise between us with a sincerity that surprised me. The moment shifted, taking on a new gravity, and the reality of our situation pressed back in. The investigation loomed over us like a storm cloud, casting shadows on the light we had just found.

As if sensing the shift, Liam's expression darkened slightly. "We should probably talk strategy," he suggested, his voice steady but serious. "What's our next move?"

"Good call." I took a deep breath, letting the laughter fade, replaced by determination. "We've made some progress with the leads, but I still feel like we're missing something crucial."

"Let's break it down." He crossed his arms, a habit of his when he was deep in thought. "What do we know for sure?"

I stepped away from the portrait, feeling the weight of my family's history behind me as I embraced the present. "We know there's a connection between the recent incidents and that old warehouse on Maple Street. Every time I dig into the records, it feels like there's something just out of reach."

Liam nodded, his brow furrowed in concentration. "And what about the owner? I remember you mentioning that he had some questionable connections."

"Exactly. It's like peeling back layers of an onion. The deeper we go, the more it stings." My heart raced at the thought of confronting the unknown. "But I think we need to confront him directly. It's the only way to figure out if he's involved."

"Right. But we need a plan. No superhero entrances." He raised an eyebrow, his lips twitching in a smile that barely suppressed his teasing tone. "No capes, no spandex."

"Fine, fine," I said, suppressing a grin. "We'll stick to stealth and strategy. But I get to wear the mask."

"Deal." His laughter was infectious, and for a brief moment, the heaviness lifted, allowing us both to breathe a little easier.

As we worked through the details, the atmosphere began to shift again. The laughter subsided, and we were drawn deeper into the complexities of our mission. The stakes were high, and a sense of urgency pulsed between us like a heartbeat.

"Do you think we're doing the right thing?" I asked suddenly, the question escaping before I could stop it. The uncertainty gnawed at my insides, a constant reminder of the risks we were taking.

Liam paused, his gaze steady. "I think it's the only thing we can do. Sometimes, you just have to plunge into the unknown and trust that you'll swim. But we'll do it together, and that makes all the difference."

A rush of emotion flooded my chest. His confidence was infectious, bolstering my own resolve. "Okay, then. Let's dive in headfirst."

The conversation shifted back to logistics, but a new current flowed between us—a blend of trust and vulnerability. We mapped out our plan, discussing details and contingency strategies, each word laced with a burgeoning excitement that almost drowned out the fear lurking in the corners of my mind.

But just as we settled into a rhythm, a loud crash erupted from the kitchen, followed by a string of muffled curses. My heart jolted, adrenaline surging through my veins as I exchanged a wide-eyed glance with Liam.

"Did you hear that?" I asked, suddenly on high alert.

"Yeah. What was that?" His voice was low, an edge of concern creeping in.

With a shared nod, we moved cautiously toward the sound, a primal instinct kicking in. I grasped the edge of the kitchen door and peeked inside, dread coiling tightly in my stomach. What awaited us could shift everything we had just built, turning our fragile moment of connection into chaos once more.

The kitchen was a chaotic tableau, the aftermath of a miniature explosion that left the air thick with flour and the faint scent of burnt toast. I blinked in disbelief, my heart hammering against my ribs, as I surveyed the scene: a ceramic bowl lay shattered on the floor, its contents spread like a powdered snowstorm across the tile. And standing amid the wreckage was my younger brother, Max, clutching a spatula as if it were a prized sword, his wide eyes mirroring my own confusion.

"What in the world happened here?" I gasped, stepping inside with cautious intrigue, half expecting him to break into a dance like a guilty cartoon character caught in the act.

"I was trying to make breakfast!" he exclaimed, defensively waving the spatula. "But the mixer got a little... enthusiastic." He looked at the floury chaos with a mix of pride and regret. "Okay, maybe a lot enthusiastic."

Liam stepped in beside me, his lips twitching in amusement as he surveyed the disaster zone. "Well, it's definitely a sight to behold. I didn't realize breakfast required a degree in culinary arts."

Max frowned, trying to muster the bravado of a chef with too many failed soufflés. "I was going for pancakes. How hard can it be? But the mixer... it attacked!"

I couldn't help but laugh, and the tension from moments before began to melt away. "Next time, I'll get you an instruction manual and some bubble wrap for the mixer. You know, for safety."

"Ha ha," he retorted, rolling his eyes dramatically. "Very funny. I just thought it would be nice to make breakfast for once. Is that a crime?"

"No, just a serious miscalculation in physics," Liam chimed in, a glint of mischief in his eyes. "But I admire your spirit. It takes guts to dive into the culinary deep end, even if you forgot your floaties."

Max puffed up, a smirk breaking through the flour dust. "Well, I'm not done yet! Just you wait—pancakes will happen, and they will be glorious."

"Let's not get ahead of ourselves," I teased, stepping carefully around the remnants of the ceramic bowl. "I'd settle for a breakfast that doesn't end with a visit from the fire department."

Liam chuckled, the warmth of his laughter filling the kitchen. But even as we bantered, the gnawing tension from earlier lingered like a stubborn shadow at the edges of my mind. We were all in this together, yet a part of me still felt adrift, as if I were watching a play unfold without knowing my role.

Max turned back to the counter, eyeing the untouched ingredients with renewed determination. "All right, round two! This time, I'm going to channel my inner pancake wizard."

As he busied himself, I caught Liam's gaze, the silent understanding passing between us that we couldn't lose sight of the real battle ahead.

"Let's clean up this battlefield first," I suggested, grabbing a broom from the corner. "Then maybe we can strategize about our next move. But first, I'll settle for breakfast that doesn't require a rescue team."

The three of us joined forces, turning what could have been a disaster into an unexpected bonding moment. We laughed as flour dust settled in our hair and pancake batter splattered across the counters. It was the kind of camaraderie I'd missed—a reminder that life could be sweet, even when it felt heavy.

Eventually, as we sat down to Max's second attempt at pancakes—which, to his credit, were surprisingly fluffy and delicious—I felt a sense of calm wash over me. The chaos of the kitchen melted into the comfort of shared laughter and playful teasing, transforming our home into a sanctuary for a brief moment.

But as the last bite of pancake disappeared, a sudden chill swept through the room. The tension that had been temporarily forgotten crept back in, and I couldn't shake the nagging feeling that something was coming. I glanced at Liam, and the flicker of concern in his eyes mirrored my own unease.

Just then, the sound of a loud thud echoed from the front of the house, followed by an ominous creak that sent a shiver down my spine. "Did you hear that?" Max asked, eyes wide.

"Yeah," Liam said, setting his fork down with a steely determination. "Stay here."

Before I could object, he was already moving toward the hallway, his posture radiating a mix of confidence and caution. I glanced at Max, who looked equally unsettled.

"I'm not staying here," I declared, my voice trembling slightly. "If something's happening, I'm going with you."

Liam paused, turning to meet my gaze, the tension between us thickening once more. "It's probably nothing. Just stay back."

"Nothing? After the last few weeks, I think I have a pretty good grasp of what 'nothing' feels like, and this isn't it." My heart raced, a storm of emotions brewing inside me. I couldn't let fear dictate my actions, not now.

He hesitated, searching my eyes for reassurance, but I could see the worry etched in his features. "Fine," he relented, a hint of exasperation in his tone. "But let's be smart about this. If it's a threat, we need to be careful."

Together, we moved cautiously toward the front door, the atmosphere charged with an electrifying mix of anticipation and dread. Each step felt heavier than the last, the shadows of the hallway stretching ominously around us.

As we reached the front room, the scene unfolded like a nightmare in slow motion. The door stood ajar, swinging slightly in the breeze, and the world outside looked deceptively calm. But there, on the welcome mat, lay an envelope—white and unassuming, yet it felt like a beacon of foreboding.

"What is that?" Max whispered, his voice barely audible.

"I don't know," I replied, stepping forward against the instinct to retreat. The envelope seemed to pulse with a life of its own, a secret waiting to be uncovered.

With trembling fingers, I reached for it, my pulse quickening. As I opened the flap, a small slip of paper fell out, fluttering to the ground. The words scrawled across it sent a jolt of fear through me:

"Stop digging, or you'll regret it."

My heart dropped as I absorbed the message, a chill running down my spine. I glanced up at Liam, who looked equally shaken.

"This isn't just a warning," he murmured, his eyes dark with concern. "This is a threat."

The weight of those words hung in the air, thick with tension. I felt the ground shift beneath me, the laughter and warmth of earlier evaporating into a cloud of uncertainty. The stakes had just escalated, and as I met Liam's gaze, we both understood: we were in deeper than we ever imagined.

Max's voice broke through the heaviness. "What do we do now?"

And as I looked back at the envelope, the looming shadows outside seemed to pulse, as if the world itself was holding its breath, waiting for our next move.

Chapter 16: A Game of Masks

The evening air was crisp, the kind of chill that made you draw your coat tighter around your shoulders as I stepped out of the car. The grand mansion loomed ahead, its stone façade bathed in the golden glow of outdoor lanterns. I could hear the soft lilt of string instruments filtering through the open doors, inviting and elusive like a secret whispered in the dark. This was no ordinary gala; it was a stage set for a game far more dangerous than the mere appreciation of art.

Dressed to the nines, I felt the shimmering fabric of my gown cling to me like an old friend, the deep emerald hue a perfect contrast to the striking gray of the mansion. My heart thrummed beneath layers of tulle and satin, each beat a reminder of the delicate balance between beauty and treachery we were about to walk into. Liam, ever the charmer, stood beside me, his dark suit tailored to perfection, a mask of confidence masking the intensity brewing beneath the surface.

"Ready to mingle with the wolves?" he asked, his voice low, a hint of mischief sparking in his dark eyes.

"Only if you promise to keep me from becoming their dinner," I replied, a playful smile tugging at my lips, though my stomach knotted with the gravity of our mission.

As we stepped over the threshold, the atmosphere shifted. The grand hall was filled with laughter and clinking glasses, the rich scent of expensive perfume mingling with the heady aroma of aged wine. Guests flitted from one conversation to another like butterflies, adorned in jewels that sparkled like stars against the velvet night. Yet, beneath this veneer of opulence, I sensed a tension that lay just beneath the surface, a current of secrets waiting to break free.

Liam took my hand, leading me through the throng of elegantly dressed patrons. His grip was firm yet gentle, an anchor amid the chaos. "Stay close," he murmured, his eyes scanning the crowd, ever vigilant, as if he were both predator and prey.

We passed a sculpture of a horse, its features so finely carved that it seemed ready to gallop away at any moment. I barely had time to admire it before Liam's attention shifted to a pair of men standing near the bar. One of them was a notorious art dealer known for his dubious connections, the other a mysterious figure whose presence felt more like a shadow than a man. I followed Liam's gaze, my heart racing as we exchanged quick glances, our silent communication sharper than any words could convey.

"Do you think they're involved?" I whispered, the words slipping through my lips like a breath of air in the suffocating atmosphere.

"They have their hands in every questionable transaction on this coast," Liam replied, his jaw tightening. "If anyone knows about the stolen pieces, it's them."

With a nod, we drifted toward the bar, pretending to engage in idle chatter about the latest trends in contemporary art. I sipped my drink, a sweet concoction that danced on my tongue but did little to quell the unease gnawing at my insides. The laughter around us felt jarring, a stark contrast to the game we were playing.

"Isn't it exciting, darling?" an older woman exclaimed, her laughter lilting above the crowd. She was clad in a gown of silver sequins, each movement catching the light like fireflies. "To think we might witness history tonight! The owner of that priceless painting has invited a select few to view it."

"Do you know who?" I asked, feigning interest, a knot tightening in my stomach.

"Rumor has it, the elusive Mr. Faulkner himself will make an appearance," she gushed, her eyes sparkling with delight. "He's rumored to be quite... persuasive."

As her words hung in the air, a chill raced down my spine. If Faulkner was indeed here, the stakes had just been raised. The tension was palpable as we exchanged glances again, this time laden with urgency.

"Faulkner's dangerous," Liam said, his voice barely a whisper, eyes darkening with resolve. "We need to be careful."

But as the evening wore on, it was Liam's demeanor that started to shift. He was no longer the charming man who had stolen my heart; the glint in his eyes turned predatory, his posture rigid and unyielding. The sweet nothings whispered in the glow of the evening light seemed to be overshadowed by something darker brewing just beneath the surface.

"Do you think I can pull off this act?" I asked playfully, attempting to break through the tension wrapping around us like a shroud.

"Absolutely. Just remember, you're a connoisseur with discerning taste," he replied, though the tension in his voice betrayed his calm facade.

I couldn't shake the feeling that the man I was beginning to fall for was at war with himself, the sides of him wrestling with a past I was only beginning to comprehend. As we moved to the center of the gala, surrounded by vibrant colors and swirling laughter, I felt the weight of secrets pressing down on us, threatening to unravel the fragile connection we had built.

A band began to play, and couples swirled across the dance floor, their movements graceful, yet I felt as if we were on a precarious edge, teetering between danger and desire. Each twirl and dip of the music echoed the unsteady rhythm of my heart. It was in the flickering candlelight that I saw the man before me, not merely as a partner in this game, but as a puzzle with many hidden pieces.

The night wore on, and my laughter mingled with the music, yet inside I felt a storm brewing, a tempest of questions and unvoiced fears. Just as I thought I could navigate this treacherous landscape, a figure emerged from the shadows—a man cloaked in enigma, his presence commanding the room with an unspoken authority.

The masquerade of glamour began to feel like a carefully crafted lie, and as I caught Liam's gaze, I wondered if the masks we wore would protect us or lead us to our own undoing. The air thickened with unspoken promises and veiled threats, and I knew we were playing a game far more intricate than I had ever imagined.

The pulse of the night thrummed with a rhythm all its own, a hypnotic blend of laughter and music interwoven with whispered secrets and veiled glances. I felt like a dancer on the edge of a stage, poised between the exhilaration of performance and the fear of an unseen trap. The chandelier above glittered like a constellation, casting intricate shadows that twisted across the polished marble floor. I caught sight of Liam in profile, his expression a mixture of intent focus and simmering tension as he surveyed the room.

"Do you ever wonder if these people even appreciate what they're pretending to admire?" I mused, my voice low enough to avoid prying ears.

"Not half as much as they appreciate the money they hope to gain from it," he replied, a sardonic smile playing at the corners of his lips. It was a brief flicker of his usual charm, but something deeper lurked behind his eyes—something that spoke of a darker game he was playing, one I wasn't fully privy to yet.

We navigated through clusters of elegantly dressed patrons, each one a masterpiece in their own right. A man with a meticulously groomed beard spoke animatedly about a recent auction, while a woman in a brilliant sapphire gown gestured widely, her diamonds sparkling like a thousand tiny suns. I struggled to keep my composure as the weight of our mission pressed down on me, heavy as the jeweled gowns swaying around us.

A server glided past with a tray of flutes filled with bubbling champagne. I took one, the cool glass a welcome distraction, and took a sip. The effervescence tickled my throat, a stark contrast to the tension gnawing at my insides. "Do you think Faulkner will actually show?" I asked, my voice steadying with each passing moment.

"His ego would never allow him to miss an opportunity to flaunt his collection," Liam replied, his gaze sweeping the crowd. "But if he does, we need to be ready. He's a master of manipulation, and he won't take kindly to being cornered."

I felt a shiver of anticipation run through me, mingled with the thrill of being part of something larger than ourselves. Yet, with each passing moment, the air felt heavier, laden with secrets yet to be uncovered. I leaned closer to Liam, wanting to breach the ever-growing distance between us. "Are you sure we can trust each other in all of this? There's so much at stake."

His brow furrowed slightly, the flicker of vulnerability caught in the corner of his expression. "Trust is a luxury in this game. But we can't afford to doubt each other now. Not when we're so close to uncovering the truth."

As the music swelled, I caught sight of a figure slipping through the crowd, his tall frame cloaked in shadows. He was dressed impeccably in a dark suit, his movements smooth, like a predator stalking its prey. I could feel my heart quicken—this had to be Faulkner.

"There he is," Liam said, his tone suddenly sharp, eyes locked on the approaching man. "Stay close, and don't let him see us sweat."

Faulkner's gaze swept the room, and for a moment, it felt as if he was searching for something—or someone. My pulse raced as he paused, studying us with an intensity that made the back of my neck prickle. There was an almost magnetic quality to his presence, drawing people into his orbit while simultaneously pushing them away.

Liam took a deep breath, his fingers brushing mine as he moved to intercept the man. "Mr. Faulkner, isn't it?" he greeted, his tone smooth, confident, as if they were old friends.

"Ah, the charming duo," Faulkner replied, his smile all teeth and no warmth. "I see you've graced us with your presence. I must say, I didn't expect to see you here tonight, especially given your... previous interests."

The air crackled between us, tension rising like the bubbles in my drink. I stood slightly behind Liam, allowing him to take the lead, while my mind raced with possible responses. I knew we had to navigate this conversation carefully; one misstep could lead us directly into a trap.

"We've come to appreciate the finer things in life," Liam said smoothly, flashing a disarming grin. "Perhaps you can enlighten us about your latest acquisitions?"

"Oh, I'd be delighted," Faulkner replied, the smile never reaching his eyes. "But tell me, do you really think you're ready to delve into the depths of the art world? It's a dangerous place, filled with more than just beauty."

"Danger is what makes it exhilarating, wouldn't you agree?" Liam countered, his voice carrying a hint of challenge.

As they exchanged verbal jabs, I felt a rising unease. The underlying current of their conversation began to swell, a battle of wits where the stakes were painfully high. I leaned in, hoping to read the subtleties of Faulkner's demeanor, searching for any telltale signs of deceit.

"You're both very bold, I'll give you that," Faulkner continued, his gaze narrowing, as if he were peeling back layers of our façade. "But I wonder, are you prepared for what lies beneath? Art can reveal the soul, but it can also shatter illusions."

There was an electric moment of silence, and I felt Liam stiffen beside me. "We're ready for anything," Liam said, his voice firm, but I sensed the uncertainty lurking just beneath.

Faulkner studied us, the glint in his eyes revealing nothing, and I could feel the walls closing in. The room, once filled with laughter and music, seemed to pulse with the rhythm of our heartbeats. I caught a glimpse of a painting hanging in the far corner, a vibrant piece that felt almost alive, and a thought struck me.

"Speaking of art," I interjected, my voice steady, "I've heard rumors about a specific piece you acquired. A particular painting that seems to have caused quite the stir."

Faulkner's expression shifted, a flicker of interest igniting in his gaze. "Ah, you must mean the Raven's Shadow. It's a masterpiece, if I do say so myself."

I pressed on, sensing an opening. "They say it holds secrets. Perhaps it's the perfect piece to spark a little... discussion?"

"Discussion?" Faulkner chuckled darkly, the sound like ice cracking. "In this world, secrets can be both a blessing and a curse."

As the words hung in the air, a shiver ran down my spine. I realized we were standing on the precipice of something monumental, and the danger we'd waded into was far deeper than I had anticipated. Just as I opened my mouth to respond, the lights flickered, plunging us momentarily into shadow before the glow returned, more ominous than before.

"Interesting choice of words," Liam said, his voice low and even, eyes locked onto Faulkner with a fierce intensity. "Maybe you'd like to share what you know about those secrets."

The air thickened around us, the tension crackling like a live wire, and I knew we were about to plunge headfirst into the abyss. In that moment, I grasped the gravity of our situation—the masks we wore might protect us for a while, but the truth had a way of unraveling even the most carefully woven lies.

The tension in the room thickened, an invisible fog that twisted around us like a serpent coiling for a strike. Faulkner's gaze flickered from Liam to me, a calculating gleam in his eyes as if he were sizing us up for a prize fight. The music swelled in the background, a seductive melody that felt starkly out of place amidst the brewing storm of our encounter.

"Secrets, indeed," Faulkner said, his voice a velvet whisper, each word laced with meaning. "But tell me, are you prepared to pay the price for the truth? It can be quite... costly."

I felt a cold rush of anxiety wash over me. "What exactly do you mean?" I asked, though the question hung in the air like a brittle thread, ready to snap.

"Oh, you know how it is in our world," he replied, his smile shifting into something sharper. "Information isn't free, especially when it comes to art—our beautiful, beguiling art. Everyone has their price, darling."

I could feel Liam's body tense beside me, a solid wall of unyielding resolve. "We're not afraid of a little cost," he stated, his voice firm, echoing the challenge laced in Faulkner's words. "Just tell us what we need to know."

Faulkner laughed, a low, rich sound that echoed through the vast hall like the tolling of a distant bell. "Bravery will take you far, my friend. But do tread lightly. Sometimes it's the fearless who fall the hardest."

Just then, the lights flickered again, dimming ominously, and the music came to an abrupt halt, as if the very air had decided to hold its breath. My pulse quickened; it felt as if the mansion itself was a living entity, aware of the drama unfolding within its walls. I caught a glimpse of a reflection in a nearby mirror—Liam, his jaw clenched tight, eyes darkened with intensity, ready to face whatever lay ahead.

Before I could voice my next thought, a sudden commotion erupted near the entrance. A woman in a stunning red gown burst into the room, her expression wild and frantic. "He's here! Someone call the police!"

Gasps rippled through the crowd, and the air turned electric with apprehension. Faulkner's demeanor shifted, the playful glint in his eyes replaced with something colder, more calculating. "It seems our little soirée has taken a turn for the dramatic," he murmured, as though the chaos were merely an amusing spectacle.

Liam turned to me, urgency flickering in his gaze. "Stay close," he said, his voice low and firm. "We need to figure out what's going on."

We moved toward the entrance, weaving through a throng of bewildered guests, confusion and fear etched across their faces. The woman in red was speaking animatedly to a group of men in suits, and the closer we got, the clearer her words became.

"There's been a break-in at the gallery! They took the Raven's Shadow!" she exclaimed, her voice quivering with urgency.

A collective gasp rose from the crowd, and I exchanged a bewildered glance with Liam. The painting we had just discussed—the very piece that could unravel Faulkner's tangled web of deceit—had been stolen right under our noses.

"Unbelievable," Liam muttered under his breath, his eyes narrowing. "We need to find out who did this and fast."

But before I could respond, the lights flickered once more, plunging us into darkness. A cacophony of gasps and murmurs echoed through the room, and in that moment of chaos, I felt a hand grasp my wrist with a force that made my heart leap into my throat.

"Come with me!" A voice hissed urgently, pulling me away from the crowd.

I twisted to see Liam's face, panic flickering in his eyes. "No!" he shouted, reaching out, but the hand that held me was strong, pulling me into the shadows just as the lights blinked back on, illuminating the chaos around us.

ARTFALL

"Who are you?" I demanded, trying to yank my arm free, but the grip only tightened.

"Shh, don't make a scene," the figure said, their voice low and urgent, tinged with an accent I couldn't place. "You're in danger. I need you to listen to me."

I could see the outline of a man, his face obscured by a mask that glimmered in the soft candlelight. Panic surged through me, but curiosity kept my feet planted, if only for a moment. "What do you know?" I pressed, forcing the words out despite the rising fear.

"There's more at stake here than you realize," he said, glancing around to ensure we weren't being overheard. "Faulkner isn't just a dealer; he's part of something much larger—a syndicate that deals in stolen art. They're ruthless, and now they know you're involved."

My mind reeled as I tried to process his words. "Involved in what?"

"Finding the Raven's Shadow," he replied, urgency coloring his tone. "And now that you're on their radar, they won't stop until you're silenced."

The gravity of his statement settled like a lead weight in my stomach. Just then, I caught a glimpse of Liam moving through the crowd, his expression fierce and determined, searching for me. "Liam!" I shouted, desperate to break free and get back to him.

The masked figure tightened his grip, pulling me deeper into the shadows. "No! You can't go back. You have to trust me!"

Before I could respond, a loud crash erupted from the main hall, and my heart nearly stopped. The sound of shattering glass echoed like gunfire, drawing the attention of everyone present. Liam's eyes widened as he scanned the room, the tension in his posture shifting to raw panic.

"Get down!" I shouted instinctively, breaking free from the masked figure's grasp.

Just as I moved toward Liam, the chaos escalated—a group of masked intruders stormed into the room, faces hidden behind balaclavas, their intentions clear in the chaos they wreaked.

"Everyone on the ground! Now!" one of them shouted, brandishing a weapon, and a cold chill shot down my spine.

In that heart-stopping moment, I saw the truth: we were no longer just players in a dangerous game of art and deception; we were caught in the crossfire of a heist that threatened to tear our world apart.

Liam was shouting my name, desperation etched across his face, but I could barely hear him over the din. I had to choose—run toward him and risk everything, or heed the warning of the mysterious stranger who had pulled me away. The stakes had escalated beyond anything I had prepared for, and as the intruders moved closer, the reality of our situation set in with terrifying clarity.

I took a breath, heart racing, as I glanced between the masked figures and the worried crowd. The game of masks was far from over, and now, the truth lay just beyond reach, draped in chaos and danger.

The world around me spun as I made my decision, the shadow of uncertainty looming ever larger.

Chapter 17: The Final Puzzle

The grand ballroom of the Harcourt estate pulsed with energy, each heartbeat echoed in the rhythm of laughter and the soft clink of crystal glasses. A cascade of glimmering chandeliers hung above, their lights reflecting off the polished marble floors, creating a celestial illusion. I stood just inside the gilded entrance, a swirl of sequins and silk enveloping me like a cocoon. My dress, a deep emerald green, hugged my curves, the fabric shimmering with every move, mirroring the chaotic beauty around me. The evening felt electric, an unspoken challenge lurking beneath the surface.

As I adjusted the mask over my eyes, its intricate lace design both concealing and revealing, I couldn't shake the feeling that this night was more than just a gala. It was a battlefield, one where alliances were forged and shattered with each whispered secret. My heart raced, not solely from the excitement of the festivities, but from the knowledge that the mastermind behind the recent art thefts was somewhere in this very room, blending in with the elite.

My gaze drifted across the crowd, spotting familiar faces: socialites in extravagant gowns, art dealers with insatiable greed glinting in their eyes, and collectors whose smiles never quite reached their eyes. The atmosphere was thick with pretense, the air laden with the scent of expensive perfume mingling with the sweetness of delicate pastries. Yet, beneath this facade of sophistication, I sensed something darker—a conspiracy woven into the fabric of this glamorous night.

I caught sight of Liam, his dark hair tousled as he engaged in animated conversation with a group of art enthusiasts. His charm radiated from him like the warmth of a fireplace on a cold winter's night. Despite the chaos around us, he held my attention like gravity pulling a star into orbit. We had become reluctant allies in this game, our shared determination to uncover the truth binding us together in ways I hadn't anticipated.

Just as I turned to approach him, a sharp voice cut through the melodic chatter, drawing my focus to a nearby conversation. "I hear the kingpin behind the thefts has been hiding in plain sight," a woman whispered, her voice a hushed melody laced with intrigue. I leaned closer, my heart pounding. "They say he's someone no one would suspect—someone we've all trusted."

My pulse quickened, thoughts racing. Who could it be? The heaviness of the air felt almost tangible as I strained to catch more. The woman's companion leaned in, his expression grave. "Rumor has it that he's even in this room right now."

I felt the ground shift beneath my feet, the laughter around me fading into a distant hum. The name echoed in my mind like a foreboding shadow—who could be so bold, so brazen? Just as I prepared to break away, a hand found my wrist, warm and firm. Liam's touch grounded me, pulling me back into the moment.

"Did you hear that?" I asked, my voice barely a whisper, urgent with curiosity and fear. His brow furrowed, eyes narrowing in concentration. "Yeah, I caught it. Let's not lose our heads just yet," he replied, his tone a mixture of concern and determination. "We need to keep our eyes and ears open, gather more intel before we make any moves."

In that moment, the air around us thickened with tension, yet I couldn't ignore the magnetic pull between us. There was something exhilarating about being on the precipice of danger together. It made me feel alive, igniting a fire within me that had long been dormant. Without thinking, I leaned closer, my lips brushing against his, igniting a spark that danced between us. It was a kiss steeped in urgency, a fleeting escape from the storm brewing around us.

When we broke apart, breathless and flushed, the world outside our little bubble rushed back in. My heart raced not only from the kiss but from the weight of what we were unearthing. The gala was no longer just a glamorous affair; it had morphed into a stage for betrayal, deceit, and hidden truths. I needed to stay focused, but Liam's presence made it difficult to think clearly.

As we maneuvered through the crowd, laughter and music fading into a dull roar, I felt my instincts sharpen. I needed answers, and the tension in my chest indicated that they were closer than I thought. "Liam," I murmured, my voice barely rising above the sound of champagne glasses clinking. "What if we corner one of the art dealers? They might have seen something, heard something. This isn't just about the paintings anymore; it's about justice."

He nodded, his gaze scanning the room. "Let's split up. You head to the east wing where the rare collections are displayed; I'll check the bar. If anyone knows anything, it'll be there." A determined glint lit up his eyes, and I found myself nodding in agreement.

I took a deep breath, steeling myself against the whirlwind of emotions. The thrill of the chase beckoned, but so did the unease gnawing at my stomach. As I drifted toward the east wing, the whispers of the crowd faded, replaced by the hushed awe of the art on display. Each piece told a story, but none held my attention as much as the unfolding drama in the air.

Once inside the gallery, I was enveloped in a different kind of beauty—vivid paintings and intricate sculptures that seemed to breathe. My fingers brushed against the cold surface of a marble bust, but my mind was elsewhere. The conversation I'd overheard danced in my thoughts. The kingpin was here, hidden among the elite, and I was determined to unmask him.

Then, as if the universe conspired in my favor, I spotted a figure leaning against a gilded frame, eyes flitting around the room with the practiced ease of someone accustomed to shadows. Something about the way he moved, the way he observed, sent chills down my spine. I edged closer, my pulse quickening with each step. Just as I was about to introduce myself, he turned sharply, and I found myself face to face with a pair of piercing blue eyes that seemed to see right through me.

"Interesting night, isn't it?" he said, his voice smooth like silk, yet carrying an undercurrent of mischief that set my teeth on edge. The tension coiled tighter as I realized the game was just beginning, and I was ready to play.

His gaze flicked over me, curiosity mingling with amusement. "Interesting night, isn't it?" The stranger's voice was smooth, yet there was a challenge hidden beneath the charm. He leaned back casually against the frame, his posture relaxed, but the intensity in his eyes suggested he was anything but nonchalant. I crossed my arms, trying to summon a confidence that didn't quite match the fluttering in my chest. "Depends on what you define as interesting," I replied, my tone sharper than I intended.

"Art thefts, a gala teeming with the city's elite, and a masked stranger practically lurking in the shadows—sounds like the setup for a thrilling plot, don't you think?" He smiled, revealing a set of teeth that seemed too perfect, almost predatory. I narrowed my eyes. There was something disarming about him, yet I could feel the weight of something deeper lurking just beneath his polished surface.

"I suppose it does, though I was hoping for something a bit less... criminal." I didn't want to play his games, but curiosity gnawed at me. Who was he?

"Ah, but isn't there a little thrill in danger? A stolen painting, a hidden agenda? It adds a dash of spice to an otherwise mundane life," he mused, his gaze unwavering. "You're not just another pretty face at this soirée, are you? You have a fire in you, a spark that suggests you're here for more than the hors d'oeuvres."

"Is that your way of saying you think I look good in this dress?" I shot back, half-joking, half-serious.

His chuckle rolled through the gallery like an echo. "I think you'd look good in a potato sack, but we're both aware that's not the point, are we?"

I could feel my cheeks heat, and I quickly regained my composure. "So, what's your angle here? You're not just a spectator in this drama, are you?"

"I'm merely an observer, taking notes from the sidelines," he replied, his smile never faltering. "But I can't help but wonder if you're playing a part as well. You're looking for answers, I can tell. What if I told you I might have some of them?"

My heart leapt at the prospect, but instinctively I held back. "And why would you share those with me?"

He pushed off the frame, stepping closer, the warmth of his presence enveloping me. "Because, my dear, the world is far more interesting when alliances are formed. Think of it as a collaboration. You want to find the mastermind; I want to see how deep this rabbit hole goes. We both stand to gain."

Skepticism warred with intrigue within me. "And what do you gain from this little venture?"

His smile widened, revealing a hint of mischief. "Oh, let's just say I have my own reasons for wanting to unravel this particular tapestry. Besides, I find you intriguing. There's more to you than meets the eye."

Just then, a wave of laughter rippled through the gallery, momentarily distracting us. I looked past him to see Liam approaching, his expression a mix of concern and determination. "There you are! I was looking for you," he said, the tension in his voice palpable as he glanced between us.

"Enjoying the conversation?" he added, a hint of possessiveness slipping through.

"Just a little discussion on art and... potential criminal activity," I replied, keeping my tone light, though I could feel the weight of Liam's gaze bore into the stranger.

"Interesting topic for a gala," Liam said, folding his arms defensively.

The stranger merely inclined his head, unfazed. "All art is, in some ways, criminal. And I think the lovely lady here knows a thing or two about that."

Liam stepped forward, a protective instinct flaring. "What's your game?"

"Just sharing insights, my friend. But don't worry, I'm not here to steal her thunder," he said, his tone dripping with faux innocence.

"Or maybe you're just waiting for the right moment to make your move," Liam shot back, the tension between them thickening like fog.

"I'm not the one with a reputation for being reckless," the stranger countered smoothly, his eyes glinting with amusement. "But if you're looking for answers about the kingpin, I think we might be able to help each other."

I shifted uncomfortably, caught between the two. "Wait, wait—how do you even know about the kingpin?"

The stranger leaned closer, lowering his voice conspiratorially. "Let's just say I have my ears to the ground. The whispers in this room are louder than you'd think."

"And why would you share any of that with us?" Liam's protective tone hadn't softened.

"Because," the stranger said, his eyes glimmering with mischief, "if you're trying to play detective, you'll need a partner who knows the territory."

"Or someone with their own agenda," Liam replied, a note of warning threading through his words.

"Perhaps. But I believe you're in over your head, and it wouldn't hurt to have an ally. What do you say?"

Liam and I exchanged glances, the uncertainty hanging thick in the air. "What's your name?" I asked, curiosity winning over caution.

"Elliot," he said with a flourish, as if revealing a secret. "And I assure you, I'm no foe. I'm simply someone who sees the potential in this little puzzle we find ourselves in."

"Fine, Elliot. What do you know?" Liam interjected, his voice steady despite the tension.

Elliot leaned against the wall, a self-assured smile playing on his lips. "I know that the person behind the art thefts isn't just a thief. He's a puppet master, and the strings run deep into the city's art scene."

"And you think we can expose him?" I asked, my heart racing with the thrill of the chase.

"With the right connections and a little bit of daring, absolutely," Elliot replied. "But first, we need to gather more information. There's a gala after-party at the St. Clair mansion later tonight. It's where the real players will be."

"Aren't you worried it'll be a trap?" Liam asked, skepticism etched on his features.

"Life is a trap, my friend. It's how we navigate it that counts," Elliot quipped. "And besides, it's the perfect chance for you two to blend in, gather intel, and figure out just who you can trust."

"Or who we can't," I added, the weight of his words settling over me like a shroud.

"Exactly. And I can help you get in." Elliot's confidence was infectious, and I felt a surge of determination rising within me.

"Fine. We'll meet you there," Liam said, the decision made.

As Elliot walked away, a sense of unease settled in my stomach. The night was only beginning, and the stakes were rising. Liam turned to me, a mix of resolve and concern in his eyes. "Are you sure about this?"

I met his gaze, feeling the gravity of our situation press down on us. "If there's a chance to unmask the kingpin, we have to take it. But I'm not doing this without you."

Liam stepped closer, the tension between us thickening once more. "Then let's get ready to play our parts. Whatever happens, we'll face it together."

His words hung in the air, a promise woven with unspoken fears and hopes. As we left the gallery, the glamour of the gala faded, and the reality of the game we were entering sank in. The night was young, and I felt the thrill of danger dancing at the edge of my consciousness. Little did we know, the final pieces of this intricate puzzle were about to fall into place in ways we never anticipated.

The drive to the St. Clair mansion was an exhilarating mix of anticipation and trepidation, the city lights flickering past us like fireflies caught in the dark. I sat in the backseat with Liam, my heart racing not just from the thrill of the chase but from the undeniable chemistry that simmered between us. The plush leather seats surrounded us in a cocoon of luxury, yet I felt acutely aware of the stakes we were facing.

"So, what's the plan?" I asked, trying to keep my voice steady despite the nervous excitement swirling within me. "Are we playing the part of the unassuming guests or the eager art enthusiasts?"

"Why not both?" Liam replied, flashing a confident smile that made my heart skip a beat. "Blend in, gather intel, and if things go sideways, we can make a quick exit."

"Is that your way of saying you're prepared to run if the opportunity arises?" I teased, but deep down, the gravity of the situation settled heavily in my stomach.

"Only if it means keeping you safe," he said, his voice dropping to a serious tone that made my pulse quicken.

The mansion loomed ahead, a sprawling estate bathed in the warm glow of strategically placed lights. It was a testament to wealth and power, the kind of place where secrets were traded as casually as the finest champagne. As we stepped out of the car, the sound of music and laughter spilled into the night, pulling me toward the entrance like a moth to a flame.

Inside, the ambiance was intoxicating. The foyer was adorned with opulent chandeliers, casting a soft light over a sea of silk and satin as elegantly dressed guests floated past. The air buzzed with the promise of intrigue, and I felt an electric charge running through me.

"Stay close," Liam murmured, his hand finding mine, grounding me in the chaos.

We navigated through clusters of well-heeled socialites, each conversation a delicate dance of wit and charm. I spotted Elliot across the room, leaning against a wall and surveying the scene with the air of someone who belonged, even in the midst of such opulence. His earlier words echoed in my mind; if he was telling the truth, the kingpin could be anywhere within these walls, hidden among the glittering facade.

"Do you see him?" Liam asked, his voice barely rising above the music.

I nodded, watching as Elliot made his way toward us, weaving through the crowd with an easy grace. "He's got that look again, you know? Like he knows more than he's letting on."

"Let's hope it's good news," Liam replied, his expression serious.

"Or we might need to come up with an escape plan sooner rather than later," I added, forcing a smile to mask my nerves.

Elliot approached, a glint of mischief in his eyes. "Glad to see you both made it. I thought for a moment you might be too scared to join the real players."

"Scared? Us?" I shot back, my bravado lifting the weight of the evening, if only for a moment.

"Right. Fearless adventurers in the wild world of high society," Liam said, sarcasm dripping from his words.

Elliot chuckled, the sound rich and deep. "Just keep your wits about you. The atmosphere is charged tonight, and you'll want to be careful who you trust. I've seen a few faces here who have more than just art on their minds."

"Any leads on the kingpin?" I asked, leaning closer, eager for any scrap of information.

"Actually, yes," Elliot replied, his expression shifting to one of seriousness. "I overheard something rather interesting in the gallery earlier. One of the patrons mentioned a shipment arriving tonight—something 'special'—and I believe it's linked to our friend in the shadows."

"A shipment? Here?" Liam interjected, the concern evident in his tone.

"Yes, and I suspect it's something that will spark quite the interest among the guests," Elliot said, a calculating gleam in his eyes. "If we can find out where they're keeping it, we might be able to expose the mastermind."

The music swelled, a crescendo that seemed to echo the pounding of my heart. "Where do we start looking?" I asked, adrenaline surging through me.

"There's a back room where they store valuables for the auction later. If this shipment is as significant as I suspect, it could be there," Elliot replied, his tone suddenly serious. "But we need to act fast. The longer we wait, the greater the chance someone will catch wind of our intentions."

"Lead the way," I said, determination burning in my chest.

As we moved through the crowd, I felt the eyes of the guests on us, some curious, others scrutinizing. The sense of being watched settled over me like a heavy cloak, and the thrill of danger danced in the air.

We made our way to a door marked with a discreet sign that read "Authorized Personnel Only." Elliot pushed it open, revealing a narrow hallway lined with priceless artworks draped in protective fabric. The air felt different here—charged, heavy with anticipation.

"There's no one around," I whispered, my heart racing as we slipped inside.

Elliot led us deeper into the hallway, and as we turned a corner, I heard the sound of voices drifting from a nearby room. I gestured for silence, my senses heightened.

"Listen," I whispered, straining to catch the conversation.

"I'm telling you, tonight is the night," a voice said, filled with a mix of excitement and urgency. "If we don't make our move now, the opportunity will slip through our fingers. The shipment is worth millions."

"What if they find out?" a second voice replied, laced with fear. "We can't afford to get caught."

"Trust me, we have everything planned. The distraction will be perfect," the first voice assured.

I exchanged a glance with Liam and Elliot, the realization dawning on us. They were planning something, and we needed to act before it was too late.

"Should we confront them?" Liam asked, his expression taut with tension.

"Not yet," Elliot replied, his eyes narrowing in thought. "Let's gather more information first. We need to know who we're dealing with."

Just then, the door swung open, and a tall figure emerged, his face obscured by the dim light of the hallway. My breath hitched as I recognized him—the very last person I expected to see.

"Liam?" The figure's voice cut through the air like a knife, filled with disbelief.

It was Marcus, the art dealer I'd once trusted, and the implications of his presence sent shockwaves through me. He stepped into the light, and I saw the unmistakable look of calculated cunning in his eyes.

"What are you doing here?" Liam demanded, his voice low and threatening.

"Funny you should ask," Marcus replied, a sly grin spreading across his face. "I could ask you the same thing."

In that moment, the air shifted, the tension thickening as the weight of his words settled around us like a storm cloud. The revelation hung in the air, a promise of danger lurking just beneath the surface. We were caught in a web of deceit, and the night was far from over.

Chapter 18: Crossing Lines

The cabin creaked softly as the ocean breeze whispered secrets through the cracks in the weathered wood. I stood at the window, gazing out at the tumultuous sea that mirrored the storm of emotions brewing within me. Waves crashed against the shore, their rhythmic pulse a reminder of the chaos outside our little sanctuary. Just a few nights ago, this place had felt like an escape, a retreat from the world, but now it felt more like a pressure cooker, with secrets simmering beneath the surface, waiting for the right moment to explode.

Liam's presence in the cabin was both a comfort and a source of tension. He moved with a grace that belied the weight of the past he carried. I watched him from my perch by the window, his silhouette outlined by the flickering light of the small lantern we had lit. He was studying the map spread out on the table, brow furrowed, lips pressed together in concentration. A part of me wanted to jump into the fray, to offer suggestions and strategize together, but another part, the part that had fallen hopelessly for him, was hesitant to disrupt the fragile equilibrium we had created.

"Any bright ideas, or are we still stuck with the old plan?" I finally asked, my voice breaking the stillness like a pebble dropped in still water.

He looked up, a spark of amusement dancing in his eyes, and the corners of his mouth tilted up into a smirk that sent warmth cascading through me. "I wouldn't say it's a 'bright' idea, but we're definitely not stuck. Just... recalibrating."

"Recalibrating?" I echoed, crossing my arms and leaning against the wall. "Is that code for 'we have no idea what we're doing'?"

Liam chuckled, a low, rumbling sound that felt like music in the dim light. "Maybe. But it's also code for—let's not throw caution to the wind and walk into a death trap."

"Fair point," I conceded, pushing off the wall to join him at the table. I leaned in, examining the map with an intensity that belied my uncertainty. "So, what's the next move? You can't just sit here looking broody while the clock is ticking."

His gaze flicked from the map to my face, and I could see the conflict swirling in his deep-set eyes. "I can't help but feel like we're playing a dangerous game, and not just with the kingpin. What if we don't make it out of this?"

The air thickened, tension crackling between us like static electricity. I reached for his hand, the warmth of his skin grounding me. "We will make it out, Liam. We're not just going to waltz in there and hope for the best. We'll fight, together."

His fingers tightened around mine, the connection sparking a current of something electric between us. The warmth spread through me, awakening all the feelings I had tried to keep at bay. I was acutely aware of the space between us, charged with unspoken words and unfulfilled desires. I had crossed so many lines in the past few days—allegiances, emotions, and the boundaries of trust. Now, standing so close, I felt the weight of everything we had both risked to be here.

"I wish I could believe you," he said softly, the teasing edge gone from his voice.

"Then believe in me," I urged, feeling bold, the adrenaline of our shared danger fueling my resolve. "Believe in us."

He stared at me, those dark eyes searching mine for something I wasn't sure I could articulate. "It's not just the fight ahead," he admitted, his voice barely above a whisper. "It's this. Us. I don't know if I can handle losing you on either front."

I inhaled sharply, the vulnerability in his words unraveling the carefully constructed barriers around my heart. "You won't lose me, Liam. Not like this. We're stronger together, and we need each other. That's what matters."

His thumb brushed over my knuckles, a tender gesture that sent my heart racing. The silence that enveloped us was thick with possibilities, a delicate dance of hope and fear.

"Do you really think we can win this?" he asked, his voice laced with skepticism yet edged with longing.

"Together, we can take on anything," I said, my confidence rising as I leaned closer, our foreheads nearly touching. "Even if we don't know the outcome, we'll face it head-on. No more running."

He let out a breath I hadn't realized he was holding, his body relaxing ever so slightly against mine. "Alright then. Let's face it together."

The intensity of the moment hung between us, and for a heartbeat, it felt like the world outside melted away. The sound of crashing waves became a distant echo, the salty breeze transformed into something softer, more intimate. I could feel the gravity of our connection pulling us closer, the space between us charged with unspoken promises and a warmth that defied the chill in the air.

But as I leaned in, wanting to close the distance, the reality of our situation crashed back like a wave breaking against the shore. We were not just two people caught in a whirlwind of attraction; we were two rivals, two players in a dangerous game that could end in betrayal or worse. The kingpin was out there, lurking in the shadows, and our feelings for each other were a complication we couldn't afford.

I pulled back slightly, the weight of uncertainty returning to my chest. "We should probably get back to planning," I said, forcing a smile, even as my heart raced with a mix of longing and apprehension.

Liam nodded, though his gaze lingered on me, as if trying to etch the moment into his memory. "Right. Planning. Let's do that."

As we turned our attention back to the map, the night stretched on around us, filled with unspoken words and lingering glances that hinted at the deeper connection between us. Each plan we laid out felt like a precarious balance between our growing feelings and the imminent threat that loomed over us. It was a dance on the edge of a blade, thrilling and terrifying all at once.

And as the moon cast its silvery glow over the cabin, I couldn't shake the feeling that whatever came next, it would change everything we thought we knew.

The air in the cabin grew thick with a tension that was almost palpable, like the calm before a storm. I could hear the waves crashing relentlessly against the shore, a haunting reminder of the chaos that awaited us. Liam was poring over the map again, tracing routes and exits with the tip of his finger, as if hoping to uncover a hidden path to safety. His brow was furrowed in concentration, but I could see the storm brewing behind his dark eyes. The connection we had forged in the heat of danger was strong, yet the weight of our circumstances threatened to crush the fragile hope we had nurtured.

"Okay, let's assume we make it past the guards. What's the endgame?" I asked, breaking the silence that had settled like a thick fog. My words hung in the air, heavy with the reality that lay before us.

Liam's gaze flicked up from the map, locking onto mine. "Endgame? You mean if we get past the guards and manage to find the kingpin? We expose him, gather evidence, and take him down. Simple, right?"

"Ah, yes, because nothing is more straightforward than confronting a ruthless criminal mastermind who's always ten steps ahead." I leaned back in my chair, crossing my arms, trying to project confidence even as the knot in my stomach twisted tighter.

Liam chuckled softly, the sound both comforting and unnerving. "You've got a point there. I just wish we had more intel. It feels like we're going in blind."

"Then we need a plan that accounts for the unexpected," I replied, my mind racing through possible scenarios. "What if we create a diversion? Something to draw attention away from us while we slip in unnoticed."

His eyes lit up at the idea, and for a moment, the tension eased between us. "A diversion could work, but we'd need something big enough to distract them—fireworks, maybe? Something to get everyone's attention."

"Or something less... explosive," I suggested, a mischievous grin creeping onto my face. "What if we stage a little party? Loud music, drinks, the works. It could lure the guards away from their posts."

"Are you suggesting we throw a rager on the kingpin's turf?" he asked, incredulous yet amused.

"Why not? It's not like we have a boring meeting on our hands," I said, leaning forward, excitement bubbling within me. "We'll charm them, keep them busy while we sneak in and do our thing."

Liam chuckled again, shaking his head. "You're something else, you know that? But I like it. Alright, let's flesh out this party plan. If we're going to do this, let's do it right."

As we brainstormed ideas, the atmosphere shifted. What had begun as a grim strategy session morphed into something lighter, infused with playful banter and teasing. The seriousness of our situation faded momentarily as we imagined the wildest scenarios, laughing at the absurdity of it all. For every insane idea I threw out, Liam countered with an equally outrageous one, and soon the weight of our reality felt a little less heavy, a little less suffocating.

But as the laughter subsided, an uneasy silence fell between us. I felt the sharp edge of reality cut through the mirth. The kingpin was still out there, a looming threat in our peripheral vision, a reminder that the game we were playing was anything but innocent. I turned my gaze to the window, where the moon hung low in the sky, casting a silvery glow over the restless ocean.

"Do you ever wonder what life would be like if we weren't entangled in all of this?" I asked quietly, my voice barely above a whisper.

Liam shifted, and I could feel the weight of his contemplation in the air. "All the time. I think about it every day. What if we could just—be normal? Find a quiet place and build a life away from all this chaos?"

"Normal sounds nice," I said, a bittersweet smile tugging at my lips. "But what does 'normal' even look like for us now? Especially after everything?"

"Maybe it looks like this," he said, motioning around the cabin, the dim light casting soft shadows on the walls. "Just you and me, figuring things out. Maybe a few less dangerous criminals involved."

I laughed lightly, but it was tinged with sadness. "Sure, let's aim for a life with less chaos. But that's a tall order when we're about to walk into a den of lions."

"True," he admitted, his expression sobering. "But you know what? I wouldn't want to do any of this with anyone else. You give me hope, even when it feels impossible."

His words hung between us, a thread of vulnerability that sent shivers down my spine. I met his gaze, and for a moment, the world outside faded away. It was just the two of us, the silence filled with everything left unsaid.

"Liam," I started, but before I could finish, the sound of a distant car engine broke through our bubble, slicing the tension like a knife. We both turned toward the sound, the reality crashing back down around us.

"Do you hear that?" he asked, the urgency returning to his voice.

"Yeah, it sounds like it's coming closer." My heart raced, a mix of adrenaline and dread coursing through me. "What do we do?"

"Quick! We need to hide everything," he said, leaping into action. "The map, the supplies—everything."

I nodded, adrenaline fueling my movements as we scrambled to clear the table, shoving everything into drawers and under the bed. The light from the car swept across the cabin like a spotlight, illuminating our frantic efforts. I could feel the weight of impending danger pressing down on us, the air crackling with tension.

As we finished hiding our supplies, Liam grabbed my hand, pulling me behind the door as we crouched low. The sound of footsteps crunching on the gravel outside echoed ominously, each step drawing closer, amplifying the tension that coiled tightly in my chest.

"Do you think they saw us?" I whispered, my voice barely audible.

"I don't know, but we need to stay quiet." His breath was warm against my ear, sending a jolt of awareness through me, even amidst the tension.

The footsteps stopped just outside the cabin, and I could feel my heart pounding in my chest, an erratic drumbeat of fear and anticipation. The door creaked open, and I held my breath, straining to listen as shadows danced across the floor.

"Where are they?" a voice called out, low and menacing.

I exchanged a wide-eyed glance with Liam, my pulse quickening as the reality of our situation settled heavily on my shoulders. We were no longer just playing a game; we were in the thick of it, the stakes higher than ever. As the intruders moved further into the cabin, I knew we had crossed a line we could never return from.

The footsteps echoed in the cabin, each crunch of gravel beneath booted feet a reminder of how quickly everything could spiral out of control. I held my breath, the air thick with tension as I pressed myself closer to Liam, the warmth of his body grounding me even as anxiety prickled my skin.

"What now?" I whispered, my heart racing in time with the intruders' movements.

"Stay quiet and stay low," he murmured back, his gaze locked on the door. The shadows danced around us, and every second felt like an eternity. I could hear the murmur of voices, low and conspiratorial, their words weaving an ominous web around us.

"Do you think they're looking for us?" I asked, my mind racing with possibilities.

"Maybe. Or maybe they're just here to check on the cabin."

"Right. Because nothing says 'a relaxing getaway' like armed intruders breaking in." I rolled my eyes, but the flutter of nerves in my stomach made it hard to maintain my usual sarcasm.

"Shh," Liam hissed, and I instantly fell silent, watching as the shadows moved closer to where we were hidden. The air felt electric, charged with fear and the unspoken realization that we were no longer in control of our fate.

"Where do you think they went?" one voice said, muffled but dripping with authority.

"They must have slipped out the back. Check the windows!"

Panic surged through me as I realized the enormity of the situation. I gripped Liam's arm, my mind racing to think of a way out. "We can't just sit here," I whispered urgently. "What if they find us?"

"Then we'll improvise," he replied, determination flickering in his eyes. "We have to be ready to make a move the moment they let their guard down."

My heart pounded in my chest as the sound of footsteps moved through the cabin, growing nearer. "Liam, what if—"

"Just trust me," he cut in, his voice firm. "Whatever happens, we'll face it together."

I wanted to believe him, but fear coiled tightly in my chest. I could feel my pulse in my throat, the adrenaline coursing through my veins heightening my senses. The footsteps stopped just outside the door, and I could see the outline of a figure silhouetted against the dim light coming from outside.

"What do you think? Should we search the bedroom?" one of the intruders asked.

"Yeah, check everywhere. We need to find them before they slip away again."

A rush of dread washed over me. The cabin was small, and there was nowhere to hide. Every moment spent waiting felt like a lifetime, and I could sense Liam's muscles tense beside me. He was ready to act, and I could only hope that whatever plan he had in mind would work.

Suddenly, the door swung open, and a tall figure stepped inside, scanning the room with a sharp gaze. My heart raced as I stifled a gasp, forcing myself to stay still.

"Clear," he called back to his partner, who followed him in, a hulking shadow filled with menace. "They must have gotten away. Let's check the beach."

"Wait!" the other intruder said, his eyes narrowing as he stepped deeper into the cabin. "I think I heard something."

Liam and I exchanged a quick glance, and without a word, we slipped silently around the corner, our backs pressed against the wall, hearts pounding in unison. The tension crackled like electricity, and I felt a surge of adrenaline as I crouched down low, ready to spring into action if necessary.

"Is this all they have?" the second intruder grumbled, throwing open a cabinet filled with dishes. "Looks like we've been duped."

The first man rolled his eyes, his frustration palpable. "Just keep looking. We'll find them."

Just then, the first man turned toward us, eyes narrowing as he took a step closer. I held my breath, every muscle in my body coiled, ready to either flee or fight.

"Check the back," he said abruptly, motioning to the door that led out onto the small porch. "I'll look here."

My heart dropped as I realized we were about to be cornered. Liam's grip tightened around my wrist, and for a moment, we were frozen in that brief heartbeat of impending danger.

"Now," he whispered, and we darted out from our hiding place just as the intruder turned his back. We bolted toward the back door, adrenaline surging as we sprinted into the night.

The salty air hit my face like a splash of cold water, and I could hear the roar of the waves crashing against the shore, urging us forward. We didn't dare look back as we raced across the sand, heartbeats drumming in my ears, desperate to put as much distance between us and the cabin as possible.

"Where do we go?" I panted, glancing at Liam as he scanned the beach for any signs of danger.

"Just keep running. We need to get to the tree line. There's cover there."

We sprinted toward the dark silhouette of the trees, the moonlight glinting off the water behind us, illuminating our path. As we neared the trees, the sound of shouting erupted behind us, the intruders realizing we had escaped their grasp.

"Over there!" one of them yelled, the anger in his voice sending a jolt of fear coursing through me.

Liam pulled me into the dense underbrush just as a flashlight beam sliced through the darkness, illuminating the sandy shore. "This way," he urged, leading us deeper into the shadows, where the trees loomed overhead like silent sentinels.

My lungs burned as we plunged into the cover of the trees, branches scraping against our skin. "What if they catch up?" I gasped, panic rising like a tide within me.

"They won't. Just keep moving," he replied, his voice steady, even as urgency laced his tone. "We need to find a place to hide until we can figure out our next move."

Just then, a rustle in the bushes made us freeze, and I could hear the unmistakable sound of footsteps crashing through the undergrowth behind us. My heart raced as I strained to listen, and the panic clawed at my insides.

"Did you hear that?" I whispered, terror lacing my words.

Liam nodded, his jaw set in determination. "We can't stop now. There's a clearing up ahead. We'll hide there and wait for them to pass."

With that, we plunged deeper into the thicket, the urgency propelling us forward. We could hear the intruders getting closer, their voices mingling with the sounds of the night, a cruel reminder of the danger nipping at our heels.

As we broke through the trees into the clearing, I stumbled, nearly losing my footing. Liam caught me, his grip firm, and we moved to the edge of the open space, crouching low behind a thick cluster of bushes.

"Do you see them?" I whispered, my breath coming in quick bursts.

Liam leaned forward, peering into the darkness. "Not yet, but they're close. We have to stay quiet."

As we huddled there, the shadows closing in around us, the footsteps grew louder, accompanied by the sound of crackling branches. My heart pounded furiously in my chest as I waited, terrified, to see if we had been spotted.

"Where did they go?" one of the intruders shouted, their voice now mingled with frustration.

"Keep looking. They can't have gotten far," the other replied, the sound of their footsteps sending chills down my spine.

The tension was unbearable, and I felt the weight of the moment pressing down on me. Liam's arm brushed against mine, a silent reminder that we were in this together, but the reality of our situation clawed at my insides.

"Liam, I—" I started, but before I could finish, the sharp crack of a twig broke the silence, followed by a shout from one of the intruders.

"There they are!"

I felt my stomach drop as panic surged through me. The moment had arrived; we had been discovered. Liam's eyes widened, and in an instant, he grabbed my hand, pulling me to my feet.

"Run!" he shouted, and we burst out of our hiding place, sprinting toward the treeline on the other side of the clearing. The night air felt electric, our footsteps pounding against the ground as the sound of our pursuers echoed behind us.

We were almost free, just a few more strides, when a flash of light illuminated the clearing. I turned my head just in time to see a figure emerge from the darkness, a shadow holding something glinting under the moonlight—a weapon.

"Stop right there!" they shouted, and my heart sank as the realization hit. There was no escape.

In that moment, everything froze—the air, the sound of the waves, the very fabric of our fate hanging by a thread. I glanced at Liam, a mixture of fear and determination in his eyes, and knew we had crossed the point of no return.

As the figure raised the weapon, I braced myself for impact, uncertainty coursing through me like a tidal wave. The world faded away, and all that remained was the deafening silence of the moment, the weight of what lay ahead crashing down like the waves against the shore.

Chapter 19: The Reckoning

The evening air hung thick with the scent of salt and secrets, the rhythmic crash of waves against the rocky shore underscoring the pulse of anticipation as I stepped onto the dock. The moonlight spilled like liquid silver over the weathered planks, illuminating a motley crew of artists, dealers, and the occasional socialite draped in finery that sparkled against the backdrop of the inky sea. Liam's presence beside me felt like a lifeline; he exuded a quiet confidence that ignited a spark of bravery in my chest, even as my heart thudded with trepidation.

"Just act like you belong," he murmured, casting a sideways glance at me. His dark hair tousled by the wind framed his face, highlighting the determined set of his jaw. "Remember, we're here for the art, not the drama."

I nodded, though the truth felt more layered than the gossamer fabric of the designer gown I wore. The gown was supposed to mask my nerves, its flowing skirt designed to draw the eye, but my mind raced with every possible disaster that might unfold. Each step toward the grand estate loomed heavy with the potential for betrayal. The event had promised art, but it felt more like a masquerade for something darker, and I was all too aware of the stakes we were navigating.

Inside, the atmosphere crackled with energy. Elaborate chandeliers cast a warm glow, and the walls were adorned with paintings that seemed to whisper tales of their own. A low murmur of conversation wrapped around us like a silken shroud as we moved through the throng of attendees, each one carefully curated, each glance a dart in a game where every player was a potential foe.

"Did you see that piece over there?" Liam gestured toward a canvas splashed with vibrant colors, its chaotic strokes concealing a deeper meaning. "I read somewhere that it's worth a fortune."

"Yeah, worth more than my sanity if this goes sideways," I replied, forcing a smile that didn't quite reach my eyes. I was suddenly acutely aware of the heaviness of my own breath, the way it mingled with the heady perfume of expensive fragrances and the rustle of silk dresses.

We meandered through the gallery, feigning interest in the artwork while keeping a watchful eye on the entrances and exits, each footstep a reminder of our purpose. Beneath the surface of glitzy conversations, a current of danger lurked, twisting and coiling like a serpent ready to strike. Liam's fingers brushed against mine, an unspoken promise that we were in this together, though the specter of fear loomed larger with every passing moment.

Then, a flicker of movement caught my attention. In a shadowed corner, a figure leaned casually against the wall, their face obscured by the brim of a wide hat. My breath hitched; there was something unnervingly familiar about the silhouette. I was struck by the realization that we were not merely players in this game; we were the hunted.

"Liam," I whispered, my voice barely a breath. "I think someone's watching us."

He turned, his demeanor shifting from casual observer to hawk-like vigilance. "Where?"

"There, by the painting of the woman with the red dress." I nodded discreetly. "Something's off about them."

"Stay close." His tone brooked no argument as he shifted into the crowd, keeping our shared goal at the forefront of his mind, even as the unease unfurled within me like a wilting flower.

As the auctioneer's voice rose above the murmurs, a tension crackled through the room, thickening the air. My heart raced; the auction was beginning, and we were on borrowed time. With each piece that came under the hammer, my anxiety deepened, until the moment arrived when the auctioneer announced the crown jewel of the evening—a rare piece rumored to belong to a long-lost collection of the underworld's elite.

The crowd surged forward, and the excitement was palpable, but I felt like a ghost drifting through a carnival of the damned. The auctioneer's gavel struck, echoing like a death knell. The auction had begun, but the true stakes lay in what we had come to uncover.

Then it happened. A commotion erupted near the back of the room. Shouts pierced the air, and I caught sight of the figure in the corner, now removing their hat, revealing a face that sent shockwaves through me.

"No," I breathed. "It can't be."

"Is that—?" Liam's voice trailed off, disbelief etching his features.

The identity of the kingpin, the very reason we had infiltrated this event, stood unveiled in the middle of chaos—Viktor, a figure from our past whose cunning had left scars deeper than any blade. The crowd recoiled, a wave of shock rippling through the assembly, and in that instant, I knew our carefully laid plans were crumbling.

"Get out!" Liam shouted, urgency spilling from him like the tide threatening to drown us. But the throng of bodies was like quicksand, pulling us deeper into uncertainty.

The room spun as I grasped at the edges of sanity, fear mingling with fury. Viktor's eyes gleamed with malice, and I couldn't shake the feeling that he had orchestrated this moment, drawing us into his web.

"Stay close!" Liam's hand found mine again, a tether amidst the chaos. "We can't lose each other in this madness!"

But the ground beneath us quaked with the chaos of the crowd, and I realized this wasn't just an auction—it was a battleground. Adrenaline surged through my veins, and with a fierce resolve, I steeled myself against the rising tide of panic. We had come too far to be swept away now.

The chaos enveloped us like a thick fog, suffocating in its intensity. As the crowd surged forward, a wild mix of curiosity and panic gripped everyone within the grand hall. The atmosphere shifted from elegant anticipation to electric uncertainty, each gasp and murmur echoing the peril we now faced. I felt Liam's hand tighten around mine, a steadying force amidst the tide of uncertainty.

"We have to get out of here," he urged, his voice firm but laced with urgency.

"Not without confronting him first," I countered, my heart pounding with a mix of fear and stubborn resolve. Viktor was here, and it felt like an unfinished chapter begging for closure. I couldn't simply turn my back on him, not when we were this close to unraveling the web he'd spun around us.

"Are you out of your mind?" Liam shot back, his eyes narrowing as he scanned the room for an escape route. "He's not just going to stand there and let us walk away. He'll—"

"Liam!" I interrupted, my voice rising above the din. "He's the reason we're here. We owe it to ourselves to at least hear him out."

Viktor had always been a master of manipulation, charming in a way that disguised the predator lurking beneath. The image of him backlit by the paintings, his smirk as arrogant as ever, sent a jolt of adrenaline through me. I couldn't ignore the chance to finally confront him.

With a quick squeeze of Liam's hand, I broke away from the throng, weaving through the crowd, my heart racing in rhythm with the pounding bass of the auctioneer's voice. The auction was still in full swing, the next piece about to be revealed, but all I could focus on was the man I once feared but now found strangely compelling in his power.

"Wait, where are you going?" Liam called after me, his tone a mix of exasperation and genuine concern.

"Stay close!" I shouted back, a playful tone masking my anxiety. "I promise to come back before dessert."

Liam rolled his eyes but followed, shaking his head in disbelief. I could see the worry etched on his face, but the thrill of my decision buoyed me forward, propelling me through the kaleidoscope of silk and satin.

As I approached Viktor, the world around me faded into a blur. He was laughing, a rich sound that sliced through the tension, as if he relished the chaos he'd created. I stepped into his line of sight, the moment stretching like a taut string ready to snap.

"Well, if it isn't my favorite little art critic," he purred, his eyes glinting with mockery. "I should have known you'd come sniffing around my masterpiece. Have you come to admire my collection, or do you have something more... confrontational in mind?"

"Surprisingly, I'm not here for a lesson in art appreciation," I shot back, refusing to back down. "I'm here to understand why you thought you could toy with our lives."

Viktor tilted his head, a lazy smile playing on his lips. "Oh, darling, it's not toy-making; it's a symphony. You and Liam, the perfect duet. I merely provided the stage."

"Symphony? More like a disaster waiting to happen," I retorted, feeling the heat of defiance rise in me. The tension in the room thickened, a palpable force that made my skin prickle.

Behind me, I could sense Liam moving closer, his presence a protective shield as he came to stand at my side. "We know what you're up to, Viktor. The art isn't just for show. You're using this auction as a front, and we're not falling for it."

Viktor chuckled, a sound that echoed mockingly. "Ah, Liam. Always the clever one. But you see, it's not about falling or rising; it's about playing the right notes. And I hold the score."

Before I could respond, a loud crash erupted from the opposite end of the hall, causing the attendees to gasp and scatter like startled birds. A priceless sculpture had toppled over, its base shattering into pieces, and with it, the tenuous grip on composure that the guests had maintained.

"Looks like the night is turning a little too dramatic for my taste," Viktor remarked, his grin widening as he took a step back, eyes darting to the nearest exit. "Perhaps it's time to reconsider your position, dear."

"Not so fast!" Liam called out, taking a step forward.

But Viktor was already slipping away into the shadows, a wolf retreating into the woods, leaving us amidst the growing chaos. The room transformed into a swirling mass of confusion, shouts ringing out as more art began to crash down in a calculated destruction that felt all too orchestrated.

"Liam, we can't let him escape," I insisted, adrenaline surging as I pushed through the chaos. The urgency in my voice was laced with a determination that surprised even me.

He hesitated, uncertainty flickering in his eyes, but then nodded. "You're right. We need to follow him."

As we maneuvered through the panicking crowd, I could feel the thrill of the chase lighting a fire in my veins. Each step forward felt like an act of rebellion against the fear that had threatened to consume me. It was no longer just about confronting Viktor; it was about reclaiming our narrative, taking back control over our fates.

Emerging from the main gallery, we found ourselves in a dimly lit corridor lined with paintings—each canvas a witness to our pursuit. The walls seemed to close in around us, thick with anticipation, and the echo of our footsteps felt like a drumroll announcing the climax of our pursuit.

"Where did he go?" I whispered, scanning the shadows for any sign of movement.

"Maybe he thought he could hide behind one of these ridiculous paintings," Liam suggested, his eyes scanning the frames.

Just then, a sharp sound echoed from a door at the end of the corridor, a distinct click that sent a shiver of realization through me. "He's in there!" I pointed, a surge of determination washing over me.

Liam nodded, his jaw set with resolve. "On three. We go in together."

I took a deep breath, feeling the weight of our resolve anchor me as I counted down in my mind. The door creaked open, and we stepped into the room, hearts racing, ready to confront the man whose strings we had longed to cut. The air was thick with the scent of varnish and wood, and as I looked around, I could hardly believe the treasure trove of art that lay before us—each piece holding the potential for revelation, and in the center, standing proudly as if he owned the world, was Viktor.

"Welcome," he said, the satisfaction curling at the corners of his mouth. "You found me. I'm flattered."

But this time, the thrill of the chase had turned into something sharper, something much more dangerous. The game was shifting, and I could feel the tension crackling in the air, poised to explode.

Viktor stood there, a smug grin plastered across his face, as if he were the conductor of a grand symphony and we were merely the unwitting audience. The room was laden with tension, each breath heavy with the knowledge that we were dancing on the precipice of something monumental.

"You've truly outdone yourself this time," he said, his voice smooth like silk but dripping with menace. "To think, the duo I underestimated would track me down to my little gallery of treasures."

"Enough with the pleasantries," Liam snapped, stepping forward with a resolve that made my heart swell with admiration. "You think you can play us against each other and walk away unscathed?"

Viktor chuckled, an unsettling sound that sent a shiver down my spine. "Oh, Liam, you misunderstand. This isn't a game of chess where I'm simply trying to checkmate you. This is more of a gallery where I curate the consequences of my decisions. And tonight, my dear friends, you are the main exhibit."

A chill raced through me, the implication of his words sinking like a stone in the pit of my stomach. "What do you mean?" I demanded, my voice steady even as dread coiled around my heart.

"Ah, the sweet sound of desperation," he replied, leaning against a nearby sculpture with casual grace, as if we weren't standing on the brink of disaster. "You see, it's not just art that's up for grabs tonight. It's your very lives—though I suppose that's just a side note."

"Lives?" I echoed, my mind racing to piece together his cryptic insinuations. "What are you planning?"

Viktor waved a dismissive hand, his eyes glinting like shards of ice. "Plan is such a strong word. Let's call it an opportunity—a chance for you to understand just how far-reaching my influence truly is."

Before I could respond, the room shook as another crash erupted outside, the cacophony of chaos reverberating off the walls like thunder. I exchanged a quick glance with Liam, and we both understood that we had to act fast.

"Whatever game you're playing, it ends here," Liam declared, stepping closer to Viktor, eyes ablaze with defiance.

Viktor's smile only widened, revealing the predator lurking beneath his charming facade. "You think you can just walk in here and dictate terms? Oh, how naïve. You're not in control; you never were."

In that moment, the gravity of his words settled over me like a heavy cloak. My heart raced as I looked around the room. Each piece of art, once beautiful and serene, now felt like a warning, their vibrant colors morphing into ominous shadows.

Suddenly, the door burst open, and a group of men in dark suits stormed in, their presence heralded by an air of authority that commanded instant attention. The murmurs in the room quieted, shifting from shock to anxious curiosity.

"Viktor!" one of them shouted, stepping forward with an authority that sent a jolt of realization through me. "You're under arrest for multiple counts of fraud and art theft."

The tension in the room snapped like a taut string. Viktor's expression morphed from amusement to fury in the blink of an eye, his facade crumbling like ancient paint from a forgotten canvas. "You think you can just barge in here? You have no idea who you're dealing with!"

"Actually, we know precisely who we're dealing with," the lead officer retorted, stepping closer, his badge glinting ominously. "And this time, your game is over."

The chaos that ensued was nothing short of a frenzy. Attendees scrambled for the exits, the art auction transformed into a scene of pure pandemonium. I could feel the air crackle with adrenaline, every heartbeat thundering in my ears as I grabbed Liam's arm.

"Now's our chance!" I shouted, urging him forward as we made our way toward the back exit.

But Viktor was not done yet. He shoved a nearby pedestal, sending a priceless vase crashing to the ground, shattering into a thousand iridescent shards. "You think you can escape me?" he snarled, his voice dripping with venom. "I built this empire, and I won't let you tear it down without a fight!"

I caught sight of the fear and desperation in his eyes, a flicker of vulnerability that gave me pause. Behind the bravado, there was a man who had fought tooth and nail to maintain his grasp on power, and losing it meant losing everything.

"Liam, let's not let him corner us," I said quickly, steering us toward a narrow corridor lined with dimly lit sconces. "We can't get trapped."

"Right," he replied, determination etched into his features as we sprinted down the hallway. The sounds of chaos receded slightly as we turned a corner, and I allowed myself a moment to breathe, my mind racing with questions.

"Where do we go now?" I asked, glancing back at the hallway we had just exited, half-expecting Viktor to appear, his wrath palpable.

"We need to find a way off this island before he gathers his people," Liam said, urgency coloring his tone. "I've got a boat docked nearby, but we have to get to it without being seen."

We continued through the maze of dim corridors, our footsteps echoing against the polished marble floors, each sound amplifying the tension hanging in the air. Just as we reached a side door that led to the back terrace, a voice called out behind us.

"Stop! You're not getting away that easily!"

We froze, adrenaline surging through me like a current. I turned slowly, dread pooling in my stomach as I faced a figure emerging from the shadows, a menacing glint in his eyes. "You didn't think we'd let you slip through our fingers, did you?"

"Liam..." I breathed, taking a cautious step back.

But there was no time to react; the door slammed shut behind us, trapping us in this sudden confrontation. The figure stepped closer, revealing a familiar face—one I hadn't seen in far too long.

"Surprised to see me?" Viktor's right-hand man, Marcus, sneered, his expression twisted with malice. "You're not leaving without a little chat."

The air crackled with tension as I exchanged a glance with Liam. This was no longer just about art or a kingpin's ambitions; it was about our lives, and it felt like we were teetering on the edge of a precipice, where one wrong move could send us tumbling into oblivion.

"Marcus, let us go," Liam demanded, stepping protectively in front of me, his presence a shield against the looming threat. "You don't want this fight."

Marcus laughed, a cold, humorless sound. "Oh, but I do. This is my moment to shine, and I plan on making it memorable."

I could feel the walls closing in, the sense of dread weaving a cocoon around us. "We'll never give in to you," I shot back, my voice steadier than I felt.

"Oh, I think you will," Marcus replied, his smile chilling as he gestured behind him. "You see, it's not just me here tonight."

Before I could process his words, the door swung open again, and a new figure stepped into the light—one who made my heart drop.

Liam's hand tightened around mine as we both stood frozen, our world tilting dangerously. The realization hit like a tidal wave, and in that moment, I understood that the true reckoning had just begun.

Chapter 20: In the Eye of the Storm

Raindrops fell in a relentless rhythm, drumming against the pavement like an urgent heartbeat, drowning out the chaos of the world around me. The air was thick with tension, an electric hum that crackled just beneath the surface. I stood there, heart pounding, caught in a whirlwind of emotions and conflicting loyalties. Liam stood beside me, his eyes scanning the dark alley, where shadows danced ominously, threatening to swallow us whole.

"Are you ready for this?" he asked, his voice steady but laced with an undercurrent of anxiety that mirrored my own.

I wasn't sure if he was asking about the impending confrontation or the emotional reckoning we both knew lay ahead. I nodded, though it felt more like a promise than an affirmation. It was impossible to ignore the flicker of uncertainty in his gaze, a crack in the armor he wore so fiercely. Yet there was also something else—a determination that ignited my own resolve.

"I've got your back," I assured him, though I felt a twinge of fear. What did that even mean in a world teetering on the edge of chaos? The flickering neon lights from a nearby bar illuminated our surroundings in fits and starts, casting long, foreboding shadows that seemed to reach out, grasping at our courage.

He smirked, a quick flash of confidence that almost felt like a shield. "Just don't get in my way."

With a scoff, I elbowed him playfully, despite the tremors of dread swirling in my gut. "I think I can manage that. Just don't forget who's the real strategist here."

The words came out lighter than I intended, a thin veil of humor masking the storm brewing inside me. The truth was, I wasn't sure who was in control. We were both players in this twisted game, yet the stakes felt higher than any wager I'd ever made. The bitter taste of betrayal lingered in the air, reminding me that trust was a fragile thing in a world where deception lurked around every corner.

The sound of footsteps echoed ominously behind us, and I felt my heart leap into my throat. A gang of Liam's adversaries emerged from the shadows, menacing silhouettes cloaked in leather and malice. My breath hitched, and every instinct screamed at me to run, to shield myself from the approaching storm.

Liam stepped forward, the tension in his body coiling like a spring. "Stay close," he commanded, his voice dropping to a dangerous whisper.

I did as he said, clenching my fists at my sides, a rush of adrenaline surging through my veins. It was as if time slowed, the world narrowing to the space between us and them. My senses sharpened, the smell of rain mingling with sweat and the distant scent of gasoline, fueling my resolve.

"Thought you'd be hiding under a rock by now, Liam," one of the men taunted, his voice a gravelly sneer. "Seems you've found yourself a little companion."

"Go back to where you came from," Liam shot back, his tone icy and unyielding. "This doesn't concern you."

I glanced up at him, startled by the intensity in his expression. It was as if a wall had fallen away, revealing a side of him I hadn't fully appreciated before—a fierce protector, a calculated strategist who wouldn't back down.

But then the air crackled with the tension of unspoken words, the promise of conflict hanging in the heavy mist. As the first blow was struck, it became a whirlwind of chaos—punches thrown, bodies colliding, the visceral thud of flesh against flesh filling the alley.

I moved instinctively, darting to the side to dodge a hulking figure barreling toward me. In that split second, I caught Liam's eye, a silent communication passing between us. He was the anchor in my storm, but as I fought alongside him, I realized I was no longer just an extension of his will; I was fighting for my own survival, for justice in a world that seemed to thrive on destruction.

Just when I thought we were gaining the upper hand, a searing pain erupted in my side, like fire igniting beneath my skin. I staggered back, gasping, my vision blurring as I registered the sharp metal glint of a knife in the assailant's hand.

"NO!" Liam's roar cut through the chaos, a raw, primal sound that echoed in the storm. He moved like lightning, closing the distance in an instant, his body shielding mine from further harm.

"Stay down!" he barked, his voice a blend of urgency and command.

I wanted to protest, to tell him I could still fight, but the world spun wildly around me, each heartbeat a reminder of my vulnerability. The storm outside raged on, mirroring the tempest inside me, a chaotic mix of fear and determination.

Liam's presence felt like a beacon, unwavering and fierce. His fierce protectiveness ignited something deep within me, a smoldering ember of affection that I couldn't quite name yet.

As he fought, I watched him, mesmerized by the way he moved—fluid and powerful, like he was dancing with the chaos, every punch thrown with purpose. The darkness didn't consume him; instead, he became a part of it, a tempest of his own making.

But with every blow he dealt, I felt the weight of my own feelings pressing down on me. It was a whirlwind of longing and uncertainty, an undeniable connection forged in the crucible of battle. In that moment, it wasn't just about survival; it was about the bond we were creating amidst the chaos, the shared understanding that we were both in this together.

Just when I thought I might drown in this storm of emotion, a new realization dawned upon me. Liam wasn't just my ally; he was my partner in every sense of the word. Together, we could face the tempest, confront the darkness that threatened to engulf us. But first,

I needed to fight back against the shadows, both external and within myself.

As the fray continued to spiral around us, I could feel the pull of destiny urging me forward. It was time to take a stand—not just for Liam, but for myself, for the justice that had eluded us both for too long. The storm would not define us; we would emerge stronger, together.

The storm raged outside, its ferocity echoing the tumult within the room. Rain lashed against the windows, transforming the world into a blurred canvas of gray and white, a fitting backdrop for the chaos that had erupted between us. I could feel the weight of tension crackling in the air, each heartbeat a reminder of the stakes we faced. The scent of damp earth seeped through the cracks, mixing with the adrenaline that surged through my veins, creating a cocktail of dread and determination.

As the kingpin's men advanced, a ruthless determination etched on their faces, I instinctively stepped in front of Liam. It was a reflex born not of heroism but of instinct; I would protect him at all costs. "You don't have to do this, you know," I called out, my voice steady despite the fear that churned in my stomach. The leader, a towering figure with a scar slicing through his brow, laughed—a deep, throaty sound that filled the room like smoke.

"Protecting him? That's adorable." He stepped closer, a predator closing in on its prey. My heart raced as I felt Liam's presence behind me, his strength grounding me even as the odds grew grim. Just as the tension reached its peak, I caught a glimpse of something unexpected in Liam's eyes—an unwavering resolve that ignited a spark of hope within me.

"Liam, we can talk our way out of this," I suggested, my voice softer now, aimed at easing the simmering hostility. But as I turned to him, I was met not with uncertainty but with a flicker of something else—confidence, perhaps even a hint of mischief.

"You really think they'd listen?" he replied, a playful glint lighting his features. "They're here for blood, not a negotiation."

I couldn't help but smile, the gravity of the situation shifting for just a moment. This was the Liam I'd come to know: sharp, clever, and never one to back down from a challenge. He stepped forward, his posture transforming from hesitant to commanding, every bit the mastermind he had been concealing.

"Listen up!" he bellowed, his voice slicing through the tension like a knife. "You've mistaken us for easy targets, but you're about to learn just how wrong you are."

Before I could process the implications of his words, chaos erupted. Liam had positioned himself between me and the advancing men, and in that moment, I realized I was no longer merely a bystander in this confrontation; I was an active participant in a game that had been set in motion long before this night.

As the first fist swung, the world turned into a blur of movement and sound. Liam ducked and countered, his agility almost surprising. He had a grace that belied the situation's urgency, weaving through their ranks like a dancer in a darkened ballroom. I followed his lead, adrenaline fueling my own movements, but in the chaos, a miscalculation sent me stumbling backward.

The impact was sharp and immediate—a searing pain erupted from my side as I collided with a table. The world around me dimmed, a flickering candle in a tempest, but even as darkness edged into my vision, I heard Liam's voice cutting through the storm.

"Stay with me!" he shouted, his urgency laced with fear. I could feel him at my side, strong and unwavering, even as the chaos swirled around us.

"I'm fine," I gasped, though I could feel the warmth spreading across my shirt, the blood pooling beneath me. It was a lie, but one that I desperately clung to. If I gave in to the pain, it might swallow me whole.

"You're not fine!" he insisted, kneeling beside me, his hands urgent as they pressed against my wound. "We need to get you out of here."

His touch was firm yet tender, grounding me in the tumult. Even amid the chaos, a strange calm settled over me, fueled by his presence. It was as if our fates were entwined, a tapestry woven with threads of hope and despair. "Just breathe," he instructed, his eyes locked onto mine with an intensity that cut through the noise.

The chaos continued to rage, but for a moment, it felt like we were in a bubble of our own—a refuge in the storm. "You should have told me," I managed, a bitter laugh escaping my lips, a mix of pain and revelation. "You could have had a whole army behind you."

He shook his head, a smile creeping onto his face despite the gravity of the situation. "And ruin the surprise? Where's the fun in that?" His humor, sharp and unexpected, lightened the air around us, even as the fight raged on.

Just as I thought we had a moment to regroup, a shadow loomed over us. The scarred leader stood at the edge of the fray, a predatory glint in his eye. "You think you can save her?" he sneered, his voice dripping with contempt.

Liam's expression hardened, and I could see the calculations shifting behind his eyes. "Oh, I don't just think I can save her," he said, rising to his feet with a grace that belied the injury I knew he was suffering from too. "I know I can—and I will."

And with that, he launched himself back into the fray, a whirlwind of fury and determination, leaving me to grapple with the realization that the man I had fought beside was not just an ally; he was a force unto himself. A fire ignited within me, fueled not just by the need to survive but by the understanding that together, we could rewrite the outcome of this encounter.

As the storm raged both inside and outside, I lay on the floor, watching Liam with a mix of admiration and trepidation. The battle was far from over, but within the eye of this storm, I found a flicker of hope. Together, we would not only face this reckoning but emerge stronger, no matter the cost.

The air crackled with tension, thick enough to cut with a knife. A low rumble of thunder rolled across the darkened sky, echoing the turmoil churning within me. As I stood alongside Liam, his determined gaze locked onto the chaos unfolding before us, I felt both a surge of adrenaline and a creeping doubt. It was as if fate had drawn the line in the sand, pitting us against an army that had long ago surrendered their humanity for power. The kingpin's men moved with a predatory grace, their silhouettes merging with the shadows like specters of our worst fears.

"I can't believe I'm about to say this," I said, my voice barely audible over the distant storm, "but we need a plan, and fast."

Liam's eyes, usually warm and inviting, now gleamed with a sharp intensity. "We've got this. Trust me," he replied, a smirk playing at the corners of his lips that somehow managed to soothe my racing heart. "I've been preparing for this moment longer than you know."

Just when the realization of our dire situation settled in, he unfurled a map from his jacket pocket—a tactic that would have seemed ridiculous had I not seen the gravity etched on his face. "What's this?" I asked, curiosity piquing through the dread that threatened to swallow me whole.

"A blueprint of their operations," he said, tracing a route with his finger. "We can outmaneuver them if we time it right. You distract the guards while I slip past and disable their communications."

"You're joking, right? You want me to just stroll up to a group of armed thugs and wave?"

With a playful raise of his brow, Liam replied, "I'd pay good money to see that. But I need you to trust that I'll be right behind you."

The storm's intensity mirrored the urgency of our situation. I had never seen this side of Liam, the strategist, the planner. But as the clouds grew darker, I couldn't help but wonder if this was merely another facade. As I prepared to take the first step into danger, a pang of fear gripped me, followed by a surge of determination.

"Okay, let's do this," I said, my voice steadier than I felt. I would be the distraction, but I would also be his shield, even if it meant putting myself in harm's way.

Liam and I moved swiftly, our actions choreographed by the unyielding rhythm of the storm. He disappeared into the shadows while I approached the guards, my heart pounding like a war drum. "Hey!" I shouted, my voice surprisingly confident as I caught their attention. "You're not supposed to be here. Aren't you guys a little out of your league?"

The guards exchanged glances, their expressions a mix of annoyance and confusion. Just as one stepped forward, Liam struck with surprising agility, disabling him before he could raise the alarm.

"Nice work," I whispered, adrenaline coursing through my veins.

As the skirmish unfolded, my focus wavered. My instincts were screaming at me, urging me to be cautious, yet Liam's presence ignited something within me—a blend of recklessness and exhilaration. However, the moment was fleeting, and in a split second, everything changed.

A sharp pain shot through my side, the world around me spinning as I crumpled to the ground. The realization came crashing down like the storm above us; I had been caught off guard. A second guard had slipped past, and before I could react, he'd delivered a blow that left me gasping for air.

"Get up!" Liam's voice cut through the haze, desperation lacing his tone as he fought off the remaining guards. I struggled, forcing myself to rise despite the nausea and the overwhelming urge to surrender to the pain.

"Liam," I managed to choke out, my voice strained. "I can't—"

"Don't say that! We're almost through this!" he shouted back, urgency thrumming in every word.

As if responding to his command, a powerful wind howled through the chaos, tossing debris around us like confetti. The rain began to pour, cold and biting, soaking through my clothes as I pulled myself back up. The guards were regrouping, and Liam was cornered, his movements becoming more frantic by the second.

"Think, think!" he muttered to himself, eyeing the remaining guards who were now closing in, emboldened by my injury.

I struggled to stay upright, my vision blurring around the edges, but I could see the determination in Liam's eyes, a fierce resolve that set my heart racing. I couldn't let him face this alone; I wouldn't.

"Liam!" I shouted, my voice cutting through the din of the storm. "The crates! We can use them!"

He turned, confusion flickering across his face before realization dawned. "Right!"

We moved in unison, dodging and weaving as we made our way to the stacked crates lining the side of the warehouse. With every ounce of strength I could muster, I began to push one towards the center of the chaos. Liam joined me, our combined effort sending the heavy crate tumbling down, blocking the path of the advancing guards.

As they stumbled back, I felt a rush of exhilaration. "Just like that," I gasped, momentarily forgetting my pain. "Now, what's your plan, mastermind?"

"Now we run," he said, a wicked grin spreading across his face as he offered me his hand.

But before I could grasp it, a sudden crack echoed through the storm—a gunshot. My heart stopped as I turned to see one of the guards aiming directly at Liam.

"Get down!" I screamed, but it was too late.

The bullet found its mark, hitting Liam squarely in the shoulder. He staggered back, his eyes wide with shock, and I felt the world spin beneath me, the storm intensifying as chaos erupted all around us.

"No! Liam!" I cried out, fear clawing at my throat as I rushed to his side. The rain mixed with the blood seeping from his wound, painting the ground a haunting crimson.

His face twisted in pain, but even through it, there was that same spark of determination. "You need to go," he rasped, gripping my hand. "I can't hold them off much longer."

"No! I won't leave you!"

But as his grip slackened, the weight of the moment pressed down on me. The storm raged around us, the lightning flashing in sync with my racing heart. I knew I had to make a choice—save him or fight back against the men who had hunted us for far too long.

With a heavy heart, I made my decision, my voice barely above a whisper, "Hold on, Liam. I'm coming back."

As I turned to face our pursuers, the world narrowed to a single focus, the storm around us a mere backdrop to the battle that lay ahead. I wasn't just fighting for my life; I was fighting for him, and I would do whatever it took to turn the tide. But as the shadows deepened, I felt a sense of dread creeping in—was this truly the end, or merely the eye of the storm?

Chapter 21: Unraveled Threads

The sterile scent of antiseptic hung heavily in the air, a constant reminder of my fragility as I lay in the unforgiving white sheets of the hospital bed. My body, a canvas of bruises and bandages, was a testament to the chaos that had unfolded. Each pulse of pain radiated from my side, a rhythmic reminder of the struggle I had barely survived. The light filtering through the blinds cast soft stripes across the room, illuminating the worried lines etched on Liam's face as he leaned against the wall, arms crossed, a silent sentinel in my recovery.

"Did you really think I'd let you off that easily?" I quipped, attempting to inject some levity into the heavy atmosphere. My voice came out a mere whisper, but the corner of his mouth twitched upwards, a flicker of amusement breaking through the worry.

"I had my doubts," he replied, his voice low and gravelly, like the rumble of distant thunder. "But honestly, I wasn't sure if you were the one fighting the kingpin or just getting into a reckless game of tag with him."

I rolled my eyes, even though it sent a sharp jab through my ribs. "Reckless? That was a meticulously crafted plan, executed with the grace of a... well, a gazelle on roller skates."

His laughter filled the room, a sound that seemed to knit the frayed edges of my heart back together. It was in moments like these, amidst the tension and uncertainty, that I felt the true depth of what we had forged together—a bond resilient enough to withstand even the darkest of storms.

But the humor faded as the weight of the situation settled back around us. The rivalry that had propelled us through a tumultuous series of events now felt like a lingering ghost, hovering just outside the sterile walls of my room. "What happens next, Liam?" I asked, my voice steadier now, threading through the emotional mire. "We can't keep dancing around this."

He ran a hand through his hair, the dark strands falling messily over his forehead, his eyes darting to the window, as if searching for answers in the bustling world outside. "I guess we have to figure out how to face whatever's left of that chaos. There are still people out there who want us dead, and not to mention, we have a kingpin to bring to justice."

"Justice," I scoffed softly, the word tasting bitter on my tongue. "What does that even mean anymore? We took down one player in a game far larger than we ever imagined. And what about the rest of it? What about us?"

Liam's gaze snapped back to me, his expression a complex blend of determination and vulnerability. "I don't know yet. But I do know that I'm not letting you go through this alone." His sincerity resonated in the silence that enveloped us, and the air thickened with unspoken fears and hopes.

The room grew heavier with contemplation, my heart racing as I faced the very real prospect of opening up. "You know, vulnerability isn't my strong suit. I'm not good at it," I confessed, the admission slipping past my defenses like the soft beeping of the heart monitor, punctuating the air with each rhythm of my heartbeat.

"Neither am I," he countered, leaning closer, his intensity igniting a spark of warmth in my chest. "But that doesn't mean we shouldn't try."

A nurse poked her head in, breaking the moment with a soft smile. "How's our patient doing?" she asked, her clipboard at the ready, pen poised to document whatever progress I had made since the last visit.

I waved her off, a playful smirk creeping onto my lips. "Just recovering from a dramatic performance. No need to worry." The nurse chuckled, a warm sound that brought a brief lightness to the heavy atmosphere.

As she busied herself with checking my vitals, I caught Liam's eye, and the fleeting connection sparked with unspoken understanding. The world outside continued to spin, indifferent to our personal tempest, but within this room, we were cocooned in our struggles, our fears, and our budding resolve.

Once the nurse exited, the weight of silence settled back in. "Can we just admit that we're not okay?" I suggested, allowing the words to hang between us like a fragile thread. "That everything feels... complicated?"

Liam sighed, the tension in his shoulders relaxing just slightly. "Complicated is an understatement. But maybe we can start unraveling those threads together?"

"Unraveling sounds like a lot of work," I retorted, half-heartedly, but beneath the teasing tone, I felt a flicker of hope.

"I think we can manage. If you can handle a kingpin, I'm pretty sure we can tackle whatever comes next," he shot back, a playful grin creeping onto his face, lightening the moment just enough to breathe.

My heart quickened, the spark of laughter igniting in the depths of my spirit. "Alright then, let's tackle this 'complicated' thing head-on, but with a bit of caution, shall we?"

He chuckled softly, leaning back in his chair, the tension between us shifting like the sun moving across the sky, illuminating the corners of our hearts that had been shrouded in darkness.

In the stillness of the hospital room, I knew we had a long way to go, but in that moment, beneath the harsh fluorescent lights, the thread of our connection wove itself tighter, creating a tapestry of resilience, laughter, and tentative trust that felt as delicate and powerful as the stitches holding my wounds together.

The clock ticked steadily, each second a reminder of my confinement to this hospital room, where the sterile ambiance stifled the free flow of thoughts. As I lay there, a sense of vulnerability coursed through me, coupled with a fierce determination to seize every moment, every word exchanged with Liam. The daylight faded outside, the golden hour spilling its warm hues into the room like a promise, a reminder that life outside continued to move forward, even if I felt anchored to this bed.

Liam shifted in his seat, his expression a mixture of concern and admiration as he watched me. "You know, you should really consider making 'hospital chic' your new style. The way you wear that gown is nothing short of revolutionary," he teased, attempting to lighten the mood.

"Oh, please! This gown is doing nothing for my figure," I shot back, lifting my arms and twisting slightly to display the shapeless fabric. "I look like a walking medical experiment. Next time, I'll demand a designer."

He laughed, the sound bright and invigorating. "Well, if anyone can pull off the 'just-got-shot-and-I'm-recovering' look, it's definitely you."

There it was again, that comfortable banter, an echo of the camaraderie that had grown between us. But as I glanced around the room, the stark white walls began to feel suffocating, amplifying the shadows of doubt that had crept in. "What if this is all there is, Liam? Just me, this bed, and an endless parade of doctors and nurses? What's waiting for us out there?"

His expression turned serious, the glimmer of mischief fading into contemplative resolve. "We take it one step at a time. You heal, and we figure out how to dismantle whatever remnants of that chaos are left. Together."

The weight of his words settled between us, a silent agreement binding our fates as tightly as the bandages wrapped around my body. Yet I couldn't shake the feeling that something deeper was lurking beneath the surface, something that could shatter the fragile foundation we were attempting to build.

The door creaked open, and in walked a nurse with a clipboard, her smile bright against the backdrop of stark white. "Good evening! How's our superstar feeling today?" she chirped, her energy unfazed by the earlier tension.

"Superstar? I prefer 'heroic figure,' but I'll take it," I replied, forcing a smile as she began her routine check.

Liam shot me a knowing look, and I could almost hear his silent laughter at my dramatic flair. The nurse completed her tasks with efficiency, oblivious to our subtle exchanges. As she left, the atmosphere shifted once more, and I turned to Liam, curiosity igniting a fire in my chest.

"Do you ever think about what happens after this? I mean, once the chaos is cleared, and we don't have a kingpin breathing down our necks? What then?"

Liam ran a hand through his hair, the weight of my question pulling him into a moment of introspection. "Honestly? I've thought about it. I want us to have something real, something outside of all this mess."

My heart raced at his words, but a new anxiety fluttered within me. "You make it sound so simple. What if we aren't who we thought we were? What if all this... us... is just a byproduct of the adrenaline and danger? What happens when the dust settles?"

"We adapt. We learn," he responded, his voice steady. "You've faced hell and come out stronger. That strength doesn't disappear because the threat does."

The sincerity in his eyes rooted me in place, yet a part of me resisted, unsure of whether I could fully believe him. "And what if we're too broken to build something new?" I whispered, the admission hanging in the air like a cloud ready to burst.

He leaned forward, intensity radiating from him. "We aren't broken; we're just... complicated. But we're still standing, aren't we? That counts for something."

His unwavering belief flickered hope through my veins, and I leaned back, allowing his words to wash over me. It felt like standing at the edge of an unknown precipice, staring into the abyss of what could be, and daring to take a step forward.

"I want to believe you, but what if—"

"Stop," he interrupted, his voice low and firm, but not unkind. "No more 'what ifs.' Let's focus on the now. Right here, right now."

His eyes locked onto mine, and suddenly the room felt alive with possibility. In that moment, the walls that had felt so confining began to dissolve, allowing a breath of fresh air to seep through the cracks.

Just then, a commotion erupted outside my door. The sound of hurried footsteps echoed down the hall, followed by muffled voices—angry and tense. My heart raced, a chill creeping down my spine. "What's happening out there?" I asked, my voice trembling slightly.

Liam rose, concern etching deep lines across his forehead. "Stay put. I'll check." He stepped toward the door, his protective instincts flaring.

"No, wait! I want to—"

But before I could finish, he had already slipped out, the door closing behind him with a soft click. I felt the weight of the silence wrap around me, amplifying the distant sounds of chaos. Panic rose within me, twisting in my gut. What if this was another attack? What if it was connected to the kingpin? My thoughts raced, weaving through a web of uncertainty and fear.

Moments felt like hours as I waited, the sterile room transforming into a cage, the walls pressing in as my imagination ran wild. Just as I began to contemplate wheeling myself out of bed to see for myself, the door swung open again.

Liam reappeared, but this time, he wasn't alone. A familiar figure stepped in behind him, a ghost from my past that I had never expected to see again. The room seemed to shrink around us as I stared into the eyes of the very person I thought was lost to the chaos of our lives—a former ally turned foe.

The figure in the doorway, partially obscured by the harsh fluorescent lights, took a step forward, revealing a familiar face that sent a rush of conflicting emotions crashing over me like a tidal wave. I blinked rapidly, convinced that the pain medication was playing tricks on my mind. "Are you really here, or is this some sort of weird hospital hallucination?" I mumbled, rubbing my eyes as if that would clear the confusion.

"Trust me, it's not a dream," came the crisp, confident voice that had once been a source of comfort. Ella stepped fully into the room, her presence filling the space with a mix of warmth and trepidation. "I had to see you. After everything, I needed to know you were okay."

Liam's body tensed beside me, his protective instincts flaring to life. "What are you doing here, Ella?" he asked, the edge in his voice unmistakable. "This isn't exactly a social visit."

"Charming as ever, Liam," she shot back, her eyes sparkling with a defiance that felt familiar yet disconcerting. "I came to talk—about what happened. We need to figure this out."

"Figure what out? You disappeared the moment things got complicated!" I exclaimed, my frustration rising like a bubbling pot on the stove. The healing process had left me raw, and seeing her now felt like a mixture of a warm embrace and a stab in the gut. "You can't just waltz back in here after abandoning ship."

Ella's expression softened, her features caught between regret and determination. "I know. And I'm sorry. But there's more at stake than just our little squabbles. You two are in danger, and I have information that might help."

The air in the room grew thick with tension. "Information?" Liam echoed, skepticism dripping from his tone. "You expect us to believe that you just happen to have the answers now, after everything?"

I felt a strange mix of anger and intrigue coursing through me. "What kind of danger?" I pressed, leaning forward despite the pain that shot through my side. "If you have something to say, say it."

Ella glanced at Liam, then back to me, her gaze unwavering. "There's still a network out there—people connected to the kingpin we didn't catch. They're hunting for you, and they won't stop until they get what they want."

A chill settled deep in my bones, the implications of her words gnawing at my insides. "What do they want?"

"Revenge. Power. And maybe something more personal," she replied, her voice dropping to a near whisper as if the walls themselves might betray us. "It's about the documents you found, the ones that implicate not just him but others in the ring. If they think you have them..."

"Then we need to find those documents," Liam interjected, his voice steady, yet I could hear the pulse of adrenaline thrumming beneath it. "What's your part in this, Ella? Why now?"

She hesitated, biting her lip in a way that reminded me of the old days when secrets hung thick in the air between us. "I have contacts. People who can help us, but I can't do this without you both."

"What makes you think we'd trust you?" I countered, crossing my arms over my chest, despite the ache that rippled through me. "You turned your back when things got tough."

"Because I'm here now," she replied, her voice rising slightly with emotion. "I'm offering you a way out, a chance to reclaim what you lost. To take control."

Control. The word lingered in the air like an echo of my own thoughts. Wasn't that what we'd been striving for all along? A way to rise above the chaos that had consumed our lives?

"And what's the cost?" I asked, suspicion tainting my words. "Nothing comes for free."

Ella's gaze dropped, and for a moment, she looked almost vulnerable. "There's always a cost, but if we work together, it will be worth it. I wouldn't have come if I didn't believe that."

I exchanged a glance with Liam, his jaw set in determination as he processed the gravity of the situation. "You need to convince us more than that. What exactly do you know?"

"I have intel on their next move. They're planning something big, something that could shake this entire city. I can get us in, but we need to act fast. The longer we wait, the tighter their noose becomes."

"Great, so we're expected to jump right back into the fray?" I asked, my tone dripping with sarcasm. "I just got out of a life-threatening situation. Do you mind if I get my strength back before we dive into another disaster?"

"Then we have no time to waste," Ella shot back, her confidence flickering like a candle in the wind. "I'll get you both out of here, but you have to trust me."

A moment of silence stretched, heavy with unspoken words and decisions that hung in the air like fragile glass. Liam stood tall, the resolute protector I knew him to be, but even he seemed caught in a web of uncertainty. "We're not just jumping in blindly, Ella. We need a plan."

"Of course. We'll gather our resources and come up with a strategy. But first, we need to get you out of this hospital."

As she spoke, a sudden noise erupted from down the hall, the sound of hurried footsteps mixed with muffled voices that sent adrenaline surging through my veins. The urgency in the air thickened as I shot a glance at Liam. "What's happening out there?"

His face shifted, alertness creeping into his features. "I don't know, but we need to move—now."

Before we could react further, the door flung open again, revealing two men in dark suits, their eyes scanning the room with predatory intensity. They looked like wolves searching for prey, and my stomach twisted into knots as they stepped inside, their presence an unwelcome shadow.

"Time's up," one of them said, a sneer curling on his lips as he fixed his gaze on me. "We've come to collect."

Panic surged through me, a primal instinct kicking in as I realized that the fragile thread of safety we had clung to was about to snap. I turned to Liam, but he was already moving, muscles coiling like a spring as he stepped protectively in front of me.

"Back off," he growled, his voice low and fierce, a warning laced with authority.

But they didn't retreat; instead, they advanced, and in that moment, time slowed as adrenaline rushed through my veins. I could feel the world tilting around me, the stakes climbing higher as danger crashed into our fragile resolve.

"Run!" Liam shouted, and just as I pushed against the sheets to get out of bed, a shot rang out, echoing through the sterile room.

Chapter 22: The Art of Forgiveness

I hadn't intended to step back into the world of art so soon, yet here I was, ensnared in its vibrant pulse once more. The gallery felt like a familiar stranger as I pushed through the heavy glass doors, the faint scent of turpentine and varnish wrapping around me like a comforting embrace. Sunlight streamed through the skylights, illuminating dust motes that danced like little fairies caught in the magic of the moment. Each piece on the wall whispered stories I had almost forgotten—screaming colors, intricate brushstrokes, and the silent, aching beauty of creativity held hostage by greed.

As I stepped further inside, my mind still buzzed with the echoes of our confrontation with the smuggling ring that had infiltrated our beloved art world. The fallout had been a cacophony of accusations, heartbreak, and a resolve that felt almost tangible, hanging in the air like the scent of fresh paint. With each passing day, my determination grew stronger, fueled by the knowledge that we were not merely restoring our own lives but also trying to salvage the dreams of countless artists whose work had been lost or stolen.

"Is it too early for champagne?" a playful voice broke through my reverie. I turned to see Leo, his boyish grin as bright as the morning sun spilling through the gallery windows. He leaned casually against a wall, one hand tucked into the pocket of his well-worn jeans. His other hand held two flutes, sparkling with bubbles that caught the light.

"Is there ever a wrong time for champagne?" I shot back, my lips curving into a smile that felt almost foreign after the tension of the previous weeks. As he approached, the familiar thrill fluttered in my stomach. It was a curious mix of excitement and trepidation—an unpredictable cocktail, much like the art we were fighting to protect.

With a clink of our glasses, we shared a moment of triumph, laughter spilling over the edges as we toasted to our chaotic endeavor.

"To finding stolen art and uncovering secrets!" Leo declared, his eyes glinting with mischief.

"Here's hoping we don't get arrested in the process," I quipped, taking a generous sip of the bubbly drink. It danced on my tongue, the effervescence mirroring the renewed energy coursing through me.

The walls of the gallery bore witness to our fervor as we began to brainstorm our campaign. It was exhilarating to be back in this world, to sift through the rubble of corruption and reclaim what was rightfully ours. We sketched out plans on napkins, creating a makeshift strategy session in the heart of our artistic sanctuary.

"Okay, so we start with the artists we know have been affected," Leo suggested, his brow furrowed in concentration. "We need their stories, the real ones—the human side of this. Once people see the faces behind the canvases, they won't be able to turn away."

"Yes, and let's not forget the stolen pieces we can track down. The more tangible the evidence, the stronger our case," I added, my heart racing at the thought of our endeavor taking shape.

Together, we crafted a narrative, one that would weave through the threads of our community, drawing in artists, collectors, and even the casual observer. We envisioned a vibrant tapestry of resilience, each thread a story waiting to be told. The thought sent a surge of warmth through me.

As the days turned into weeks, our partnership blossomed amid the chaos. We shared countless late nights in the gallery, the air thick with the scent of oil paint and creativity. Our laughter echoed off the walls, mingling with the soft sound of jazz from a nearby café that floated in through the open windows. I found solace in these moments, the chaos of the outside world fading into a distant memory.

Yet, for every triumph, there were setbacks that felt like punches to the gut. Artists hesitant to share their stories, collectors unwilling to confront the dark realities of the industry, and the constant threat of the very criminals we aimed to expose. Each obstacle was a reminder of how far we had to go, but it only strengthened my resolve.

One evening, as we sat on the gallery floor surrounded by canvases and scattered papers, Leo looked up from his scribbles, his expression suddenly serious. "You know," he began, his tone heavy with unspoken words, "we can't just focus on the fight. We have to remember why we're doing this. It's not just about the art; it's about the people behind it."

His gaze held mine, and I could see the sincerity radiating from him. It was a reminder that amidst the whirlwind of our mission, there lay a deeper connection—a friendship forged in the fires of adversity, brimming with uncharted territory and a tension that crackled like static in the air.

"I know," I replied, my voice barely above a whisper. "Sometimes it's easy to lose sight of that."

"I just... I don't want to forget what this all means. You know?"

His words hung in the air, and for a moment, we were enveloped in a silence that spoke volumes. I could feel the shift in our dynamic, an undercurrent of something more profound stirring beneath the surface, threatening to spill over.

"Leo," I started, but the words caught in my throat, tangled in the complex web of emotions we were both navigating. Instead, I reached for my glass and took a long sip, the bubbles fizzing away the tension.

"Let's not forget the joy of it all, too," I finally said, my heart racing at the uncharted path that lay before us. "This journey can be fun, right?"

"Absolutely," he grinned, the spark returning to his eyes. "We're reclaiming art and having a blast doing it. Who knew fighting corruption could be so exhilarating?"

With that, the mood shifted once more, laughter cascading over us as we resumed our planning. But beneath the laughter, I couldn't shake the feeling that our mission was evolving into something far more complex than either of us had anticipated, weaving together threads of friendship, ambition, and perhaps, something deeper yet. The city outside continued its relentless hum, but within the sanctuary of the gallery, a new rhythm was beginning to emerge, one that would resonate long after our campaign reached its crescendo.

The relentless rhythm of the city seeped into our work, each heartbeat a reminder of the urgency that thrummed beneath the surface of our efforts. With the gallery as our headquarters, we transformed its austere walls into a canvas of activism. Posters adorned with vivid colors and evocative imagery began to plaster the once-blank surfaces, proclaiming our mission to reclaim art and support the artists whose voices had been stifled. Every morning, we met under the warm glow of the skylights, a sense of purpose igniting our creativity.

I found myself entranced by the endless possibilities that unfolded in our discussions, the way Leo's ideas sparked new angles in my mind like firecrackers on a summer night. One afternoon, we sat cross-legged on the floor, surrounded by a chaotic array of materials—paintbrushes, canvases, and a wild assortment of sketches that spoke to our determination.

"What if we held a benefit auction?" Leo proposed, tapping a pencil against his chin. "We could invite local artists to donate their work. The proceeds could go to a fund dedicated to supporting the artists affected by the smuggling ring."

I couldn't help but smile, the idea blooming in my mind. "And we could showcase pieces that have been recovered as part of our campaign. Make it a celebration of resilience."

"Exactly!" he exclaimed, his eyes lighting up with enthusiasm. "We'd turn the gallery into a vibrant showcase, a testament to the strength of our community."

The thought of filling the gallery with art and laughter sent a thrill through me. I envisioned the space alive with energy, the hum of conversation mixing with the clink of glasses, artists mingling with collectors, all bound by a shared passion for preserving the beauty that art brought into the world.

As we finalized our plans, our conversations drifted into lighter territory, a playful banter developing that became a staple of our time together. "You realize, if we succeed, we'll need to give speeches at this auction, right?" I teased, nudging him with my shoulder.

"Speech-giving is not included in my skill set," he replied, feigning horror. "What if I trip over the microphone and end up with a face full of cake?"

"Then it would just be an unforgettable evening!" I laughed, picturing him floundering in front of an audience, his signature charm somehow intact despite the embarrassment.

"I think I'd rather stick to painting," he shot back, raising an eyebrow. "I can hide behind a canvas much better than a podium."

Our laughter echoed through the empty gallery, wrapping us in warmth as the sun began to dip below the skyline, casting a golden glow over the city. The light glinted off the framed art pieces, illuminating the passion that swirled within their colors. It felt as though the entire universe was conspiring to breathe life back into the dreams we had nearly lost.

As the days sped by, we poured ourselves into the preparation for the auction. The gallery transformed, each inch imbued with the hope of reclaiming the past and nurturing the future. Artists began to arrive, their faces a mixture of curiosity and trepidation, bringing with them stories of stolen dreams. Each conversation became a thread woven into the tapestry we were crafting.

On a particularly vibrant afternoon, an artist named Mia stepped through the gallery doors, her presence instantly magnetic. She had an air of quiet defiance, her hands stained with paint as if she had just emerged from a canvas.

"I heard about what you're doing," she said, her voice soft but resolute. "I want to help."

The sincerity in her eyes tugged at my heartstrings. I felt a kinship with her, an understanding that ran deeper than mere words. "We'd love for you to contribute a piece," I replied, gesturing toward a blank wall. "This space is yours as much as it is ours."

Her smile illuminated the room, a spark igniting between us as we discussed her work, a series of paintings that expressed the fragility of identity and the longing for authenticity. "Every stroke has a story," she explained, her passion infectious. "Art can heal, even when it feels like everything is lost."

I could sense that this was only the beginning. As word spread about our auction, the gallery transformed into a sanctuary for artists yearning to reclaim their voices. Each donation felt like a battle won, a step toward restoring the vibrancy that had been drained from the art world.

One evening, after a long day of setting up and organizing, Leo and I collapsed onto the gallery floor, surrounded by sketches and empty pizza boxes. "I can't believe how far we've come," I mused, glancing around at the chaotic beauty we had created together.

"Me neither," he replied, a content smile playing on his lips. "But I have to admit, I'm starting to feel the pressure."

"Pressure? What pressure?" I challenged, feigning a dramatic gasp. "The pressure of being an art hero?"

"I'm serious!" he insisted, laughing. "What if nobody shows up? What if we end up talking to an empty room?"

"Then we'll just have to fill that room with laughter," I said, unable to hide my grin. "And pizza. Lots of pizza."

"I like your plan," he chuckled, shaking his head. "Maybe we'll just become the world's greatest pizza connoisseurs instead."

As we joked, a comfort settled over us, the kind that thrived in shared vulnerabilities. Yet, beneath the surface, the current of tension that had lingered between us crackled, unspoken but palpable. There was an electricity in the air, one that felt like it could shift the very foundation of our friendship.

The days turned into nights, each moment layered with purpose and passion, the stakes rising higher as the auction drew closer. The anticipation was intoxicating, mingling with the bittersweet reality of what we were trying to reclaim. But just as the excitement reached a crescendo, a shadow loomed on the horizon, one that threatened to unravel everything we had fought for.

One evening, as I stood in the gallery alone, lost in thought while arranging the final pieces, I received an unexpected call. The voice on the other end was cold, filled with an urgency that made my heart race. "You need to know that they're onto you," it warned. "If you're not careful, everything you're trying to do could come crashing down."

I hung up, a chill running down my spine. The stakes were higher than ever, and the very foundation of our mission felt precarious. I turned to the canvases lining the walls, each one a testament to the struggle for authenticity and truth. The battle was far from over, and I was determined to fight back—one brushstroke at a time.

The gallery buzzed with an energy that was almost electric, a tangible excitement that hummed beneath the surface as we moved ever closer to the auction. Artists had poured their hearts into their contributions, each piece a testament to resilience and hope, their stories etched into the canvas. I found myself lost in a sea of colors, brushing my fingers over the edges of a vibrant painting that depicted a sunset over the city—its hues a kaleidoscope of orange and pink. It seemed to pulse with life, much like the excitement surrounding our endeavor.

Just as I began to lose myself in the artistry, Leo's voice cut through the haze, smooth and teasing. "Are you contemplating a career change? Because I can already see you as a gallery cat, lounging among the paintings."

I turned, half-amused and half-annoyed. "And what would that make you? The pretentious curator who only drinks overpriced coffee and critiques my nap skills?"

"Please, I'd be the one you'd have to convince to leave the warmth of the sunbeams for a night out," he shot back, laughter dancing in his eyes. "You know, the whole 'mysterious artist' vibe is really taking off."

We shared a laugh, the kind that echoed against the walls and momentarily washed away the worry creeping into the back of my mind. Yet, the call I had received loomed large, an ominous shadow that refused to dissipate. Just as I was about to shake off the feeling, the door swung open with a loud thud, a gust of cold air rushing in, sending a shiver down my spine.

In walked Mia, her usually vibrant aura dimmed, replaced with an urgency that made my heart race. "We need to talk," she said, her voice edged with anxiety.

"What's wrong?" I asked, instinctively stepping closer, drawn into her worry.

"I overheard something at the café," she whispered, her eyes darting around the room as if she expected someone to jump out from the shadows. "They're aware of your plans for the auction. The people we're trying to expose—they're coming for you."

My heart dropped, the weight of her words anchoring me in place. "What do you mean? How do they know?"

"I didn't catch all the details, but there were conversations about a 'disruption' at your event. They think you're getting too close, and they're not going to let that happen."

The world around me seemed to tilt, the colors of the gallery bleeding together in a swirl of dread. Leo stepped forward, concern etched on his face. "We can't let them intimidate us, Mia. We've come too far."

"I'm not suggesting we back down," she replied, a fierce determination lighting her eyes. "But we need to be careful. Maybe we can change the venue or make some adjustments to keep things under wraps until the auction."

"What if we do a decoy?" Leo suggested, his mind racing. "We could create a distraction—something that will pull their focus away from the auction while we execute our plan."

"A distraction?" I echoed, my mind swirling with possibilities. "Like a pop-up exhibition? Something loud and chaotic that draws attention away?"

Mia nodded slowly, her brow furrowed in concentration. "If we can create enough buzz about something completely unrelated, it might give us the time we need to execute our original plan."

I felt a spark of hope ignite within me, the thought of turning the tables making my pulse quicken. "I love it. We can showcase the art of emerging artists—something unexpected that will have everyone talking."

Leo's eyes sparkled with mischief. "And if we invite a few local influencers? We'll blow up social media with live updates, turning our auction into the talk of the town."

As we brainstormed, the tension in the air shifted, transformed into something creative and invigorating. Together, we began to weave a tapestry of plans that felt both daring and essential. Each idea we tossed around brought us closer together, the camaraderie deepening, blending our fears and hopes into a singular vision.

Yet, just as we began to settle into a rhythm, a loud crash echoed from the back of the gallery, causing us all to jump. My heart raced as I turned to face the sound, a gnawing fear settling in my stomach.

"Mia, stay here," Leo instructed, moving towards the sound, his footsteps firm against the polished floor.

"Be careful," I called after him, my voice barely above a whisper.

Mia and I exchanged wide-eyed glances, the air thick with unspoken anxiety as we waited in tense silence. Moments stretched out like an eternity, and just as I felt the urge to follow, Leo reappeared, his expression a mix of confusion and alarm.

"There's a message," he said, holding up a piece of paper that fluttered in his hand like a flag of surrender.

"What does it say?" I demanded, my heart pounding as I stepped closer, the words dancing just out of reach.

He unfolded the paper, his brow furrowing deeper as he read aloud, "If you want to keep your precious event, you'll follow the rules. We'll be watching."

The message felt like ice water poured over my head, chilling me to the bone. "They're watching us," I whispered, fear tightening around my chest.

Mia moved closer, peering at the note. "This isn't just a warning. It's a threat."

My mind raced, thoughts colliding as panic began to claw at the edges of my resolve. "We can't let this stop us. We have to move forward with the auction. We can't let them win."

"But how can we ensure everyone's safety?" Leo countered, the conflict evident in his gaze. "What if they really do try to disrupt it?"

"We adapt," I said, my voice steadier than I felt. "We become unpredictable. We turn this into our advantage. Let's amplify our plan. The bigger the distraction, the less they'll focus on us."

Mia nodded, her determination mirrored in her eyes. "Then we need to act fast. We can't let them undermine what we're trying to accomplish."

As we regrouped, a sense of urgency fueled our every decision. The gallery became a whirlwind of creativity, our laughter mingling with a newfound tension that underlined our every word. Each moment felt charged, the stakes rising with each brushstroke of our plans.

Yet as we threw ourselves into action, the feeling of being watched lingered like a specter at the edge of my consciousness, always there, always looming. Just when I thought we had begun to gain ground, I noticed a shadow flit past the gallery windows—a fleeting figure that disappeared just as quickly as it had appeared.

"Did you see that?" I asked, my voice trembling with disbelief.

"What?" Leo glanced toward the window, then back to me, confusion etched on his features.

"I think... I think someone's out there," I stammered, dread creeping back into my veins.

Suddenly, the power flickered, plunging the gallery into darkness. The buzz of the city outside faded, replaced by an ominous silence that swallowed us whole. The air thickened, and I felt a shiver run down my spine.

"Mia, get behind me," Leo commanded, instinctively shielding her as I felt my heart pound in my chest. "Stay close."

I gripped his arm, adrenaline surging through me. The world outside our sanctuary had suddenly become a threatening unknown, a harbinger of chaos just waiting to erupt.

"Is this how it ends?" I wondered aloud, my heart racing as we stood in the darkness, the shadows closing in around us.

Before Leo could respond, a loud bang echoed through the space, the sound reverberating off the walls like a gunshot. My breath caught in my throat, panic rising as the reality of our situation crashed down on us.

Then, the sound of footsteps—heavy, deliberate—approached. Each step sent a jolt of fear through me, and I squeezed Leo's arm tighter. I knew we were at a crossroads, teetering on the brink of something profound, something dangerous.

"Whatever happens, stay together," Leo whispered, his voice steady despite the chaos.

With my heart pounding in my chest, I nodded, ready to face whatever darkness lay ahead, determined that we would not back down. Not now, not ever.

Chapter 23: A Brush with Destiny

The gallery thrummed with a heartbeat of its own, a living entity wrapped in the scents of polished wood and fresh paint mingling with the heady aroma of gourmet hors d'oeuvres. I stepped into the radiant expanse, the walls adorned with pieces that had once been buried in obscurity, now glowing under the soft spotlight, each canvas a testament to resilience, passion, and a love that blossomed amidst rivalries and repartee. My heart raced as I adjusted my dress—a cascade of deep crimson that clung to my form, reflecting the fire of the night, and my mind flitted nervously through the rehearsed lines I'd crafted to describe our journey, our transformation from adversaries to partners.

Liam stood across the room, his tall silhouette a confident presence amidst the swirl of patrons. He wore a tailored navy suit that accentuated the sharp angles of his jaw and the playful glint in his eyes. There was something unshakeably magnetic about him, an energy that pulled people in and set their imaginations alight. As I caught his gaze, a thrill of anticipation ran through me; this was our night, our moment to shine, a culmination of stolen moments and whispered dreams painted into reality. I knew he was watching, his expression a mix of admiration and something deeper, something electric that shot through the air like the brush of a fine artist's strokes on canvas.

"Do you see that one?" I pointed to a piece, a chaotic blend of colors that spoke of turmoil and hope, a chaotic dance of brush strokes that resonated deeply within me. "That was my first piece after we—well, you know." I felt a warm blush creep up my neck as I recalled the arguments and challenges we had faced. "It was like the colors were arguing just like we did."

Liam chuckled softly, his voice warm and smooth as melted chocolate. "You mean the 'Who Can Be More Stubborn' competition? I think we both won that one." His smile was infectious, and I couldn't help but laugh, the sound ringing through the gallery like music, light and free.

"Ah, but you were the reigning champion, my dear," I shot back playfully, raising an eyebrow as I stepped closer, weaving through the crowd, reveling in the energy surrounding us. Every patron seemed enraptured, immersed in the stories that each piece of art whispered. The buzz of conversation blended harmoniously with clinking glasses and soft laughter, wrapping us in a comforting cocoon of creativity.

As I turned to scan the room, I caught sight of some familiar faces—friends, critics, and collectors whose admiration felt tangible in the air. They were drawn not just to the art, but to the story behind it, the narrative of two passionate souls whose paths intertwined against the backdrop of rivalry. My eyes landed on Eleanor, a prominent art critic whose opinions could either make or break an artist's career. She stood with her arms crossed, lips pursed in contemplation as she studied a piece, the cool gleam of her pearl earrings catching the light.

"Do you think she'll like it?" I murmured to Liam, my voice low, tinged with a hint of anxiety.

"She's got an eye for depth," he replied, his gaze serious but softened by the smile still dancing on his lips. "Just like you." He turned to face me, his expression earnest. "Remember, this is our moment. Whatever she thinks won't change what we've created together."

His words settled over me, a reassuring warmth amidst the swirling anticipation. I took a deep breath, the tension slipping from my shoulders, and straightened my posture. "You're right. We did this. Together."

As the evening unfolded, I found myself swept into a whirlwind of conversations, laughter echoing in the gallery like a gentle tide. I spoke passionately about the pieces we had recovered, each story a thread in the rich tapestry we had woven together. With every word, I felt the tension of the past fade, replaced by an electric excitement for the future.

But then, an unexpected hush fell over the room, a collective intake of breath that rippled through the crowd. I followed the gazes of those around me, my heart thudding as I saw a figure standing at the entrance, silhouetted against the soft glow of the gallery lights. It was Victor, the rival whose shadow had loomed over our past, the man whose ambitions had driven a wedge between us before. My stomach twisted with a mix of disbelief and dread as he stepped forward, his presence commanding attention.

"Ah, what a lovely gathering," he announced, his voice smooth yet laced with an undercurrent of condescension. "I must say, I didn't expect to see such a... vibrant display of mediocrity." His eyes flicked over the artwork, a smirk playing at the corners of his mouth.

The room shifted, a tension crackling in the air as I felt Liam tense beside me. "What are you doing here, Victor?" I demanded, the strength in my voice surprising even me. I had learned to stand tall against his barbs, my confidence having blossomed through the very struggles he had tried to exploit.

"Oh, just taking in the spectacle," he replied, his eyes glinting with mischief. "After all, I do have a vested interest in the art world. Wouldn't want to miss the opportunity to witness my former protégé floundering in her new endeavor."

Liam stepped forward, positioning himself protectively beside me, his jaw clenched. "This isn't about you, Victor. This is about the work, the community we've built."

Victor raised an eyebrow, seemingly unfazed. "Ah, but community can only thrive when talent is recognized. And let's be honest, darling," he turned to me with a derisive smirk, "you've always been more of a footnote in my story."

Anger surged within me, hot and fierce. I had fought too hard to let him diminish the achievements we had crafted together. "I may be a footnote in your story, but this is my narrative now," I said, my voice steady, each word ringing clear with determination. "And it's time you learned to read between the lines."

Victor's expression faltered for a moment, surprise flickering in his eyes. The audience was silent, tension palpable as they observed the exchange. Liam's presence beside me felt like an anchor, grounding me in this moment where I stood tall and unyielding.

The corners of Victor's mouth twitched, as if he were trying to mask a grin beneath layers of indignation. "Touché," he said, raising his glass in mock salute. "But do remember, the art world is fickle, my dear. It will be interesting to see how long your little love story holds up."

And with that, he turned and strolled out, leaving behind a wave of murmurs that washed over the gallery like an unexpected storm. The silence hung thick in the air, but beneath it, a newfound strength pulsed within me.

Liam's hand found mine, fingers intertwining as he leaned closer. "You were incredible," he whispered, his voice warm against the cool air. "Don't let him get to you. We're just getting started."

A smile broke across my face, buoyed by his words, and as the conversation resumed around us, I felt the night blossom anew, vibrant and full of possibilities. This was our canvas, and together we would paint it with the colors of our dreams, undeterred by the shadows of the past.

The atmosphere shifted with the lingering echoes of Victor's departure, leaving a wake of murmurs and whispers that danced like fluttering butterflies through the gallery. I could feel the tension dissipate slowly, replaced by a vibrant energy that thrummed beneath the surface. Patrons resumed their conversations, laughter bubbling up again as they turned their focus back to the art, but I felt the sharp edge of the moment still pricking at my consciousness.

"Okay, let's be honest," I said to Liam, a smirk pulling at my lips as I surveyed the room. "If this was a movie, Victor would have made his grand exit, and the crowd would erupt in applause for my fierce comeback."

Liam chuckled, a sound that wrapped around me like a warm blanket on a chilly evening. "Well, I'm definitely applauding in my head. That was Oscar-worthy."

"Good to know my dramatic flair is appreciated," I teased, nudging him playfully. "But let's focus on more important matters. Like the buffet. I need sustenance to balance out the adrenaline."

"Lead the way," he said, bowing slightly as if he were my personal knight in shining armor, ready to escort me to the banquet of culinary delights.

The buffet table was a feast for the senses, adorned with an array of colorful dishes—miniature quiches bursting with flavors, delicate pastries that shimmered with glaze, and vibrant fruits glistening under the soft lighting. I grabbed a small plate, my eyes darting over the options as if I were scanning an artist's palette. "This is the real art," I declared, selecting a piece of goat cheese wrapped in roasted peppers.

Liam chuckled beside me, mirroring my choices. "Forget the critics; this is where the real masterpieces lie." He raised his glass of sparkling water, clinking it against my wine glass in a toast. "To art, love, and the occasional culinary delight."

"To all of that and more!" I replied, taking a sip that tingled delightfully on my tongue.

We settled into a cozy corner of the gallery, the chatter around us melding into a comforting background hum. Between bites, we exchanged glances, and the way his eyes sparkled made my heart flutter. It was impossible not to feel the depth of our connection, like threads woven together in a beautiful tapestry.

"What's next for you?" he asked, genuine curiosity dancing in his tone. "What's the next big piece you want to tackle?"

I paused, considering the question as I looked around at the art that surrounded us. "I've been toying with the idea of exploring the theme of duality—how light and shadow coexist, how beauty can emerge from chaos."

"Sounds like a perfect metaphor for our relationship," he replied, a teasing lilt in his voice. "You bring the chaos; I'll supply the light."

"Only if I can paint you in all your gloriously chaotic glory," I shot back, laughter spilling out effortlessly.

Just then, Eleanor approached us, her expression poised yet curious. "I couldn't help but overhear your conversation," she said, a hint of intrigue in her eyes. "Duality, you say? That's a compelling direction. I'd love to see how you interpret it."

"Thank you," I said, feeling a flush of pride creep into my cheeks. "I'm still in the brainstorming phase, but it's definitely brewing."

"I'd recommend exploring the emotional landscapes involved," Eleanor continued, her voice smooth like silk. "Art often transcends visual appeal when it resonates on a deeper level."

As she spoke, I felt a spark of inspiration ignite within me. Eleanor had a knack for pushing artists to dig deeper, to explore the very core of their emotions. "You're right. It's the rawness that captivates, isn't it?"

"Exactly," she affirmed, her smile genuine. "If you're willing to share those vulnerabilities, your work will shine."

"Easier said than done," Liam interjected lightly. "But I suppose we're in the business of making the difficult look effortless."

Eleanor's gaze shifted between us, a flicker of understanding passing through her. "You two have a remarkable partnership," she observed, her tone shifting slightly. "The energy is palpable."

I exchanged a quick glance with Liam, our eyes reflecting a shared understanding. This was more than just art; it was our lives, intertwined and vibrant. "Thank you," I replied, feeling a swell of gratitude. "We've certainly learned to embrace the chaos together."

Before Eleanor could respond, a sudden commotion erupted at the entrance, pulling my attention away. A group of enthusiastic college students burst through the doors, their energy crackling like a live wire, clearly drawn in by the artistic allure. They were the kind of people whose excitement was contagious, a refreshing burst of youth that invigorated the room.

"Is this where the magic is happening?" one of them exclaimed, his voice ringing out like a joyous melody. He had a shock of bright blue hair and an artistic flair that spoke of boundless creativity.

"Only if you're ready to embrace the chaos," I called back, a grin spreading across my face.

"Chaos is my middle name!" he shot back, winking.

Liam leaned closer, a conspiratorial grin lighting up his features. "Looks like we've found our fan club," he whispered.

The group meandered toward the art, their laughter mingling with the soft music playing in the background. I felt an undeniable warmth at the sight—this was the essence of art, after all. It was a bridge connecting people, sparking conversations that ignited the imagination.

Just as I was about to engage with the students, Victor reentered the gallery, this time with an entourage that included some notable figures from the art world. My stomach sank as I caught his eye; the confidence he exuded felt like a dark cloud drifting back into our sunny space.

He sauntered over, his entourage behind him, their eyes glinting with curiosity. "Ah, the raucous crowd I expected," he announced, as if he were delivering a performance. "But I must say, the real spectacle lies here." He gestured grandly at the art, an exaggerated flourish that dripped with disdain.

Liam stiffened beside me, his protective instinct flaring again. "What do you want, Victor?" he asked, his tone edged with irritation.

Victor leaned closer, a conspiratorial whisper that rang false. "Oh, merely to witness how the other half lives," he said, glancing disdainfully at the students. "Isn't it charming, watching the young and naive embrace mediocrity?"

I could feel my pulse quicken, my cheeks flushing with indignation. "They're not naive; they're excited about art. Something you've clearly forgotten amidst your elitist views."

Victor raised an eyebrow, amusement dancing in his eyes. "Touché again. But let's not forget, excitement doesn't always equate to talent."

With every word, I felt a growing fire within me. "Art is subjective, Victor. You should know that by now."

The students, sensing the tension, began to whisper amongst themselves, their innocent enthusiasm suddenly dampened. I could feel Liam's hand squeeze mine, a silent reminder that I wasn't alone in this moment.

Victor opened his mouth to retort, but before he could spew more of his condescension, Eleanor stepped forward, her presence commanding attention. "I believe art challenges us, Victor. It pushes boundaries, whether you like it or not."

Her words hung in the air, and I could see the shift in the crowd's energy. What had started as a warm glow of excitement had transformed into something much more powerful. The students stood taller, their confidence bolstered by Eleanor's words.

"Exactly!" the blue-haired student chimed in, emboldened. "Art should be about expression, not just what's 'in' or 'out.'"

Victor's expression faltered for a brief moment, surprise flickering across his face. He was losing ground, and I could see it.

"Indeed," Eleanor pressed, a smirk dancing on her lips. "Perhaps it's time you embraced that notion."

With that, Victor huffed and turned, storming off with his entourage, leaving behind a charged silence that crackled with newfound determination.

The gallery erupted into spontaneous laughter, the tension melting away like frost in the spring sun. I felt buoyed, a rush of exhilaration surging through me. "Can we have a round of applause for Eleanor?" I shouted, and soon the gallery was filled with claps and cheers, uniting everyone in this moment of triumph.

"Now that was a proper exit!" Liam declared, his laughter infectious.

As we basked in the aftermath, I realized that this exhibition was more than just a display of art; it was a celebration of our journey, a testament to the resilience of the creative spirit. I glanced at Liam, his eyes sparkling with mischief, and felt the warmth of our connection radiate through me.

"Let's make a pact," I said, my voice filled with determination. "No more letting Victor steal our joy. We'll rise above and create art that matters, that resonates."

"Deal," Liam replied, a playful smile lighting up his features. "And we'll make sure to sprinkle a little chaos in there, just for fun."

As the laughter and chatter enveloped us, I felt a surge of hope—this was just the beginning. With each brush stroke, we would continue to craft our narrative, a vibrant tapestry of love, art, and resilience woven together, forever unyielding in the face

The energy in the gallery crackled with a newfound vitality, the aftermath of our collective victory against Victor reverberating like a pulse beneath the surface. I felt buoyed by the laughter and applause, a warm glow radiating through my chest as I reveled in the shared triumph. The students' spirits had lifted the atmosphere, transforming it into a vibrant celebration of creativity and expression.

"Did you see their faces?" I asked Liam, unable to contain the excitement bubbling within me. "It's like we sparked something in them!"

"Definitely," he replied, his eyes alight with enthusiasm. "It's the beauty of art, really. It inspires and unites." He grabbed my hand, intertwining our fingers, and together we navigated the thrumming crowd, weaving through clusters of guests engrossed in animated discussions.

As we approached a particularly striking piece—a sweeping landscape that seemed to pulse with life—I couldn't help but notice the way Liam's thumb brushed against my knuckles, an electric current that seemed to echo the vibrant colors on the canvas. "You know," he said, leaning closer, "if we ever had a gallery of our own, I'd want it to be filled with pieces like this. Art that tells a story."

"And that story would involve an ongoing saga of our chaotic yet charming romance?" I teased, nudging him with my shoulder.

"Absolutely. Every piece would be a chapter in our life together. Some would be wild and bright, others dark and moody, reflecting our fights over who left the cap off the toothpaste."

"Hey! That's a serious issue!" I laughed, picturing the many evenings spent bickering over trivial things that felt monumental at the time. "But I'd prefer my art to reflect the best of us. Like this one," I gestured to the painting, where a sunset exploded in vivid oranges and purples, the horizon kissed by the last light of day. "This captures beauty even in the chaos."

His gaze shifted from the canvas to my face, an intensity in his eyes that made my heart race. "You have a way of seeing things, you know? I'm not sure I would have thought of that without you."

Before I could respond, a sudden commotion erupted near the entrance, and I turned just in time to see Eleanor engaging in a heated conversation with one of Victor's associates, a woman with sharp features and an even sharper tongue. The tension in the air thickened again, a crackle that drew attention like a magnet.

"Great, another showdown," I muttered, half-amused and half-anxious.

"Should we intervene?" Liam asked, his brow furrowing slightly.

"Let's give Eleanor a moment. She's quite capable of handling herself," I replied, curiosity piqued as I watched.

The discussion escalated, voices rising above the chatter of the crowd. "You think your little exhibit can overshadow the legacy of Victor? This is a joke!" the woman exclaimed, her tone dripping with disdain.

Eleanor stood her ground, arms crossed, her posture unwavering. "Art is not about legacy; it's about connection. Something you clearly wouldn't understand."

"Touché, Eleanor," Liam whispered to me, his lips curving into a sly smile. "She's on fire tonight."

As the exchange unfolded, I felt a sense of solidarity with Eleanor, admiration swelling within me. She was a force to be reckoned with, unyielding in her defense of artistic integrity.

But then, without warning, the atmosphere shifted again. The gallery doors swung open, and in walked a tall figure, silhouetted against the light—Alexander, a prominent art dealer with a reputation for changing the game. Murmurs rippled through the crowd as people recognized him, excitement and anxiety intertwining in a swirling wave.

"What's he doing here?" I whispered, my heart racing. "He doesn't just show up at random events."

"Probably looking to snag a new talent," Liam replied, his tone tinged with skepticism.

I watched as Alexander sauntered over, a predatory glint in his eyes as he surveyed the room, stopping briefly to chat with Victor's associate. They exchanged words that were too low to hear, but the body language was unmistakable—collusion, a conspiring energy that set my instincts on edge.

"I don't like this," I said, a knot forming in my stomach. "He's too calculating. He wouldn't come here unless he had something in mind."

"Let's keep an eye on him," Liam suggested, a frown etching itself onto his features.

As we maneuvered closer to the source of the tension, I couldn't shake the feeling of impending change, like a storm brewing on the horizon. Alexander raised his voice, silencing the crowd with a mere glance. "I must commend the effort put into this exhibition," he began, his tone dripping with charm. "But I wonder, where is the true artistry? Is it in pieces that linger in the shadows of forgotten rivals, or is it in the boldness of innovation?"

The tension in the room grew palpable, each patron exchanging glances, the weight of his words hanging heavily in the air. It felt like a gauntlet had been thrown, a challenge that stirred the competitive spirit within everyone present.

"Is he really trying to provoke us?" I whispered to Liam, incredulous.

"It sure looks like it," he replied, jaw tight. "We can't let him undermine everything we've worked for."

Eleanor stepped forward, unwavering. "Art is subjective, Alexander. What may resonate with you may not resonate with everyone else. You can't dictate its value."

"Oh, but I can, darling. I have the connections and the influence to shape narratives," he retorted smoothly, a calculating smile on his lips. "You may have this moment, but the future? That's a different story entirely."

A collective tension rippled through the crowd, the air thick with uncertainty. My heart raced as I realized this was more than just a battle of words; it was a confrontation that could define our careers, our lives.

"Are we really going to let him just walk in here and challenge our worth?" I felt the heat of my own defiance rising. "We need to show him what we're made of."

Liam squeezed my hand. "Together, we can turn this around. Let's use this moment to rally everyone. Remind them why they fell in love with art in the first place."

With resolve coursing through my veins, I turned back to the crowd. "Everyone! Let's not forget why we're here," I called out, my voice ringing clear. "Art is about passion, connection, and resilience! It's about the stories we tell through each brush stroke, each color, each experience!"

The crowd began to respond, murmurs of agreement swelling as patrons nodded, eyes lighting with renewed purpose.

"I want you all to think about what this art means to you!" I continued, my heart racing. "It's not about what anyone else thinks—it's about the joy it brings, the emotions it stirs! It's the heart of creativity, the essence of our community!"

Just then, the lights flickered slightly, casting a brief shadow over the gallery, an unsettling shiver running through the crowd. The murmurs turned to whispers, an undercurrent of apprehension replacing the initial excitement.

"Something feels off," Liam murmured, glancing around.

As I opened my mouth to respond, a sharp sound pierced the air—a crash, like glass shattering, followed by a gasp from the crowd. The gallery seemed to hold its breath, and all eyes turned toward the source of the commotion.

My heart raced as I spotted it—one of the artworks had fallen from the wall, a precious piece that had been the centerpiece of the exhibition, now lying shattered on the ground. A collective gasp echoed through the gallery, and chaos erupted.

Before I could process what was happening, the lights flickered again, plunging the room into darkness for a heartbeat before they stabilized. In that moment, I felt a cold chill run down my spine, a sense that something much larger than an art exhibition was at play.

"What's happening?" I breathed, panic creeping into my voice as I clutched Liam's hand tighter.

But as we stood there, rooted to the spot, the chaos of the gallery swirling around us, I knew we were on the cusp of something monumental. Little did I know, the fallout from that shattered artwork would unravel the threads of our lives in ways we could never have anticipated. And as the dust settled around us, I realized that the brush with destiny had only just begun.

Chapter 24: New Beginnings

The salty tang of the ocean air mingled with the fading warmth of the sun, wrapping around us like a well-worn blanket, familiar yet comforting. I watched as the waves rolled in, their frothy edges tumbling over one another, crashing rhythmically against the shore, each swell a promise of something new. The dawn painted the sky in hues of coral and gold, a stunning backdrop to the silent conversation that passed between Liam and me. He stood close, his presence grounding, yet I could feel the restless energy vibrating off him, like the anticipation before a storm.

"I thought the exhibit would never end," I said, breaking the serene silence that surrounded us. My voice danced over the sounds of the ocean, carrying a hint of laughter that bubbled beneath the surface. "Did you see Mrs. Henley's face when she realized her prized piece was hanging next to yours?"

Liam chuckled, his deep, throaty laugh resonating with the rhythm of the sea. "If looks could kill, I'd be a goner. I might need to start wearing a bulletproof vest to future exhibitions."

I nudged him playfully with my shoulder, the warmth radiating from his skin igniting a spark of mischief within me. "And here I thought the only danger was the art world's high stakes. It's the middle-aged collectors that'll get you."

He turned to me, a playful glint in his eyes. "Careful, or I might just let them know you're the true mastermind behind my success."

"Ah, yes. The 'mysterious muse' trope. How very romantic," I teased, rolling my eyes dramatically. "Next, you'll say I should wear flowing gowns and sit on a pedestal, sipping wine while gazing longingly at you."

"Honestly, that might not be a bad look for you," he said, his gaze shifting to the horizon, where the sun was slowly rising, casting shimmering paths across the water. The moment hung in the air, thick with unspoken feelings and electric tension.

As I studied him, the way the morning light danced in his tousled hair, I felt a pang of something akin to fear tugging at my heart. It was unsettling how effortlessly we fell into this rhythm, like the ocean and its waves, but I couldn't ignore the nagging question that hovered in the back of my mind: What would happen when the tides changed? I squeezed his hand tighter, the warmth of our connection anchoring me against those turbulent thoughts.

"I've been thinking," I started, my voice steady despite the uncertainty roiling inside me. "About what comes next for us."

"Next?" he asked, turning back to face me, his expression a mix of curiosity and concern. "Like, in terms of art, or—"

"More like... life," I interrupted, the weight of my words heavy between us. "We've come so far, and I just wonder—are we really ready for the next chapter?"

His brow furrowed, and I could see the gears turning in his mind. "Are you asking if we're ready to take a leap of faith?"

"More like... do we know how to fly?" I replied, my heart racing as I spoke. The metaphor hung between us, heavy with meaning. "We've fought so hard for this moment. It feels like we're standing on the precipice of something beautiful, but what if we're not ready?"

Liam stepped closer, the ocean breeze tousling his hair, and his gaze bore into mine with an intensity that sent shivers down my spine. "We've already flown, haven't we? We've soared through the chaos of our pasts, through the highs and lows of this exhibition. Look at what we've accomplished."

"True," I admitted, a smile creeping onto my face despite the swirling fears. "But flying doesn't mean we know how to land gracefully."

He laughed, and it was a sound that wrapped around me, warm and inviting. "Isn't that the thrill of it all? The risk of falling? I don't want to just walk through life—what's the fun in that? I want to leap, to dive, and if we fall, then at least we do it together."

The sincerity in his voice sent a rush of warmth through me, and I found myself laughing along, a mix of exhilaration and fear bubbling within. "Okay, you have a point. Together, we can make quite the mess or quite the masterpiece."

"Exactly," he said, a playful smirk appearing. "So, what's the worst that can happen? We land in the sand instead of the sky?"

"Fine, but if we end up stuck in a sandpit, I'm blaming you," I teased, nudging him again. The sun broke free from the horizon, spilling light across the ocean, illuminating the world around us and washing away the shadows of uncertainty.

The laughter faded, replaced by a contemplative silence. As the sun rose higher, I let my worries drift away with the tide. With each crashing wave, a weight lifted, and a sense of clarity emerged. I realized that life was a series of waves, each one offering an opportunity to ride the current or sink beneath it. And with Liam by my side, I felt more like a surfer than a swimmer—ready to catch the next wave, come what may.

"I'm glad we're in this together," I said softly, feeling the soft grain of the sand beneath my feet, the coolness of the ocean lapping at my ankles. "Whatever happens next, we'll navigate it side by side."

"Side by side," he echoed, his voice a gentle promise as we stood there, the sun illuminating the path ahead, endless and uncharted.

A sudden gust of wind tousled my hair, sending a few rebellious strands whipping across my face. I tucked them behind my ear, glancing sideways at Liam, who was busy trying to catch the morning light reflecting off the waves with his phone camera. "You'd think we were on a tropical vacation instead of the shores of our own chaotic lives," I quipped, watching him fumble with angles and shadows, his brows furrowed in concentration.

He lowered his phone, casting me an amused look. "What's wrong with capturing a little slice of paradise? This could be our 'we made it' moment, a digital trophy to hang on our metaphorical wall of achievements."

"Oh, right. A highlight reel of our most impressive sunrises and awkward beach selfies." I rolled my eyes, though my heart warmed at his enthusiasm. "Because nothing screams 'we're adults now' like grainy photos of us squinting against the sun."

Liam feigned shock, placing a hand over his heart. "You wound me! The world deserves to see our glamourous transition from art world wannabes to actual artists." He waved his phone dramatically, like a conductor before an unseen orchestra. "Step right up, folks! Witness the transformation!"

I laughed, the sound mingling with the rhythmic crash of the waves. The atmosphere felt charged, alive with possibility, and for a fleeting moment, I wished we could bottle this energy and carry it into whatever awaited us next. But just as quickly, a shadow of doubt crossed my mind, dimming the light of my optimism. "What if the reality is more mundane than we hope?" I asked, my voice dipping low, almost swallowed by the sound of the ocean.

He stepped closer, brow furrowing as he processed my question. "Mundane? Are you saying you'd rather not wake up to this every day?" He gestured to the sun-drenched shore, the sweeping horizon beckoning us forward. "Look at this place! We're standing on the edge of the world, and you're worried about... what, going back to spreadsheets and meetings?"

"It's not just that," I replied, biting my lip. "It's the unknown. The rush of excitement is thrilling, but it can also be terrifying. I don't want to stumble back into the shadows of our pasts. We've fought so hard to step into the light."

His expression softened, understanding replacing the teasing glint in his eyes. "Hey, every sunrise brings a little uncertainty with it. But that's what makes it beautiful. Embracing the unknown means we're alive, and it means we have the chance to shape our story."

I looked into his eyes, feeling the truth of his words settle in my chest, warming me from the inside out. There was power in vulnerability, and it took courage to face the unknown together. "You're right," I admitted, feeling lighter. "But I still think we should have a contingency plan in place—like a safe word if we get too overwhelmed."

"Safe word? Is this a 'we need to talk' kind of safe word?" he teased, arching an eyebrow. "Because I was thinking more along the lines of 'pineapple,' for emergencies only."

"Pineapple it is. We can't risk confusion in case we ever find ourselves surrounded by decision-making anxiety," I shot back, laughter spilling between us like the surf at our feet.

Just then, the atmosphere shifted as a group of beachgoers strolled by, dragging surfboards behind them, their laughter ringing out like music against the crashing waves. A rush of exhilaration washed over me, and I felt the magnetic pull of the sea beckoning us to join in the adventure, to plunge into the unknown like those fearless surfers.

"Let's do it," I said, my voice steady and resolute. "Let's embrace this. I want to ride the waves, not just stand on the shore."

"Now you're speaking my language!" Liam replied, a broad grin spreading across his face. "Are you ready to make some serious memories?"

With a sudden surge of energy, I pulled him toward the water, splashing through the cool surf. It was a stark contrast to the lingering warmth of the sand beneath our feet, and each wave that rolled in sent delightful chills racing through my body. "If we're going to get soaked, we might as well go all in!" I shouted over the roar of the ocean, my laughter mingling with the sound of crashing waves.

As we plunged deeper, the coolness enveloped us, a refreshing contrast to the warmth of the sun above. The world shrank to just the two of us, splashing and laughing like carefree children. In that moment, worries faded away, swept out to sea with the ebb and flow of the tide.

"You're crazy!" Liam called out, dodging a wave as it surged between us, the water sparkling like diamonds under the sun. "But I think I'm starting to like this crazy version of you!"

"Crazy is my middle name!" I retorted, launching myself at him, tackling him into the surf. We tumbled into the water, laughter erupting between us like fireworks, a celebration of the new beginnings we were forging together.

Emerging from the water, we both gasped for breath, the salt of the ocean clinging to our skin, the taste of freedom lingering on our lips. "Okay, okay, truce!" Liam laughed, holding up his hands in mock surrender. "I can't be responsible for any more of your wild antics if it leads to me ending up fully soaked!"

I grinned, brushing the wet hair from my face. "Well, that ship has sailed, my friend. We're all in now. Besides, I think it suits you—more rugged, more adventurous."

"Rugged, huh? I'll take that as a compliment," he said, giving me a mock-serious look. "But only if you promise we'll keep doing this. The crazy, the unexpected. I want to ride this wave together."

"Deal," I said, our eyes locking in an unspoken understanding. "As long as you don't mind a few splashes along the way."

"I thrive on splashes!" Liam declared, pulling me closer, his voice warm and confident. "Bring on the waves, I say."

And just like that, amidst the laughter and the salty air, I knew we were ready. The ocean stretched endlessly before us, vast and inviting, a world of possibilities waiting to be explored. Together, we would ride every wave, face every storm, and navigate the beautiful chaos of our new beginning.

The sun climbed higher in the sky, casting a golden glow that shimmered across the water, turning the ocean into a canvas of sparkles. Each wave that rolled in whispered secrets to the shore, urging us to stay just a little longer, to embrace the magic of this moment. The salty breeze tousled my hair, and I felt as if I could take flight, buoyed by the promise of adventure that lingered in the air.

With a sudden burst of energy, I grabbed Liam's hand, dragging him further into the surf. "Let's see who can hold their breath the longest!" I challenged, playfulness bubbling to the surface like the foam of the waves around us.

"Not fair!" he shouted, mock indignation coloring his voice. "You're part fish!"

"Only on Tuesdays!" I laughed, diving beneath the water before he could respond, the cool embrace enveloping me in a refreshing cocoon. Time suspended as I swam, my heart racing with exhilaration. I could hear the muffled sounds of the world above, the laughter, the crashing waves, and Liam's playful taunts as I kicked toward the surface.

When I finally broke free, gasping for air, I spotted him a few feet away, his hair slicked back and droplets of water cascading down his sun-kissed skin. "You'll have to do better than that!" he called, and I couldn't help but grin at his competitive spirit.

"Challenge accepted!" I yelled, before launching myself at him again, splashing water with both hands like a child in a puddle.

He laughed and returned fire, sending waves of water flying my way. It was a simple game, but the pure joy radiating from him sent warmth through my chest. The world around us faded into a blur, leaving only our laughter and the playful splashes of water.

But as I gazed into his eyes, I felt a flicker of something deeper, an understanding that this moment was more than just fun—it was a stepping stone toward the future we were beginning to build together. "What if we took this energy and channeled it into something bigger?" I suggested, the idea bubbling to the surface of my mind like the foam cresting on the waves.

"Bigger? Like a mural on the side of a building? I could totally see us painting a giant octopus or a tropical paradise," he replied, his voice rich with enthusiasm. "But I might need a lot of snacks for that kind of project."

"Snacks? I think that's your secret ingredient," I teased, nudging him with my shoulder. "But what about something more profound? We could organize an art retreat—an immersive experience for aspiring artists. Teach them what we've learned."

Liam's eyes sparkled with interest. "You mean like a hands-on workshop? I like the sound of that. It's perfect! Plus, we could feature local artists, create a community space—"

"Yes!" I interrupted, excitement building. "We could even incorporate environmental themes. Think about it! Art that raises awareness about ocean conservation or sustainability. It could be amazing."

"I love it," he said, his enthusiasm palpable. "But wait—who would actually sign up for our retreats? We're not exactly famous yet."

"Not yet," I corrected him, confidence surging through me. "But we could change that. We've come this far; why not keep pushing ourselves? We have the talent, the passion—why not invite others into our journey?"

He grinned, a glimmer of admiration in his eyes. "You really believe we could do this?"

"Absolutely. Together, we can turn dreams into reality." The weight of my words hung between us, electrifying. In that moment, I realized we were no longer just two individuals navigating life; we were a team, ready to face the world.

"Then let's do it! Right here, right now," he said, raising his arms triumphantly. "We'll draft a plan while standing in the ocean like true visionaries!"

I laughed, the sound echoing across the water. "I can already see the headline: 'Two dreamers conspire to change the world while wet!'"

As we splashed and bantered, the tide shifted, and I felt a sense of peace wash over me, blending seamlessly with the thrill of possibility. This was what it meant to be alive—immersed in the moment, dreaming big, and laughing loudly.

But just as I turned to suggest we wade deeper, I spotted a figure on the beach, standing alone near the rocks, watching us intently. My heart lurched. It was a woman, her silhouette striking against the vibrant morning sky. Something about her seemed familiar, yet unsettling.

"Liam, do you see that woman?" I whispered, my playful mood deflating like a punctured balloon.

He turned, squinting against the sunlight. "Where? The one with the... green dress? She looks lost."

"She's not just lost," I murmured, my mind racing. "I think I've seen her before. At the gallery."

"Really? Did she work there?" he asked, tilting his head as he examined her.

"I'm not sure. But she was there when everything went down—when we had to confront those people about the art theft," I replied, a chill creeping up my spine. "What if she's here for a reason?"

Liam's playful demeanor shifted to one of concern. "You think she's connected to what happened?"

"I don't know, but I have a bad feeling about this," I said, my voice tight. "We should—"

Suddenly, the woman lifted her arm, pointing directly at us. I felt my heart skip a beat as a sense of dread coiled tightly in my chest.

"What is she doing?" Liam murmured, his brow furrowing.

Before I could respond, the woman started walking toward us, her expression unreadable, but her intent clear. The atmosphere shifted, the warmth of the sun turning cold as a heavy tension enveloped the beach.

"What do you want?" I called out, forcing my voice to remain steady, but uncertainty thrummed beneath the surface.

As she drew closer, the playful waves behind us faded into the background, replaced by an electric stillness. I exchanged a quick glance with Liam, the earlier joy of our shared moment evaporating like mist under the glaring sun. The horizon, once a promise of new beginnings, now loomed ominously ahead, shrouded in uncertainty.

And just as the woman opened her mouth to speak, the unmistakable sound of a phone buzzing echoed from my pocket, cutting through the tension like a knife. I fumbled for it, my heart racing as I glanced at the screen. A message flashed ominously across it, sending a chill down my spine:

"We need to talk. You're in danger."

The world tilted on its axis, the waves crashing around me suddenly feeling more menacing than inviting, and I realized that our lives were about to take a turn we never saw coming.